Rave Reviews for Andrew McGahan

"Andrew McGahan writes with understated brilliance. A sort of inside-out Aussie odyssey that features two luckless but likable guys trapped on a colonized, bleak peninsula, *1988* is a ruthlessly truthful look at the impossible dream of refusing to grow up."
—Michael Drinkard, author of *Disobedience*

"*1988* is a sometimes suspenseful, sometimes painful, sometimes hilarious story of a young man's six-month journey of self-discovery into Australia's Northern Territories. Andrew McGahan is a wonderful writer, with a sure voice, a great eye for detail, and a gift for storytelling. I couldn't put this book down."
—Daniel Lyons, author of *The Last Good Man*

"They're a shambling mess, heading into the desert without water or a map, but they are also classic Australian adventurers...too stoned to realize they've been driving in first gear for hours. McGahan's laconic wit and casual sniping at human nature is stylish and seductive. Addictive stuff."
—*Good Weekend,* Australia

"*1988* is a telling, unassuming, and oddly cheering book. McGahan's account is moving and clear, from the inside, on just how meager are the rations provided for young men setting out on adulthood."
—*The Australian*

"Anomie Australian style is a stepping off point for beguiling journeys of self-discovery."
—*Time,* Australia

On his first novel, *Praise*

"*Praise* became a bestseller, and McGahan, much to his horror and amusement, became the poster boy for Australia's so-called grunge writers. The twenty-somethings have added McGahan to their purchases of Bukowski, Burroughs, and Kerouac."
—*Sunday Age,* Melbourne

"Dark honesty...a good first novel with an honest ending."
—*Publishers Weekly*

"A bold novel, distinct voice, and impressive debut."
—*Kirkus Reviews*

1988

Andrew McGahan

ST. MARTIN'S PRESS ❧ NEW YORK

The author would like to sincerely thank the Australia Council
for the awarding of a Category B Fellowship which greatly
expedited the completion of this novel.

Library of Congress Cataloging-in-Publication Data

McGahan, Andrew.
    1988 / Andrew McGahan.
        p.   cm.
    ISBN 0-312-15043-1
    I. Title.
    PR9619.3.M3234A15   1997
    823—dc21   96-44519
                                                        CIP

First published in Australia by Allen & Unwin Pty Ltd

First U.S. Edition: January 1997

10   9   8   7   6   5   4   3   2   1

AUTHOR'S NOTE

The locations mentioned in this book are real. The Cobourg Peninsula. The Gurig National Park. Cape Don. The groups and organisations mentioned are also real. The Bureau of Meteorology. The Northern Territory Conservation Commission. The Cobourg Aborigines. However, this is a work of fiction. It is not intended to be an accurate portrayal of any of these locations. Nor is it meant to be an accurate portrayal of any of these organisations, or of their policies. Most particularly it is not meant to be a portrayal of any actual persons who live in these locations, or who work for these organisations. Any resemblance to actual people, living or dead, is unintentional.

ONE

There was an argument in Chinese outside my door. It happened often and in many ways I was beginning to hate the language. I rolled over and considered the digital clock. Nearly midday. Time, maybe, to get out of bed. I lay and listened for a while, looking down at my white round belly. It was hot in the room, a stale air of sweat and old sheets. The morning asthma weighed in. I groped around for the Ventolin, found it, sucked in the drug. Outside the voices rose, fell, moved along the hall, came back again. Maybe it wasn't an argument. Maybe it was just a loud discussion.

I got up and shuffled around. Five foot, eleven and half inches of me, running to fat. I wrapped a towel around my waist, opened the door. Five of the Chinese were in the hall. I knew some of their names, but only some. They stopped talking and looked at me.

'Morning boys,' I said.

'Good morning,' some of them answered. There were nods and smiles from the ones who spoke no English.

'Any luck today?' I asked.

1

Shakes of the head, negatives. One of them laughed. He said 'You always get up very late.'

I nodded, began edging my way through.

Another laugh. 'You like sleep. Sleep very late.'

'You got that right.'

I moved towards the shower.

It was a four bedroom house, in James Street, New Farm. Brisbane. I'd lived there about six months. I'd chosen it because I needed a cheap room and I vaguely knew the owner. His name was William. He dealt marijuana and worked part-time installing dishwashing machines. When I first moved in the other two rooms were occupied by female university students. I never knew them well. Shortly after I moved in, they moved out. As far as I could gather it was nothing personal. Still, we were left with two rooms to fill. Which was where it all began.

William placed an ad with the local alternative radio station. 'Relaxed smokers of either sex wanted. No bond.' We waited. Over the following weeks there were only a few calls and none of them, upon seeing the rooms, were interested. It wasn't much of a house. The walls and windows were dirty, and the floor had fallen through in several places. William's plan was to renovate one day and sell at a profit.

In the meantime the lack of rent was a problem. William needed it to pay the mortgage. And I was in no position to pay extra, I was only a casual worker myself. More time passed. William gave up on selective advertising and went to the mainstream newspaper. 'Two rooms available. No bond.' Again, for some time there was no interest. Then two Chinese males arrived at the door.

Their names were Li Ping and Michael Wan. Each was carrying a suitcase. They'd just arrived, they said, from Shanghai. They were in Australia to study English and

Engineering. The English they already had wasn't much good, but it was understandable. William showed them the rooms. They were the smaller two of the house. Unfurnished. They were also slightly cheaper than mine. Forty-five a week, compared to fifty. Li and Michael said that was fine and could they move in straight away. William said yes. He pocketed the first two weeks' rent in advance and smiled at them.

'You wanna go and get all your stuff?' he asked.

Li and Michael held up the suitcases. 'This is it.'

There were a couple of old mattresses under the house, and a derelict wardrobe. It was enough to get them started.

I showered for a long while. It was a fine shower, the spout set high above a large, rusty claw-footed tub, the water strong. One of the few good points of the house. I was grateful for that. Mornings were a bad time and a good shower helped. No matter whether I'd been drinking the night before or not, I always awoke feeling hungover and ill. There were many explanations for it. My asthma was severe, and some of the drugs I took for it caused nausea, especially on a morning's empty stomach. Others caused throat infections and foul breath. I also suffered chronic hayfever and took vast amounts of antihistamines. They knocked out the hayfever, but took me along as well, made the night's sleep dead and deadening.

After the shower I threaded my way back through the Chinese to my room and dressed. Then it was to the kitchen. The kitchen floor was one of the bad spots in the house. A whole corner of it had fallen through and needed to be avoided. Otherwise the room was small and hot and dirty— an overflowing compost bin in the corner, milk cartons and beer bottles and unwashed dishes on the benches, stiffened tea bags and rancid butter on the cutting-board. A small black-and-white television sat on the windowsill. It was the only TV in the house and for some reason William refused to put it in the living room. He liked to watch TV in the kitchen, propped up in a chair amidst the mess, sweating and drawing in periodic belts of his home-grown heads. There was nothing I could do. It was his house and his TV.

I dug around and found bread, put two slices in the toaster. There was a pot of fishhead soup on the stove. I stared into it while I waited. The Chinese made the soup regularly, it was easy and the ingredients were cheap. I'd tasted it a few times and liked it well enough, but now it was cold and congealed. I thought about dead fish. When the toast was ready I buttered it, Vegemited it, and sat down. I stared out the window. It was a bright sweltering day, nothing to see but the glare from the neighbours' tin roofs and from the sky. Summer in Brisbane. I contemplated options.

It was a day off, that was one thing. Exactly what date I didn't know. Early February. The ninth or the tenth or the eleventh. It didn't matter. I worked four days a week at a pub across the river. Fridays and Saturdays and two other days more or less at random. Shifts between four and eight hours. I disliked the work, so a free afternoon was something. At least it would've been, had I anything else to do. I had nothing else to do. I sat there, thinking about time. It was 1988. Australia's Bicentennial year. The country was two hundred years old. I was twenty-one.

They were, I knew, significant numbers. Something should have happened in my life by then. But I'd already made my big move, and it hadn't worked. It was two years earlier, when I was nineteen. I was at uni then, studying literature. I dropped out. I was to write a novel. A horror novel. It was supposed to be a best-seller. A money-maker. Somehow it all went wrong. I wrote the novel but no-one wanted it. I threw it away. I started others, got bogged down, gave them up. Things got slow. After a while I was barely writing at all. I'd never quite made it back to uni either. Now it was mostly pub work, and sleeping late, and the wasting of days. A steady decline. Happy Birthday then, Australia.

One of the Chinese came into the kitchen. He was better dressed for the heat than me—as most of them usually were—naked except for a pair of white Y-front underpants. This one was tall, lean, dark-skinned and quite beautiful, as again, most of them were. William and I were constantly shamed by them. Both of us were pale and overweight, patched red with rashes from sweat. We took to keeping our shirts on, no matter how hot it got. The two of us, western decadents.

He said, 'You will be home all today?'

'Probably. Why?'

'We all going out. You take messages?'

'What messages?'

'Work. Jobs.'

'I see. Yes, I'll be home all day.'

'Thank you.'

He was gone. There were more discussions in Chinese in the hallway, then the front door slammed and it was silent. The house to myself. It was a rarity. I sat there. Just past midday. There were at least twelve waking hours ahead of me. I sneezed. Once, twice, three times. My eyes watered. The familiar, first itch of hayfever settled. I headed for the antihistamines.

The first couple of weeks of Li and Michael's residence had passed painlessly. Indeed, William and I were aware that the living arrangements offered no small opportunity for cross-cultural interchange. After all, neither of us knew much about China. And Li and Michael, it was clear, knew equally little about Australia.

On their first night thus we introduced them to Fourex beer and the one-day cricket on TV. Our intentions seemed sound, but it wasn't a great success. The cricket meant nothing to them, and they found the Fourex merely amusing. It seemed the Fourex stubbie was identical in shape to a bottle used for some foul Chinese laxative. After that we asked them about the political situation in China. 'Not good,' they replied, and showed no interest in commenting further. They asked us about job prospects in Brisbane.

'What sort of jobs?' we asked.

'Anything.'

'We thought you were here to study.'

'Yes, but we have no dollars.'

'Oh.'

'Getting here *very* expensive.'

'Of course.'

'Rent here *very* expensive.'

The conversations never really improved. William and I ran out of polite questions about China, and Li and Michael offered nothing more themselves. Their prime concern was finding work. They had paid in advance for the private college that would teach them English and Engineering, but for day-to-day living they needed cash. Every morning they rose early and went out searching.

They tried Chinatown in the Valley first, but hundreds of other Chinese students were already after the limited jobs there. They asked William if there was any work going in the dishwasher installation trade. He said there wasn't. They asked me if there was any work in the pub trade. I thought about my boss, and his attitude to Asians, Blacks, The Unemployed, Anyone. I said it was unlikely. They looked further afield, out of walking distance. They came to me for help in deciphering bus timetables. I was of no use. I had my own car. I'd barely caught a bus in my life.

Finally they came to William.

'We cannot pay this rent,' said Michael, 'Not without a job.'

'That's a pity,' said William.

'We have two friends. They just come from Shanghai. They need rooms.'

'Yeah?'

'Between four we could pay.'

'You mean two to a room?'

'Yes. Same rent, but between four. Or else we have to leave.'

William thought for a moment. I knew what he was thinking. Basically there were the house repayments to meet, and if Li and Michael left, then there were all those empty weeks while we looked for someone else.

'Okay,' William said, 'Sure.'

They moved in that afternoon. Our two new housemates were named Xo and Robert. Robert's English was bad and Xo had none at all. They were also from Shanghai, also English and Engineering students, and also in need of work.

Time passed. The Chinese, now that there were four of them, kept mostly to themselves. In the evenings the kitchen was used to cook two separate meals. Mine and William's, and the Chinese's. Not that William and I cooked many meals. There was a takeaway down the road and we often ordered our meals there. The Chinese cooked every night. They made their dishes out of cheap leftover cuts from the markets. William and I rarely asked, or were invited, to join in. Within a few weeks communication between East and West had come down to little more than the odd nod when we bumped into each other in the kitchen, or on the way to the toilet.

Then one day the four of them came to William. None

of them had found any work yet. 'We cannot afford this rent,' they said.

Two more of their friends moved in. Students, fresh from Shanghai, no money and no work. I didn't bother learning their names.

The day showed no signs of picking up. Even TV was no help. Bad midday movies and poor reception. I settled on the back steps. I sneezed a few more times. Hayfever made the light painful. The antihistamines swung in. I stared at the mango tree in the back corner of the yard. Over-ripe mangos littered the ground beneath it. Somewhere, several houses away, someone was playing a record that sounded like Cossack dance music. I could hear the faint clapping and stamping of feet, the sound drifting across the roofs. No dancing here, I thought.

I got up and headed back to my room. I looked at the computer on the desk. I'd purchased it to help with my writing, in the more hopeful days. Before that I'd written on an electric typewriter. Before that it was an old manual, and before that again it was with a fountain pen on finely-crafted paper. One thing I'd learned from it all—the method didn't matter when you had nothing to write about. The computer was coated with dust. I thought about switching it on. Didn't.

Drinking then. There was nothing in the house, but the Queen's Arms Hotel and its bottle shop was just down the road. The only problem was that I took no joy in drinking alone, either in bars or at home. I didn't know why. All it meant was that to drink I had to find at least one partner. That often involved spending time with people I had no real interest in seeing, or them me. It made the drinking dull and pointless, but it was better than not drinking at all.

I ran through my list of friends and acquaintances. There

was only one who I thought might be interested on a slow weekday afternoon. His name was Leo. He was a bank teller who'd quit work and was waiting now to start university. I dialled his number.

'Leo,' I said, 'It's Gordon.'

'Gordon. What's news.'

'Nothing. You interested in a few drinks this afternoon?'

He was yawning. 'Well . . . what'd you have in mind?'

'Just a beer or two.'

'Where?'

'Here. Or down at the pub.'

'What about coming over here? My parents are away for the week, I've got the house to myself.'

I thought about it. Leo lived with his parents, out in the suburbs. It was a large, two-storey brick house. Inside was scrupulously neat. Somehow I never felt relaxed visiting there, parents or no parents.

I said, 'You're not interested in coming over this way?'

'I'd just as soon hang around here.'

'Well, I don't feel much like moving myself.'

'That's that then.'

'Guess so.'

'I don't really like drinking at your place all that much Gordon. It's always so bloody crowded.'

'The Chinese are out at the moment.'

'They'll be back.'

'I guess they will.'

'It's a shitful day for it anyway.'

'Yeah.'

We talked a while longer, hung up. I thought about a few other people I could try, lost interest. It *was* a shitful day for it. I got up and made for the toilet. Leo was right about the other thing too. The house was too bloody crowded.

In the end we had nine Chinese students living there. The floors of their two rooms were covered with mattresses, and they took the sleeping in rotation. They paid ten dollars each in weekly rent. During the day they filled up the living room and the kitchen, cooking, talking, poring over the job columns. Nine lean, dark, Y-fronted bodies. William had lost control. He sat on his chair and smoked endlessly and stared at the television. He'd never been a talkative man, now he said nothing at all.

I spent the days wandering about the house, dodging the Chinese, ignoring them and ignored by them. Eleven people in residence and I felt as if I was living alone. I wasn't even sure this type of mass-rental was legal. But although a few of the Chinese did manage to find part-time work, they remained desperately poor. Even ten dollars a week was a burden to them. Where else were they going to go?

At least their social lives were improving. They started bringing women home. Female Chinese students. The boys pooled their resources and bought six-packs of beer and extra cigarettes when they entertained. An ancient Chinese woman began appearing whenever the girls did. Some sort of chaperone, I assumed. Several times she took it upon herself to clean our kitchen, shooing William and his marijuana out with her broom. The Chinese, both men and women, apologised. They said they didn't like the old woman, didn't even want her there. They asked William to make her go away. He only looked at them, then took his television off to his bedroom and brooded.

Increasingly I retreated to my room. I stopped using the kitchen. I ate meat pies and fish cakes and chips from the takeaway. Greasy wrappers and small piles of salt gathered around my bed. I switched on the computer from time to time, switched it off. I lay and stared at the ceiling, listening to the Chinese outside my door. Went to work at the pub, came home. Nothing much else happened. December passed into the New Year, the New Year into late January. And then it was February. The ninth or the tenth or the eleventh.

I stared into the toilet as I pissed. The water in the bowl was a dark yellow, the smell of urine enough to make me gag. That was the Chinese again. They only flushed for shits. I understood that. Shanghai was a massive city with water-supply problems, you didn't waste water on unnecessary toilet flushing. It was small of me to be squeamish. It showed a lack of cultural tolerance. But still, eleven people had pissed in that bowl. I finished, pressed the button and got out of there.

Someone was knocking on the front door. I moved down the hall and opened it. It was a Chinese man, young, unfamiliar.

'Hello,' he said.

'G'day.'

He held a suitcase in one hand, and a piece of paper in the other. He lifted up the paper and read out a street number. 'Is that here?'

'Yes.'

He grinned. 'I come from airport. I told I live here.'

'You live here?'

'My friends live here, yes?'

'I guess they do.'

'Then I live here.'

We looked at each other. He laughed nervously. It was a new country and a new town and he was all alone. I wasn't giving much of a welcome.

I sighed. 'Come on in.'

He followed me down the hall. I showed him the bedrooms. 'In there. They're all out at the moment.'

'They will be long?'

'No idea.'

I sat on the living room couch. He put his suitcase just inside one of the bedrooms, then stood, looking around. Finally he sat on the edge of one of the other chairs, hands on his knees. We were silent for a minute, avoiding each other's eyes.

'This is nice house,' he said, and smiled at me.

'Yes,' I said. I didn't smile back.

It was time, I decided, to move.

TWO

I saw Wayne a few days later.

At the time I barely knew him. He was a struggling artist, and I had no real interest in art, struggling or otherwise. But we had a friend in common, a woman named Madelaine. She was an advertising copywriter. Both Wayne and I had been through brief affairs with her, about a year before. Possibly she had a thing for failed artists and writers. Possibly they had a thing for her. She was generous and good-natured, lived in a nice house in Nundah, and her fridge was always full.

There was a party at Madelaine's house. It was Friday night and I'd just finished an eight-hour shift at the bottle shop. I arrived in my black pants and white shirt, my legs aching, a bottle of bourbon tucked under my arm. It wasn't a big crowd, a dozen or so people. University students, a few unemployed, some of Madelaine's fellow workers. They weren't my regular friends, but I knew most of the names and faces, enough to be at home.

Wayne was there. He was older than me, somewhere in

his mid-twenties. I'd seen him three of four times before, around Madelaine. He certainly *looked* like an artist. His clothes were always soft and loose, his skin was pale almost to the albino stage, and he was tall, narrow-faced, with a head of untidy, bright blond hair. It was hard to say if he was attractive or ugly, but you could imagine him at the canvas, slapping the paint on. Either way, I'd never said more than a few words to him, or him to me.

I sat on a couch, let the first few bourbons seep down to my feet. It was good to be finished with work for the day, even better to be away from my house and its population explosion. I still didn't know what to do about it. Move certainly, but there was more wrong with my life than just where I lived. I was bored. Failure was the problem. I'd always expected success at something, sooner or later. I was sick of waiting.

Madelaine flopped down beside me.

'Gordon,' she said.

'Madelaine.'

'How are the Chinese?'

'I'm leaving them.'

'Really? Where're you gonna go?'

'No idea yet.'

'It's a pity. I like visiting your house. They're interesting people. Amazing stories about Shanghai.'

'I've never really got that far with them.'

'You just have to ask.'

I shrugged. 'Do you know anyone who has a spare room?'

She thought. 'Not really. But I'll ask around. I'll find you something.'

We talked about other things. I liked Madelaine, without really understanding her. She was a round, curly-haired, motivated woman. Twenty-seven-years old. Apart from working at the ad agency she also studied literature part time at uni. That was how we'd met. We'd been in a tutorial together, then one day she asked me out to a pub. We'd got ourselves drunk, and got along. Then I'd left uni and started writing, but we still met from time to time. And when the writing started to die she was sympathetic. About the writing, and about other things.

That was how the fucking had started. I was lonely and losing it a little, and she'd known that. She'd also known that I'd go home quietly each morning, after the asthma attack, and cause her no trouble. So she'd taken me to bed. But sex was a problem with me. Madelaine was the fourth woman I'd tried it with, only the second with whom it had lasted more than a couple of nights. I was clumsy and shy. My penis was very small and I always came quickly. I was ashamed of it. Ashamed of my whole body.

Nor did I have any real idea of what to do with *hers*—her big breasts, her wide legs, her clitoris, anything. In all our time together she never came. She was very friendly about things, but that only made it worse. I didn't seem to learn anything or get any better. There was more to sex, I knew, than just pricks and cunts, but somehow the rhythm of it, the whole fuck that was supposed to be there—I couldn't get the hang of it. I didn't know why. After about a month I suggested that maybe we should stop. I was still lonely, and I still craved sex, but there was a terrible knowledge there too. *I was no good in bed.* I masturbated all the time, despairingly. There'd been no one since Madelaine.

Finally she moved off to circulate. I stayed on the couch, talked with other people. The bourbon slid down. I grew drunk. Joints were being passed around but I didn't take any. Despite living with William and his eternal supply, I smoked very little. At least, not in company, and not when drinking. It made me paranoid and sleepy. It came to me that I was living a dull and innocent life. No sex of late and not many drugs. All I could claim was a weakness of character, a poor diet, and alcohol.

Wayne sat down next to me.

'I hear you wanna leave town,' he said.

'Who told you that?'

'Madelaine.'

'I wanna move *house*, that's all.'

He was disappointed. And maybe a little stoned. He stared blankly around the room. 'Oh.'

Wayne, in fact, had been Madelaine's partner immediately prior to me. Exactly how things had gone with him, and why it didn't last, Madelaine had never said. She still liked him though, and in particular liked his paintings. I'd never seen any.

I said, 'Why?'

'I'm looking for someone to come to a lighthouse with me.'

I considered this. I knew about lighthouses. Windswept coastlines. Rocks. Treacherous fogs. Men in thick seafarer's sweaters.

I said, 'What do you mean, a lighthouse?'

He dragged his hand through his hair, glum. It was a long, slim, artist's hand. 'You know, a lighthouse.'

'Where?'

'The Northern Territory.'

'Jesus.'

'Yeah.'

'What are you supposed to be doing there?'

'I don't really know. It's a job my father organised.'

'Ah.'

There was a pause.

Wayne sat up. 'It's not in the actual lighthouse. The lighthouse is automatic. But there's a weather station there too. I'm gonna be running that. But it's a two-man job, I need someone else.'

I thought. 'Do you know how to run a weather station?'

'What *is* a weather station? Do *you* know?'

'No.'

He nodded. 'The jobs vacant, and my father's friendly with the administration, that's all I know. I'm supposed to go up there and paint. My parents think the solitude will be good for me. It's a very lonely place, apparently.'

'And no one wants to go with you?'

'I've asked everyone. Then Madelaine mentioned you. And I thought, since you're a writer . . . '

'I haven't written anything in years.'

'Oh. Okay.'

We sat. I sipped on the bourbon, watched the party. It was looking tired. I felt tired. Drunk. I thought about the bottle shop, my life in general. About the Chinese, ten of them now, waiting for me at home.

I said, '*You* don't even wanna go, do you.'

'No. But my parents have been supporting me for years. I don't have much choice.'

That was something, at least. I could live with most things, but not enthusiasm.

I said, 'How long would we be there?'

Wayne looked at me. 'Six months.'

We spent the night plotting details. A lighthouse. A weather station, thousands of miles away. For six months. I drank steadily. With alcohol it all made sense. Meanwhile, the party dwindled around us. The bourbon ran out and I moved on to some leftover wine. We kept talking.

This was the only problem. There wasn't any. Wayne had spent weeks trying to find someone for the job, now there were only nine days left before he was due to start. The first step was getting to Darwin. There was supposed to be a day's training there, with the Bureau of Meteorology. To learn how to run the weather station.

'Have you got a car?' Wayne asked.

'Yes.'

'I don't wanna take a bus or anything. You mind driving?'

'No. Sure. We can drive.'

And we could. It seemed fitting. We'd drive, we'd traverse the continent. Not that we could go all the way by car. Wayne didn't know exactly where the lighthouse was, but he *did* know that it was somewhere remote, not accessible by road. The only way in was by plane or boat. And it seemed that once we'd arrived, we'd be stuck there until the six months were up. There was no transport for holidays or weekends off. Only, maybe, for emergencies. Critical injuries, heart attacks, death.

Somehow it didn't matter. I tossed down the wine, agreed to everything. Then it was five in the morning and the wine was finished. I wrote down Wayne's phone number, called a cab and rode home. I watched the Brisbane streets roll by. Suddenly I was worried. The Northern Territory? A lighthouse? Me?

I made it home and went to bed. I lay there, thinking. I calmed down. It would be fine. Later on I'd wake up sober and decide to dump the whole idea. I slept. Got up late. The Chinese were still there. The dust on the computer was still there. The mess in the kitchen was still there. And the heat and the hayfever and the long, tedious day.

It was settled then.

To the lighthouse.

THREE

The first thing was to quit my job at the bottle shop. I worked my Saturday night shift then explained things to the boss after closing. He didn't seem too concerned.

'How long will you be gone?' he asked.

'Six months.'

'Well, the way people come and go around here, there might be a spot for you when you get back.'

I was moved. He was from the old guard of pub-owners. Alcoholic and cynical, hateful of staff and customers alike. For him it was an affectionate goodbye. And maybe I'd earned it. I'd worked for him two years, diligently and without complaint. I was polite to customers, kept the fridges fully stocked, never called in sick or skipped shifts.

No wonder I hated the place.

Then there were things like gathering a six-month supply of asthma drugs. One of my deepest fears was being trapped somewhere inaccessible without my medication. I used far more than was necessary. I sucked on the Ventolin puffer every hour or so, automatically, whether I was short of breath or not. I hid this fact from the doctors. They were evangelical about asthma and about how to control it. I preferred not to get lectured—it was my disorder, not theirs. I visited the necessary chemists, stocked up.

Most important, though, was the collection of writing material. I'd decided it was time I started another book. More than time. Wayne's parents had the right idea about the lighthouse. Isolation was the key. The computer, however, was too big to take. I'd long ago sold my old typewriter. It would have to be pen and paper again.

I found a stationer's. I went to the shelves and selected a ream of finest quality writing paper. Five hundred pages. I thought about that for a moment. Then I took another ream, and then two more. Two thousand pages. Just how much writing might I get done in six months? I took another ream. And another one. I had six of them, stacked up in my arms. I paused. What was I doing? Three thousand pages? I put two of them back. Then picked one up again.

I moved to the counter. The clerk looked at me, at all the paper. 'Planning *War and Peace* are we?'

'You never know.'

'Anything else then?'

'Ink cartridges for a Parker fountain pen.'

He dug around under the counter and came up with a pile of small boxes. 'There're five cartridges to a box,' he said, 'How many you want?'

'Twenty boxes.'

He laughed. 'Are you kidding?'

'I'm gonna be out of reach of shops for the next six months. I don't wanna run out of ink.'

'You wouldn't use that much in six years. Even if you *were* writing *War and Peace*.'

'I still think I'll take the twenty.'

He started packing them up. 'Your money.'

He was right. It was getting expensive. I had only a few hundred dollars saved. With petrol and other expenses, I'd be broke by the time I hit Darwin. And what about food? How did we get food out at this lighthouse? Did we have to take six months' worth of that as well? And what about alcohol? Where was *that* going to come from?

Unknowns. There was nothing to be done about them.

Madelaine rang me.

'So you're really going!' she said, 'I knew I'd sort things out. How do you like Wayne? Think you'll get along?'

'I don't know. What else does he do except paint?'

'Nothing. It's tricky for him, his parents keep demanding he gets a real job. They don't think he's motivated enough. That's why he has to go, to get them off his back. They want him to paint enough stuff for an exhibition. He can hardly say no, seeing they usually have to help him out with cash . . .'

'Is he any good?'

'He's fantastic. Just a little obscure, that's all. People don't know what he's on about. You know what Art's like.'

'I thought I might try writing again.'

'That's *great*. A novel for you and an exhibition for Wayne. This lighthouse'll end up being famous. When are you going?'

'Tuesday.'

'Are you having a going-away party?'

'It's only six months. No one'll even notice we're gone.'

'*I'll* miss you.'

'Thanks Madelaine. That's very kind.'

Monday night I began clearing out my room. I'd given William two weeks' rent as notice. He wasn't happy about it, but he understood. I packed gear for the trip. When it came to clothes I went through my stuff, selecting warm weather gear. I was heading for the tropics. I needed shorts and T-shirts. Hats and thongs.

I came to my leather jacket. It was heavy and stiff, with lots of zippers—a motorbike jacket. I'd bought it about a year before. I'd worn it only twice and both times I'd felt like a fool. It took a certain style to wear a leather jacket. I didn't have it. And it'd be hot up north. I'd have no possible use for it. I threw it on the discard pile, then took it out again, packed it for Darwin.

Afterwards I gathered up everything I wouldn't be taking and ferried it over to my sister's house. Louise had plenty of storage space downstairs.

'So,' she said, 'A lighthouse. That's very romantic Gordon.'

'Romance is the last thing I need.'

'It's just a pity you're going to miss everything.'

'Like what?'

'The Bicentennial. All the special events. Expo. Everything.'

She was right. Brisbane, like the rest of Australia, had a big commemorative year planned. But Brisbane in particular had the International Exposition Expo '88. It was almost ready to open. I'd seen the massive construction site, read all the brochures. Laser shows and monorails and hundreds of thousands of visitors. People couldn't wait.

I said, 'I think I can live with the loss.'

'Really? I hear that while Expo is on all the pubs in town'll be open twenty-four hours a day.'

I considered that.

'I didn't say it would be easy.'

Tuesday morning I loaded the last of my things into the car. I checked the oil and the water and the spare tyre. Everything was operational. I went back inside. Several of the Chinese were wandering around my empty room, discussing its potential. At least now they'd have some space. And I'd left them my mattress. I wished them luck with Australia. They wished me luck with the Northern Territory. They'd heard plenty about the Northern Territory. It was much closer to home for them than Brisbane was.

'Crocodile Dundee,' one of them said.

'That's me.'

I went looking for William. He was in the backyard, under the mango tree. He was inspecting the rotten mangoes.

'I'm off,' I said.

'You got some dope to take with you?'

'No.'

'Shit. I'm almost out, or I'd give you some.'

'It's fine.'

'Six months at a fucking lighthouse, straight? You call that fine? Maybe you can get some in Darwin. I hear it's in good supply up there.'

'Maybe. Well, I hope it goes okay with the house . . .'

He gave me a stare. 'They've already got another two lined up.'

There was nothing more to say. I climbed back up the broken stairs. William continued his inspection. Peering down. Prodding. Dead fruit and the Chinese. I left him to it.

I fired up the Kingswood. HZ sedan, canary yellow, just on ten years old. I sat there for a moment, warming the engine. Three days. That's all it had taken to snap off my life in Brisbane. I supposed it could have been quicker. Maybe it should have been. Change, that was the hard part. It was supposed to be healthy, but who really knew. It was too late now. I slipped the shift into drive, got on my way.

It was only a few minutes. Wayne was living with his

parents, in Hamilton. We'd talked some more on the phone
and I had the address. I drove around the hill, up in to
the luxury area, found the house. Wayne was waiting in
the front yard, with a woman I assumed was his mother.
Next to them was a huge pile of wood, canvas, cardboard
boxes and suitcases. It was a mountain.

I walked over. 'You're kidding.'

'Is it too much?' said Wayne's mother, 'I told him it was
too much.'

I looked it over again. 'No wonder you didn't wanna go
by bus.'

'It's what I need,' he said. Then to his mother, 'If I'm
supposed to be painting up there.'

'Yes dear,' she replied, 'But will it fit in Gordon's car?'

We started loading. The boot overflowed and we moved
to the back seat, piling it all up. I looked in some of the
boxes. There were paints and brushes and papers. Dozens
of art magazines and books. A portable stereo and lots of
tapes. Two easels, wooden frames, rolls of canvas. The boy
was an artist alright. The stuff reached to the roof.

Wayne's mother was concerned. 'Will you be able to see
out the back?'

'I've got a side-mirror.' I looked at Wayne. 'Well?'

'Right.' He turned to his mother. 'See you then.'

'Goodbye Wayne.' She kissed him, rubbed a tear from her
eye. 'Don't worry, I won't cry.'

'It's alright Mum.'

I climbed in behind the wheel, Wayne into the passenger
side. He slipped his feet up on to the dash, long legs bent.
He was in old shorts and a paint-spattered singlet, white
skin showing everywhere.

'Sure you got everything?' I asked.

'Yeah. Get us out of here.'

I turned the key, pulled out into the street, headed west.

FOUR

We had six days to reach Darwin. Neither of us had ever been there before, and we had no maps. It wasn't a problem. All we had to do was head out west until we hit Central Australia, then turn north, up to the coast. Darwin was up there somewhere—it was the *only* thing up there—we could hardly miss it.

Today though we only had to make Dalby. It was a country town, about three hours out of Brisbane. My home town. My parents still lived there, on the family farm. I'd arranged for Wayne and I to spend the night. It meant we wouldn't cover much ground on the first leg, but six days seemed like time enough. The serious driving could wait.

Wayne was surprised to hear I'd grown up on a farm. He'd assumed I was a city kid.

'So what sort of farm is it?' he asked.

'Grain. Wheat and sorghum mainly.'

'What about horses?'

'No, no horses.'

'Can you ride a horse?'

'I've never even touched one.'

'Some farm boy you are.'

I'd heard it all before. Wheat farms weren't very exciting. You planted the stuff, watched it grow, cut it down. People seemed to find that a disappointment.

We cleared Brisbane. I eased the Kingswood up to one hundred and ten, let it sit there. It was a fine, hot day. We hung our arms out the windows, stared. There didn't seem much to talk about, now that we were on our way. We were strangers. On the other hand, we would be alone together for the next twenty-five weeks. We had to start somewhere.

'What about you,' I said, 'Always lived in Brisbane?'

'Yeah.'

'Been anywhere else?'

'Sydney and Melbourne. You?'

'Just Queensland.'

I wasn't widely travelled. A few trips up the coast to Rockhampton, Townsville, Cairns, that was about it. On the other hand, I'd been doing the Brisbane to Dalby stretch for years. The Kingswood had clocked-up the miles. These days I could just switch off and let it follow the road. Out through Gatton and Grantham, then up the Great Dividing Range to Toowoomba. Four-lane highway most of the way, one or two spots notorious for radar traps.

It wasn't all that scenic a road. Wayne gazed out the window for a while, then he dug an art magazine out of the back seat and flicked through it. I glanced across at the pages. The articles looked long and dense. I thought about how many artists I knew, how much I knew about art. It wasn't a lot.

Wayne pulled out a packet of Winfield Blues. 'Mind if I smoke in the car?'

'Not at all.'

He lit up, then offered me the pack.

'I don't smoke.'

'I thought all writers smoked.'

'I'm an asthmatic. It never seemed that good an idea.'

'I know a few asthmatics. They all smoke. I didn't think asthma was that serious.'

I glanced across at him. 'It varies.'

He nodded, exhaled out the window, began playing with the radio. It was the Holden original, AM only.

'Don't you have a tape deck?' he asked.

'No.'

He shook his head, blew out more smoke. 'It's gonna be a long drive.'

Toowoomba arrived. We stopped at a pub for lunch—sausages and onion gravy and beer.

'So this farm of yours,' Wayne asked eventually, 'Is it big?'

'Not very.'

'I thought it must've been huge. Madelaine said there were ten kids in your family.'

'Uh-huh. I'm number nine.'

'You gotta be Catholic then.'

'My parents are. I wouldn't say I was.'

'Private schools?'

I nodded. 'You?'

'Catholic parents. Private schools. Middle class.' He held up a pale arm. 'And very, very white.'

'So how many kids in your family?'

'Just me.'

We got back to Madelaine, how each of us knew her. Wayne had met her at an exhibition, gone home with her that night, and the sex had started straight away.

'How'd *you* meet her?' he asked.

'Through university.'

'You did a degree?'

'I dropped out.'

'Yeah, I spent a couple of years at Art College, didn't finish. Madelaine's like that, befriending lost souls.'

'How long were you a couple?'

'We were never a couple. We just always wound up fucking at the end of the night. You know, after everyone has gone home and there's just the two of you sitting there—what else are you gonna do?'

I nodded. What else.

'Ever done anything apart from painting?'

'For money?'

'For money.'

'I get the dole usually. My parents help out sometimes. I haven't had much luck with jobs. The last one I had was dishwashing. That lasted two nights. I was hopeless. Before that I tried being a pizza-delivery boy. That was one night. I kept getting lost.' He thought. 'Before that it was a 7-Eleven. I couldn't get the hang of the cash register.'

I was impressed. A man beaten by a cash register. 'So the painting's full-time?'

'I suppose. I haven't done much lately. That's what the lighthouse is for.'

'Same here.'

Something else we shared then—great expectations. But that seemed about it. We got on to movies and books and music and there was nothing to talk about. Wayne was into the experimental and the new, I wasn't into anything. Wayne spent many of his days hanging around the State Library, reading. I'd never been there. I had a fondness for watching rugby league and cricket. Wayne didn't.

But there were no impossible differences either. Neither of us were right wing, or new age, or religious. Or even vegetarian.

It was enough for the time being.

From Toowoomba it was out onto the western plains, grain-growing country. The sun beat down on the paddocks. Things were dry, dusty. There was nothing to see. We hit Dalby after less than an hour. Wayne stared out at the town, taking in the agricultural equipment lots, the muddy creek, the boys with their panel van, hanging out at the Shell service station.

'You *grew up* here?'

'It wasn't so bad.'

I watched the old streets slide by. I had nothing at all against Dalby. I'd enjoyed my years there. Still, I had no regrets about having moved on. I doubted the town had any regrets about it either. Ten thousand people, none of whom I knew anymore. I drove straight through without stopping. On the far side I took the northbound road. In ten minutes, we'd reached my parents' place.

You could see it all from the road, the farm, and it wasn't much to look at. Dead flat, treeless, a square block of dirt. It was very good dirt however, agriculture wise. Productive. The twelve of us had never been desperate for money. I turned off into the driveway, pulled up outside the house.

Wayne looked around.

'Big house,' he said.

It was. Big and ugly. It'd been extended over the years and size had always been more of a concern than aesthetics. There were three living rooms. Three bathrooms. Ten bedrooms. Fifteen beds. Most of my older siblings were married, so there were extra mattresses for inlaws and grandchildren as well. The kitchen was huge and the dining room had three tables. But the family wasn't in residence often anymore. We children had moved on to Brisbane, or interstate, or overseas. Not one of us had stayed on the farm.

I took Wayne inside, introduced him to my father and

mother. We settled at the kitchen table. Coffee and biscuits were arranged. Wayne sat there, upright and stick thin. His hair had blown vertical from all the wind in the car, his face and lips burnt faintly pink. My parents watched him.

'So you're a painter,' my mother said.

'Uh-huh.'

'What style do you work in?'

Wayne looked around at the paintings on the walls. My mother was a collector, on a small scale. Still lifes. Abstract landscapes.

'Nothing like anything here,' he said, 'Uh . . . these are nice though.'

'Well I like them,' my mother said.

A pause.

I started talking with my father about the trip. He was worried about the Kingswood. It'd been one of the family cars originally, and it was still registered in his name. Would it make it to Darwin?

'It has before,' I said.

This was true. Some years previous one of my older brothers had driven the Kingswood up there, looking for work. He'd gone in the wet season and used the backroads. The car had never really been the same since. He claimed to have collided with a crocodile while crossing a flooded creek.

My father wasn't convinced. 'What about spare tyres?'

'I checked it. It's okay.'

'You're only taking *one?* What about water?'

'Water?'

'If you overheat. There won't be service stations every ten miles out there.'

'Okay, we'll take some water.'

'And a spare fanbelt, you can always use a spare fanbelt.

I've got one over in the shed that should fit. What sort of map have you got?'

'Uh . . . we haven't.'

He shook his head, got up from the table, went off. It was clear we didn't have a clue what we were doing. He was easygoing enough, my father, but I was hardly his most practical son. He came back with a map and spread it out on the table. 'How fast do you want to get to Darwin?'

We studied the route. It was a big tourist map. It had little snippets of information on the towns and regions along the way. Looking at it you had a good idea of distances. It was a long way indeed to Darwin, right across the country. We discussed roads and destinations. Wayne took no part. He was bored.

'Do you know anything more about the actual job yet?' my mother asked him.

'Not really.'

'What will you be living in up there? The lighthouse?'

'No, I think there's a house for us.'

'What does it have? Do you need to take your own cooking gear? And sheets?'

'I don't know about cooking stuff, but mum made me pack sheets.'

She got up. 'I'll get some pots and pans together, and a few plates, and knives and forks.'

I said, 'The car's already overloaded.'

'You'll have to eat.'

'Got books to read?' my father asked.

'A few.'

'Six months is a long time.'

'And what about other things to do?' said Mum from the cupboards, 'Are you taking a pack of cards?'

'I guess we could.'

'What about some board-games? Monopoly or something.

And insect repellent. There'll be mosquitos everywhere up there.'

It went on until everything seemed to be covered. Wayne shifted about in his seat, looked blank, but there were necessities that couldn't be ignored. Afterwards I took him off and showed him the room my mother had ready. Most of the house was shut down, vacant. My parents used barely a quarter of it. We walked around, ended up in the main living room, in front of the TV.

I said, 'I could take you over to the sheds. Show you all the big machinery.'

'I don't think so. I don't like engines.'

We sat there until dinner, then returned to the TV for the rest of the evening. My parents went off to bed around ten-thirty. Wayne and I were left with the late-night movie. Wayne'd hardly spoken all night. From time to time he'd walked outside to smoke cigarettes, come back in. I felt I should be entertaining him. This was my home after all. I couldn't think of anything. As kids, my brothers and I had spent most of our nights out hunting rats around the sheds. It didn't sound like Wayne's style.

I'd always enjoyed it though. They could be crafty, rats, and mean when cornered. It'd been a pleasant life, the farm. I still came home to help out around harvesting and planting times, when things were busy. I even looked forward to it. It was satisfying sort of work, certainly better than the bottle shop. Still, it could only hold your interest so long. I was no farmer. I was home when I first hit Brisbane, and I knew it.

We packed it in around midnight. We were due for an early start. On the way to bed I went to the cupboard where all the family games were kept. I sorted through for anything that might be useful. Monopoly was there, but I couldn't really imagine Wayne and I playing it. The rest seemed to be kids games. Then I came across an old Scrabble set. I hadn't played Scrabble since I was ten or twelve years old, and even then only a couple of times. But then there *were* going to be a lot of long hours to fill at that lighthouse. I went out to the car, stowed the game in the boot.

FIVE

My father woke me early next morning. I rolled around in the bed, squinting painfully at the sunlight streaming through the window. My father wasn't sympathetic. 'You wanted an early start didn't you? I've already made breakfast. You can get Wayne.'

I rose and showered, then woke Wayne. He was no happier about it than me. 'What the fuck is this?'

'The West awaits.'

We were set to go by nine. We'd crammed a small drum of water into the boot, along with a spare fanbelt. My parents came out, wished us farewell and good luck. I slipped on my sunglasses, started the car. I was awake now and felt good. It was a bright, clear morning, and even my asthma and hayfever were behaving. They always did, away from Brisbane. We hit the road, headed north until the first crossroads, then turned west.

Wayne was studying the map, getting the folds all wrong. 'So how far're we going today?'

'What about Longreach?'

He looked it up. 'Is there anything interesting to see along the way?'

'What does the map say?'

'Wheat, sheep and cattle.'

'That sounds about right.'

He tossed the map aside. Lit a cigarette.

'There'll be landscape,' I said, 'Do you paint landscapes?'

'No.'

We drove. We were on the backroads, cutting across to join the main highway, and we had them to ourselves. It was all sorghum paddocks, patches of scrub, long brown grass by the roadside. The Kingswood stretched out, heavily laden but strong. It was running beautifully. From Dalby to Darwin, by road, it was around three thousand, three hundred kilometres. It was nothing.

The morning went well, speed steady at one hundred and ten. Wayne played with the AM dial, stared out the window. He read from time to time. Midday found us in Roma. Population 6000, according to the map. The map also said that Roma was the site of the trial of the infamous Captain Starlight. I didn't know anything much about Captain Starlight, other than that he was a bushranger of sorts. We pulled in at a road-house on the fringe of town, filled up with petrol and ordered food in the cafe.

It was my third or fourth visit to Roma. My one clear memory of the place was playing football there as a child— under-11 or under-12 rugby league. The field had been hard, devoid of any life except for patches of bindi-eyes and hundreds of bull ant nests. We lost the game, scratched and bitten, and came away feeling soft. The Roma boys were tough. Most of them played with their feet bare.

It was also as far west as I'd ever been. From now on it was all new territory. We watched the trucks come and go, finished eating, walked back out into the carpark. Wayne gazed up at the sky. It was hot, a dry, clean heat.

'What about a drink?' he said.

'Already? What about Longreach?'

'We can't do this thing sober.'

We found a pub in the main street, went in. There were only a couple of drinkers, old men, staring up at the TV. Ceiling fans pushed dry air around the bar. We took a table. Wayne bought the first round. We slugged it down and stared out the window. There wasn't a lot happening. A few cars parked in front of the shops, a few people out on the footpaths. Everyone moving slow.

We finished the first round. I bought the second. Then it was on to the third. Our pace was similar, with neither of us pressing it. That was good, our drinking habits were compatible. Time passed. Wayne played with his drink, shifted, stared around the bar. There was still just the two old men.

'I thought there'd be pig shooters,' he said.

'Pig shooters?'

'You know, pig shooters. I thought there were always pig shooters in pubs like this. Aren't there herds of feral pigs out here?'

'How much TV do you watch?'

'Why?'

We drank on. Four beers, five, six. On the seventh it was Wayne's turn at the bar. The barman took the order, looked Wayne over. 'Where you boys from?'

'Brisbane,' said Wayne.

'And where you headed?'

'Darwin.'

'Darwin eh. Hope you make it.'

'Why wouldn't we? We've got this far alright.'

The barman laughed. '*This* far? Right.'

Wayne came back.

'What's that guy's problem?' he asked.

I said nothing. Wayne didn't realise how much he stood out in the surroundings. That long body of his, the skin, the hair. Then there were the white shorts, the bright yellow singlet. He was from the city alright. It was different with me. I was solidly built, there was nothing unusual about my hair or my face. And I was dressed correctly. Black shorts and a long-sleeve King Gee work shirt, the sleeves rolled-up. It was my standard gear, even in Brisbane. I was still that much, at least, a country boy.

We finished the beers, decided it was time to go. We headed back to the car.

'Can I drive?' said Wayne.

I gave him the keys. He started up and we moved out of town. A few hundred yards along we pulled over. I watched while Wayne dug through his gear in the back seat. He came up with a large bag of marijuana.

'Did you bring any of this?' he asked.

'No.'

'It's okay. I've got three of these bags.'

He rolled a joint, lit it. We started up again. I stashed the bag in the back seat, then took drags when the joint came my way. I coughed a lot of it out again. I always coughed. Virgin lungs.

Wayne eased the Kingswood up to speed. It was getting towards mid-afternoon. I consulted the map. Mitchell was the next town, and after that some small place called Morven, where we'd turn and start heading north-west. I put the map down, stared out the window. The country was all reds and dull greens, scrub and ant-mounds. There wasn't much traffic. The odd car, a few semitrailers. Farm houses baked under the sky.

I remembered that we'd bought batteries for Wayne's

stereo at the roadhouse in Roma. I dug around on the back seat, found the batteries, the stereo, and a box of cassettes. I inserted the batteries, then inspected the tapes. They were all outside their cases, most of them battered and spotted with thumb prints in various colours of paint.

'I don't recognise anything here except for Neil Young,' I said.

'Put the Big Black tape on.'

I found it, slipped it in, pressed play. It was loud and harsh and full of bass. It seemed appropriate. I leaned back. The joint moved in, mixed with the alcohol. Time drifted by.

I thought about things, forgot them. I stared at the blur out the window. It was strange. The trees seemed to move in close, then swerve away. I blinked, sat up. It was Wayne. He was swinging the car back and forth across the road. I watched. He was crouched over the wheel, leaning with it as he turned. I decided he was ugly, almost hideously so. The angled elbows and knees, the sunburn, the tangled clumps of blond hair. He was *disgusting*.

Something flashed on the dashboard. It was the alternator light, blinking on and off. Then I saw the temperature gauge. It had swung right over to the red. I considered what that meant for a moment.

'Wayne,' I said, pointing.

He started, looked down. 'Oh.'

The car didn't slow. A few seconds passed.

I said, 'Don't you think you'd better stop.'

'Oh. Okay.'

He slowed, stopped, switched off the engine. I turned down the stereo. We listened to the hiss and splutter of the radiator boiling over.

'I have to admit,' I said, looking around, 'I did think we'd make it further than this.'

Wayne popped the hood and we climbed out to examine things. Water and steam were gushing out from under the radiator cap. The fanbelt was broken.

'Lucky we've got a spare one,' Wayne observed.

I found myself annoyed.

'Don't you ever look at the dashboard?'

'Sorry.'

'You didn't notice that the alternator light was on and that the temperature gauge was in the red?'

'How was I to know your car overheats.'

'It doesn't. How fast were you going anyway?'

'Not fast. I could barely even get up to a hundred. It drives very heavy.'

I thought, Heavy?

I said, 'What gear were you in?'

'It's an automatic.'

I went round to the driver's seat and looked in. Wayne hadn't put the shift in Park when he pulled up. It was still in the same gear he'd been driving in. It wasn't Drive or even Second. It was in Low.

'Have you *driven* an automatic before?'

He thought. 'I'm not sure. I drive my mother's car a lot, but it's a manual. Why?'

'You were going a hundred in first gear. Revving the absolute shit out of the engine. You're lucky it didn't explode.'

'No kidding.'

'Why didn't you notice?'

'Why didn't *you*. You're the machinery man.'

Why indeed?

'Well anyway,' I said, 'I bet that's why the fanbelt broke.'

'Is it hard to put on a new one?'

'Not if you've got a spanner.'

We went to the boot, unloaded everything, and searched

in the recesses. We found the spare fanbelt, and a spanner. We tried the spanner on the tension bolt. It was too small. The bolt wouldn't move. We tried stretching the fanbelt over the wheels anyway. It was too tight.

'That's one thing your father didn't think of,' said Wayne.

I threw the spanner away. 'I guess he assumed that even an *artist* would know how to drive.'

'What now?'

'What d'you think? We flag someone down.'

We waited. Wayne sat in the car, the stereo on again. Big Black didn't seem so impressive anymore. I sat on the hood, staring up and down the road. It was twenty minutes or so before a semitrailer appeared, coming towards us. A petrol tanker. I stood on the road and waved. It slowed and stopped, air brakes hissing. A thin face looked down from the cab.

'What's your problem?'

'Fanbelt. We need a spanner to put on the new one.'

He nodded. 'Got a set here somewhere.' He climbed down. He was small and wiry, dressed in shorts and a large black hat. Wayne and I stood there and watched while he changed the fanbelt. It was a two minute operation. No one spoke. When he was finished he repacked his spanners. 'There you go,' he said. He looked us over, Wayne mostly.

'You boys from Brisbane?'

'That's right.'

'Where you headed?'

'We're exploring the outback,' said Wayne.

Another long look. 'Hope you get there.' He headed back towards his truck.

'Thanks,' I said, after him.

Then he was in the cab, and pulling away.

'I don't think he liked us,' said Wayne.

'I don't think he cared.'

'Well isn't this the outback?'
'No.'
'Where the hell is it then?'
'I think I'll drive from here.'
'Fine.'
We refilled the radiator and climbed in. Wayne dialled
up the stereo. I put the car firmly in Drive, and we moved
on.

By nightfall we were four hundred ks further along,
approaching Longreach. Wayne was driving again. We'd
sobered up and straightened out completely over the hours.
We were very bored.

We eased into town and drove up and down the wide
main street, checking things out. Longreach, population
over three thousand, birthplace of Qantas, and Gateway
(so a community road sign said) to the Outback. I pointed
out the sign to Wayne. He nodded, said nothing. We drove
back to a motel we'd seen on the outskirts. At the check-in
desk we asked for a double room.

'You mean a twin,' said the woman.

'What's the difference?'

'It would be illegal for me to rent two males a double
room. Double rooms only have one double bed. *Twin* rooms
have *two* beds. You can have a twin room.'

'What if we were two women, and we asked for a double?'
said Wayne.

'That'd be no problem.'

'Tricky being gay in Queensland, isn't it.'

The woman gave us a dark look. 'I wouldn't know anything about that.'

We signed in and went to the room. Two single beds,
plain motel decor. Nothing to see. We shut the door and
drove back to the main street. We found a takeaway and
bought burgers and chips. Then it was to a pub across the

street. We sat in the bar, drinking beer. There were about a dozen other men there. They checked us out briefly, forgot us.

I began to feel better.

'So *are* you gay?' I asked Wayne. It seemed a reasonable question, despite the fact he'd been sleeping with Madelaine. Even I knew sex wasn't always a straightfoward thing.

He leaned forward. 'Do you think this is a good place to use the word gay? In this town? In this bar? Amongst all these pig shooters?'

'You really don't know anything about pig shooters do you.'

'I hear they're very rugged.'

We sat there and considered the bar. I remembered that there had, in fact, been an arrest of two men for homosexual behaviour in Longreach. It was a big case in the media. There was talk of the law being outdated and inhuman. The National Party Government wasn't so sure. Civil rights wasn't one of their strong points. And this was National Party territory.

Whatever our sexual orientations though, it didn't look as if anything would be happening with them that night. After a couple of beers we picked up a bottle of bourbon, some coke, and headed back to the motel. We sat on the beds, switched on the TV, and drank.

There was some tourist information beside the bed. I read through it and came across Captain Starlight again. In 1870 he and some compatriots had rustled a thousand head of cattle from the area. They'd herded them across thousands of unexplored kilometres, all the way to South Australia. It was considered such an impressive feat that even when captured and tried, no one wanted to convict him. He was a hero, a pioneer.

Australian history, I didn't know any of it. Wayne was

rolling a joint. We smoked it. The night dissolved. Just on eleven we heard a bus pull up outside and a hubbub of voices. I looked out the window. It was a tour bus unloading. Most of the passengers seemed old. Pensioner couples.

Wayne came to the window. 'Geriatrics,' he said. 'If there's one thing that makes you wanna die young, it's that. Knowing your future will be staring out the windows of a great big bus . . .'

He went back to the bourbon. I watched the old people. They all seemed happy. No doubt they had a tour guide, and no doubt they knew more about Captain Starlight than I did. I looked at the small window at the front of the bus that would say where it was headed. It said Darwin.

SIX

Next day we rose late and repacked the car. The bus, with its passengers, was already gone. I went to the office and payed the bill. It was a man behind the counter this time.

'Headed north?' he asked.

'Darwin.'

'Holiday?'

'Work.'

'Be back this way?'

'Not for six months or so.'

'Be worth stopping. The Stockman's Hall of Fame will be open by then. You must have seen it. That big shed they're building, on the way in.'

I nodded. There was indeed a big shed being built on the outskirts of town.

'It's a Bicentennial Project,' he added.

I nodded. 'Like Expo in Brisbane.'

'That's right. Me and the wife are going to that, too. Already got the season passes.'

I made for the door. Back at the car Wayne was in the passenger seat, studying the map.

'Which way now?' he said.

We looked. Mt Isa seemed the next obvious stop, seven hundred ks away. According to the map there were two ways to get there. One was the highway, which was the most direct. The other was a road that looped away southwards. It was longer, but something about it looked encouraging. A thin red line on the paper, compared to a big fat black one. We fuelled-up at a roadhouse, fed ourselves, and got on our way.

It was a hot, dry, cloudless day. It was our third in the car, and the Kingswood was beginning to attain a well-travelled air. Food wrappers, soft drink cans, newspapers. The ashtray was full. We followed the highway to Winton. Population 1300, said the map. Gateway to the Channel Country, and home of fossilised dinosaur footprints. We headed straight through. The scrub began to thin out, leaving wide patches of bare red sand. We came to the turn for the southward loop, and took it.

It was a secondary road. The bitumen narrowed to a single strip, rutted lanes of gravel on either side. A sign informed us the route was subject to flooding. I'd heard about the Channel Country. About muddy walls of water coming down from the northern wet, the Diamantina River running ten miles wide. We crossed through some gullies and creek beds, then the bed of Diamantina itself, but everything was bone dry. Eventually the country widened into an open, arid flat. The scrub failed completely. Stony ridges reared in the distance. Heat shimmered across the road and blazed through the windscreen.

I was impressed. It was as close a thing to a real desert as I'd ever seen. I looked out at the low clumps of brown grass, the red soil. There were no other cars. No houses. No trees. Just us and the Kingswood, under the sun, carving our way across the plain.

Finally we came to two sheer and naked hills. The road passed directly between them. I gazed up at the peaks. I slowed the car, stopped, killed the engine. I climbed out. I looked up on either side. It was silent and still, the sky above the hills a profound blue.

Wayne was still in the car. 'Why've we stopped?'

'I'm looking.'

Wayne got out, lit a cigarette, glanced around. I wandered away from the car.

'I think I might climb up,' I said.

Wayne studied the hills. 'Why?'

'Just to see.'

'What?'

'I dunno. We can't just drive straight through without looking at *anything*.'

'But there's nothing here.'

'That's the point.'

I headed off.

'Okay,' said Wayne, and followed.

We climbed. The hill on the right had the gentler slope, littered with broken rock. We scrambled upwards for five minutes, ten. I was already out of breath. Just below the peak we found a small cave. There were a few rags in it, and the area smelled of shit and piss.

Wayne looked in. 'What were you hoping for, cave paintings?'

We kept climbing. We came out on a rocky platform at the top. Wayne sat down and lit another cigarette. I puffed on my Ventolin, looked out across the land. Nothing. The air was hazy. It made the plain formless, just a wide blur to the horizons. I sat there and sweated. The stone beneath us was hot. There was no shade. I wasn't sure what I'd been hoping for, but this didn't seem worth the climb.

I looked back down into the pass, at my car parked

beside the road, a small blob of yellow amidst all the red. It was further away than I'd thought. Wayne nodded eastwards.

'Car.'

I followed his eyes. A vehicle was coming along the way we had, windscreen glinting. We watched it approach. It was the first we'd seen since leaving the highway. It was an old utility, with iron framework on the back and a spotlight on the roof.

'Pig shooters?' asked Wayne.

I didn't answer. The utility approached my car, slowed and pulled up behind it. Nothing happened. Then both doors swung open and two figures climbed out. Men. Hats, black jeans. The two of them walked around my car. One of them bent and peered in the window. I noticed what looked like rifles, racked up on the frame of the utility. Finally one of them opened the passenger door, sat inside.

'Didn't you lock it?' I asked Wayne.

'I thought you weren't supposed to do that in the country. Everyone's so trustworthy.'

'Jesus.'

The other man was now climbing in the driver's side. I thought about all the things they could simply take, if they wanted to. Then I remembered that you didn't even need a key to turn the ignition. The car was anyone's. What would happen if they took it? There might not be any other cars for days. I could see the newspapers, the photos of the bodies. 'Albino artist and unpublished writer found dead in desert.'

Both men got out, shut the doors. Then they moved away from the car, walked to the other side of the road. They seemed to be looking up our way.

'Think they can see us?' Wayne asked.

'Who knows.'

We didn't move.

They walked back to their own vehicle. A moment later we heard the engine start up, and they were on their way. We clambered down, got to the car, looked inside. Nothing was missing. Nothing seemed to have even been touched.

I started up. I felt like a fool. Not so much for worrying about having my car stolen, but for stopping and climbing the hill in the first place. It was unnecessary. A ten minute walk away from the road—what was I expecting? To master the outback? I wasn't Captain Starlight. I put the Kingswood in gear, left the hills behind.

We arrived at a place called Middleton. The map gave no information about it at all. It consisted of a small pub by the roadside, a windmill, and nothing else. We pulled in. I was in a low mood. It was time for drinking. That, at least, I knew how to do.

Inside, the place was just as small as it looked from the outside. It was empty. We sat at the short counter, looked around. The room was crammed with western paraphernalia—cattle horns and skulls, battered broad-brimmed hats, old road signs. The walls were painted white, but covered with signatures, short poems, witticisms, stickers and impromptu works of art. It all seemed fairly deliberate. I had a feeling I'd seen photos of the room, or one like it, in old magazine features.

A woman emerged from a back room. She suited the bar. Old. Small. Wearing a faded floral dress.

'Morning boys,' she said.

We ordered pots of beer.

'Sorry. No beer on tap. Stubbies do?'

They did. We cracked them open and drank. We answered questions about where we'd come from and where we were going.

'Why'd you pick this way?' she asked me.

'We thought it might be a better drive.'

'It's longer, that's all I know. So what'll you be doing in Darwin?'

'We've got a job on a weather station up there.'

'The weather? You do that in Brisbane too do you?'

'Not exactly.'

Wayne said, 'I'm a painter, he's a writer.'

The woman fixed on me. 'A writer! I'm a writer too.'

'Really?'

'Nothing else to do around here. I've almost finished my first novel.'

'What's it about?'

'It's historical. You wouldn't believe some of the things that have happened out here. You know anything about it?'

'No, not much.'

'I should show you the first chapter, see what you think.'

'I'm not really a writer. I mean, I've never had anything published.'

'What do you write.'

'So far, horror stories.'

'Oh. I don't read that sort of thing.'

'Fair enough.'

We sat there with the beer for a while. Then she turned to Wayne. 'Maybe you wanna paint something on the walls. Everyone else does.'

Wayne glanced around.

'They look pretty full already.'

Silence again. We finished the beers and ordered two more. She went to the back door. 'Charlie,' she called, 'Get these boys two beers. I'm gonna have my lie down.'

She disappeared. Charlie came through. He looked about my age, with a wide, tanned face and lank, black hair. He got us our stubbies, then leaned on the bar and watched us drink them. We went through the source/destination routine.

'Had a look at your Kingswood,' he said at the end of it.

'Yeah?'

'I used to have one like it. What's it done?'

'Hundred and ninety thousand.'

'Original engine?'

'No. Second.'

'What'd you pay for the new engine?'

'It wasn't new. It was reconditioned. Eight hundred, fitting included.'

'Ripped off. I could've got you one for two hundred and fitted it for another fifty. Where was the mechanic. In Brisbane?'

'Dalby.'

'You were still ripped off.'

'I guess so. I don't know anything about cars.'

'How's the transmission?'

'Fine, as far as I know.'

'Those Holden three-speeds last forever.'

'That's encouraging.'

He looked at me. Laughed. We drank on.

'Anyone else ever come in here?' Wayne asked.

'Plenty. You hang about and see what it's like tonight. Friday nights the place is packed.'

'Where do they come from?'

'Around.'

Wayne didn't sound convinced. 'You stay here all the time?'

'I go to Winton every few days. Or to Isa. I've even been to Brisbane a couple of times. Shitty hole. But I can't leave the place too long. The old girl's mad as a hatter.'

'She really writing a novel?'

He was suddenly serious. 'Yeah, she's writing a novel.'

We ordered more beer. The conversation limped on. Charlie started on shots of rum to keep us company. The old woman never reappeared. Finally there was the sound of a truck pulling up outside. Wayne and I purchased a six-pack takeaway and departed just as the driver was coming in. Maybe it was the beginning of the Friday rush.

Back out in the car Wayne took the driver's seat, opened one of the beers and rolled himself a joint. We smoked it, staring out at nothing. Heat rolled down from the sky.

'Why doesn't anyone like us?' Wayne asked after a time.

'We know nothing about cars.'

'What's there to know about cars?'

I looked at him. He shrugged, started up. The road slid away beneath us.

It was a long, hazy stretch. I was stoned and drunk again. The stereo was dialled up loud. Neil Young. Sonic Youth. Wayne drove fast. Every time I glanced at the speedo it hovered between one thirty and one forty. At least nothing was overheating. The road was mostly straight. Occasionally it switched from bitumen to loose gravel. Wayne didn't appear to notice the difference. He maintained speed. The car fishtailed from time to time, and a small note of fear would sound somewhere inside me, then fade away.

Another small pub passed by, then Boulia, population 300. It was sunset, suddenly. We'd spent too long at the Middleton pub. I took over the driving and we swung north again. Night fell. We were into hill country now. The beer was all gone. I was sobering up, feeling tired. Two hours came and went. Then a glow of lights became visible on the horizon. It increased, cast red shadows across the hills. Eventually we could catch glimpses of some industrial structure, vast and lit with orange. A mine, a smelter, who knew. The road passed it by. Gradually another glow grew on the horizon. Towers emerged, stacks, plumes of steam. Then streetlights.

We entered Mount Isa. I didn't bother getting details from the map. It was a famous town. Kids were taught about it in schools. Silver, zinc, lead. Shafts kilometres deep. We followed the main road in, gazed up at the mine complex itself. It was big, a pile of black steel and spotlights, looming over the city. Men were walking up to its gates. King Gee shirts and shorts, boots. Workers. *Miners.* Twenty-four hour operations, deep underground. We passed it all by. Down the highway we found a cheap motel and checked in.

Across the road was a pub and a Chinese takeaway. We went over and ordered food, then stood out on the footpath, surveying Friday night. A few men were hanging around outside the public bar, drinking beer. People came and went from a video store. Steady traffic flowed along the highway. Not much else. With the mine hidden from view, it felt like suburban Brisbane. On a particularly dry, hot night.

'Should we go out?' I asked.

'We should,' said Wayne, 'But I don't think I could be bothered.'

I agreed. We collected our Chinese, bought another six-pack, then went to our room. We sat on the beds and ate. We watched TV. From time to time there came yells from the street, and the sound of loud fast cars. I forced a beer down, thought about another, rejected it.

'I didn't think it'd be like this,' said Wayne.

'I know what you mean.'

'It'd be different if we knew someone here.'

We didn't. I went and showered. When I came out Wayne was staring out the window. 'Look at this,' he said.

In the car park was a bus, unloading old people. The sign at the front said Darwin.

'It can't be,' I said.

'Looks like it.'

It did. It was the same one. I checked the time. Almost eleven.

Wayne was shaking his head. 'What the hell have they been doing? Where've they been all day? They left Longreach long before we did.'

The old folk were laughing, collecting bags from the luggage compartments. The driver moved among them, slapping backs.

'They're on a tour,' I said, 'They've probably been stopping everywhere along the way. Seeing the sights.'

'I guess,' said Wayne.

I left the window, looked at the room. I cleared the remains of the Chinese away from the bed, threw the empty stubbie into the bin, and climbed under the sheet. I was wearing shorts. So was Wayne. No naked bodies for either of us. Shy boys.

I tried to sleep. Wayne rolled and grunted. The room was hot. Periodically there came more yells from the street. And from time to time the long squeals of burning rubber.

SEVEN

Next morning Wayne took the first shift at the wheel. There was a certain excitement to the first shift. The morning air, the fresh car, the unknown road ahead. It never lasted long. We got out of the Mount Isa hills and back onto the flatlands. Patches of scrub. Dust. Heat. We arrived at Camooweal. A hundred people or so, said the map. We refuelled and sat for a moment, drinking Coke. There was just the one street. The pub was open and people lounged on the verandah. One car passed through heading west, one car passed through heading east. Nothing else moved. Camooweal, I thought.

We stayed about ten minutes, then got back on the road. Shortly afterwards we passed a sign that informed us we had just crossed from Queensland into the Northern Territory.

A new state. We drove on. The quality of the road improved, but otherwise the country was as drab and empty as it had been in Queensland. No houses, no sheds, no cars. Only the sun, red soil, dead grass. An hour went by. We saw nothing, said nothing. I grew drowsy. Yawned. I noticed a dog, sitting by the roadside.

We went straight past it. The dog turned its head, watched us steadily. It was a cattle dog. It seemed very calm. Wise. It knew things about us. Where we were going, what would happen when we got there. And what it knew wasn't good. I sat up suddenly. I'd been falling alseep. A dog? I turned, looked back. It was still there. Just sitting by the road. Dwindling. Still watching us. There appeared to be nothing and no one that it could've been attached to. Not even a fence or a windmill.

'Did you see that?' I said.

'Yes,' said Wayne.

We drove on, silent. Something was strange. I couldn't explain it. The dog had affected us. It was a sentinel. A warning.

'We should go back,' Wayne said, 'See if it's alright.'

'Do you think it'd still be there?'

He thought. 'No.'

'Do you think it was a real dog?'

'No.'

We drove on.

It was a long straight road to Tennant Creek, and we did it sober and straight. There was nothing along the entire stretch but one road-house at roughly the halfway point. Tennant Creek itself arrived just on dusk. Population 3000, once a station on the famous Darwin to Adelaide telegraph line. The map knew everything. We cruised along the main street, looking at motels and selecting the cheapest. It wasn't that cheap, but it had a restaurant attached. We checked in, dumped our gear in the room, then went to eat.

It was a nicely set-up place. It even had a cocktail lounge. We were the only customers. We lounged and sipped cocktails. Martinis. Margaritas. We didn't know much about cocktails. We moved to a table. A husband and wife team were serving us, the wife cooking, the husband waiting and mixing the drinks. It emerged that they were the new owners, up from Adelaide and in possession of the motel for all of three weeks.

'We're hoping things will pick up,' the husband told us.

'This is quiet?' I asked.

'It's the wrong time of year. Tourist season is a couple of months away yet. No one comes through in summer. It's too hot down here, and too wet up in Darwin.'

'You don't have a bus-load of old people booked in here tonight do you?'

'No. Why?'

'No reason.'

We ate a fine dinner, steak, and drank with the owners for a time. They seemed decent people, but apprehensive. They'd invested their lives in the motel. Their dream. The cocktail lounge had been their idea. To date, not a single local had used it.

'So what's happening in town,' Wayne asked, 'It's Saturday night, after all.'

'There're the pubs,' said the wife, 'Two of them have discos.'

'Discos? Do you really mean discos?'

'They don't call them that anymore, do they? But you can hardly call them nightclubs.'

'I think I heard some act from Brisbane was playing,' the husband said, 'In one of them.'

It was decided. Wayne and I finished our drinks and went back to the room. We showered and dressed. I was in jeans and a white long-sleeve shirt, black shoes. Wayne was in loose black slacks and a cream silk shirt. I looked plain, he looked very impressive indeed. It was the silk shirt.

'What about that leather jacket of yours,' he said, looking me over.

'This is hardly the time or the place.'

'Then why'd you bring it?'

'I don't know.'

We left the motel and walked down the main street. A group of kids were hanging around outside a takeaway. They didn't share my opinion of Wayne. They hooted and laughed as we went by. 'What the fuck *is* that?'

Wayne ignored them. He knew he was looking smooth. We passed on. The first pub on the left seemed to be the one we'd been told about. A blackboard by the door said 'Hawaiian Night! Live From Brisbane! Danny Ray!' Behind the sign a flight of stairs led upwards. We headed in. At the top a man demanded a two dollar cover charge. We paid and passed through. It was about nine-thirty.

I looked around. They'd spared no expense on the Hawaiian theme. There were cardboard cut-out palm trees positioned around the room. And in one corner, behind the small stage, there was a painted beach scene with women in grass skirts and bikini tops. On the stage itself was a DJ's turntable and two large speakers. In front of the turntable was a sign that said 'Danny Ray. Who *is* he?!'

We were the only ones there. We got to the bar and ordered bourbons.

'You're early,' the barman said.

'Yeah?'

'Wait till after ten. That's when the other bars close. Things'll pick up.'

We selected a table and sat down to wait.

'Wild,' said Wayne.

I shrugged. I rarely went to nightclubs in Brisbane, mainstream or alternative, so it seemed pointless to cast judgement on this one. We drank, leaning back in our chairs. The PA was playing standard top-forty stuff, a little out of date and not very loud. I watched the sign that said 'Danny Ray. Who *is* he?!'

I found I was depressed. And bored. It wasn't enough, after all the driving, sitting there in a bland nightclub waiting for the DJ. In three days the only memorable thing we'd seen was a dog. I didn't even know why it was memorable. It didn't mean anything, dogs were everywhere. Surely life on the road was supposed to be something more.

We sat there and drank, talking about nothing. I was beginning to get drunk. When I finally looked around I saw that the room had filled a little. The crowd was in. I counted seven people. Five men, sitting in two separate groups. And two women, sitting together. The men appeared to be locals, judging by the moleskins and western shirts and boots. From time to time they checked out the two women. The women could have been from anywhere. They talked and drank amongst themselves. From time to time they looked at Wayne and me.

Then the background music cut out and there was a pause. One of the western boys laughed, sharp and loud. The lights on the stage went up. I looked at the sign to remind myself. It still said 'Danny Ray. Who *is* he?!' Then he hit the stage. He was short, dressed in white, and bursting with energy. He bounced in behind the console and said 'Hello Tennant Creek!'

The western boys yelled back. It sounded like abuse. Wayne and I, the city boys, just sat there. We had nothing to say.

Danny Ray was peering out, assessing the crowd. 'I've been touring the West,' he said, 'And the West *rocks!*'

No one said anything. The silence was ominous. We all knew who he was now, and we knew we'd paid two dollars to see him. Live. From Brisbane. He started on his songs. It was standard top-forty. Louder than the PA, a little more contemporary, but that was about all. No one was dancing. Eventually Wayne and I turned back to each other.

'There must be something else,' I said. 'Let's get out of here.'

Wayne nodded. We headed downstairs. On the way we got ourselves stamped on the wrist by the doorman. Out on the street Tennant Creek was quiet. We walked down to the next pub. It was closed. An old drunk was wandering around outside it. He didn't notice us. The next hotel was a little further down. We looked in. It was packed. There were pool tables and a tiled floor and tall bar stools. The music here was country and everyone looked local. There were yells, laughter, dancing.

Wayne and I eyed each other, our clothes. There was no point in going in. It was their town and their night, not ours. We turned and headed back. Up the stairs to Danny Ray, our fellow Brisbanite.

He was still going. Spinning songs and trying to buck enthusiasm in between. The crowd had swelled to about a dozen in our absence. Wayne and I found our old table and set to drinking. Nothing else was going to happen for us. I descended into it, became very drunk.

At some stage, much later, the two women we'd seen before came over and sat at our table. I watched while Wayne talked to them. I couldn't hear anything over the music. Wayne smiled and laughed. I was dimly surprised. I barely recognised him. He didn't seem drunk. He seemed charming. Now and then the women would look at me. They asked me questions. I answered without any interest in what I was saying. They annoyed me.

Then the two women and Wayne were up dancing. They were the only ones on the floor. Danny Ray yelled at them, incomprehensibly. I stared. The women danced well. So did Wayne. His shirt was on fire under the strobe. It all seemed so easy. And beautiful. And horrible. I couldn't dance, had never been able to.

Then they vanished. I looked around, couldn't see them. It was just me, sitting at the table, stubbornly forcing the bourbon down. Feeling stubborn and slightly bitter, all round. I studied Danny Ray, up behind his turntable, and decided I hated him. What was he even doing there? What was I? Finally I stood up and left. I thrust my stamped wrist at the doorman on the way out, lurched into the street. It was dark. Blurred. I was too drunk. There were groups of people hanging about on the footpaths. More yells. More laughter. I swayed back towards home. On the way I passed another motel, and in the car park was the bus with the Darwin sign.

'Bastards,' I said to it.

I found our own motel and our room and went in. I switched on the TV. Nothing there either. Then I had an idea. I hunted through Wayne's luggage until I found one of his bags of pot. I rolled a joint, very slowly, very carefully, and very badly. I lit up what I had and smoked it. I coughed and lay back and let it move in. The room spun. My stomach spun. I felt ill, and then very ill.

I stumbled into the bathroom. I saw the shower and decided it might help. I undressed and climbed in, turned the water on hot and heavy. It didn't help. I vomited. Gushes of bourbon and thin strands of steak. I pushed the solid bits down the drain, then leaned against the wall, breathing hard. I vomited again, bile. I lay on the cubicle floor, panting, until the worst of it passed. It passed slowly. Finally I crawled out. I towelled off, moved back into the room.

It was still empty. I thought about Wayne and despised whatever he was doing. I found my bed. Single mattress. Cold, stiff motel sheets. I got in, switched off the light and listened. There was no sound at all. I waited for Wayne to come home.

EIGHT

The hangover and the asthma woke me. It was daylight. I lay still for a moment. The air wheezed along my throat. It was bad. I'd forgotten to take any of the asthma drugs the night before, and the smoking wouldn't have helped. I sat up. The coughing began. It always sounded terrible, the coughing, but it was a good sign. It meant the air was getting through and the phlegm was on the rise. What I truly feared was the death rattle, the spasm in the chest that locked everything down for good.

I reached for the Ventolin, sucked in the gas. I looked around. Hotel room. Tennant Creek. Wayne sleeping in the other bed. I sat there until the crisis passed. Then I got up, pissed into the bowl, and stood under the shower. Things got no worse. I climbed out, towelled off. I thought about cleaning my teeth and decided against it. I went back out into the room.

Wayne was awake. He was slumped on the end of the bed, watching TV and smoking a cigarette. He didn't look any healthier than I was. His skin was patched red, his eyes swollen into a squint. Maybe he was allergic too, in some way. He wasn't taking in much of the nicotine.

'Ready to move,' I said.

He slumped even further. 'God. This is endless.'

I started dressing. Wayne moved off to his own recovery in the shower. By the time he returned I was sitting on the bed, the morning glow gone. I needed painkillers.

'Where the fuck is Darwin anyway?' he said.

'Somewhere up there.'

'Do we have to go today? I don't feel up to driving.'

'You really wanna spend another day here?'

He thought. 'Guess not.'

I left him to it and took my gear out to the car. It was another bright, utterly clear day, already hot. The Kingswood sat there, streaked with dust. A journeyed car. You had to hand it to the Holden designers. The more shit you covered a Kingswood with, the better it looked.

I took the map from the front seat and studied it. Darwin was up there alright, at the end of a long, very long, straight road. We wouldn't make it. Not today. Which left only Katherine, two-thirds of the way. I went back in to Wayne and explained the proposal. We would still reach Darwin by Monday.

'Fine,' he said.

'So what exactly is the plan, once we're in Darwin?'

'We call the guy at the Conservation Commission. He'll tell us what to do.'

'I thought it was the Met. Bureau.'

Wayne shrugged. 'Dad's friend is in the Northern Territory Conservation Commission. He's the one we go to first.'

'Is he expecting us?'

'He should be.'

By a little after ten we were back in the car, striking northwards. It was more of the same. Scrub, dirt, dust.

Whatever natural wonders brought all the tourists out this way, none of them were visible from the highway. We sat and watched the white lines—when there were white lines—sliding away under the bonnet. Wayne was very quiet. I waited, brooding.

Finally I said, 'So where'd you end up last night?'

He looked across at me. 'Nowhere. Just back at the hotel.'

'But where'd you and the women go? I was sitting by myself for hours, there in the pub.'

'Oh. That. We went outside for a smoke. One of them had a few joints with her.' He thought. 'That was Sarah, I think.'

'It was a long smoke.'

'I don't really remember. We would've asked you, but you were just sitting there getting pissed off at everyone. You were gone when we got back.'

I sorted through the memories of the nightclub, the table, the women. 'I wasn't in the best of moods.'

'No. Sarah and Kate thought you were a bit of a dickhead.'

'I didn't think I was that bad.' I considered the scenery. Then, after a while, 'So what were they like?'

'Oh . . . fine. They're backpackers. From Adelaide. They've been in Darwin for a few weeks, they're on their way back.'

'How long did you stay at the Hawaiian Room?'

'Till it closed. You had a smoke last night yourself, I noticed.'

'It seemed the only hope.'

'What'd you do with it?'

'Threw up several times.'

He laughed. 'You've really gotta take up smoking tobacco. It's the only way to get your system attuned.' He pulled out a Winfield Blue and lit up. The smoke blew across. I'd always liked the smell of burning tobacco. I liked the look of the whole thing. The drawing out of the cigarette, the cupping of the hands, the flick of the lighter, the first drag, then the easy drift of the hand away from the face . . .

Who was I kidding.

'Why?' said Wayne, 'Did you think I was back at their room fucking one of them?'

'Maybe both of them.' It was true. Maybe I was sick. I always had to assume sex was involved. I didn't even know why I cared. Jealousy. It was a cruel and pointless use of the imagination.

Wayne was offhand. 'Well, I suppose, if they'd offered. But they were just backpackers. It wasn't really on my mind.'

I said nothing. It was on mine.

We crawled along. Every two hours or so there were small settlements by the road. They earned no descriptions on the map. Generally they weren't much more than a road-house, bar attached, and maybe a motel. Sometimes there was a small shantytown behind. I was surprised by the towns—the run-down shacks, the junk littered around, the people, mostly black, sitting in the shade. They were unlike anything I'd ever seen. They came and went at speed, but they left an impression of something. I wasn't sure exactly what.

The afternoon lengthened. We traded stints at the wheel, drank water and persevered. We avoided the bars at the roadhouses. Katherine presented itself around sunset. It was just in time. The driving and the hangover had taken their toll. I needed a bed, and airconditioning, and sleep. We did the usual tour of the town, looking for the cheapest motel. Apparently the Sunday night session at the pubs had just finished. There seemed to be a lot of drinkers pouring out onto the footpaths. One man lay passed out on the street. We looped our way around him.

We found a motel. It was a budget affair, off the highway, twenty-seven dollars a room. For that we got two bad beds, a tiny TV and a ceiling fan. We went out again and a found a pizza place. Then it was back to the motel. I lay on the bed. The mood was low, it was Sunday evening. Maybe Katherine just *seemed* worse than anywhere else.

I thought about the lighthouse. It was close now. Next day we'd be in Darwin and Wayne would make his phone call. Things would start happening. Lying there in the second-rate motel room it all seemed depressing and unlikely. I thought about my finances. I had roughly one hundred dollars left. Wayne, as far as I know, was even worse off. It was nowhere near enough to get ourselves and the car back to Brisbane. Petrol costs alone, so far, were standing at over three hundred.

Wayne came out of the shower, a towel around his waist. I was stuck with him now, whether I liked it or not. 'Look at this body,' he said, 'It's ruined.'

I looked. He was right, all the sun of the last few days was killing him. His arms and legs and face, everything was burnt.

'It gets worse.' He opened the towel, turned around for me. Where his shorts and singlet had been was pure white, the rest was deep red. It was painful to look at, grotesque. Even his pubic hair was almost white, and his prick was whitest of all, hanging down smooth and pale. 'I couldn't have gone to bed with those women last night. They would've been sick when they saw this.'

He stood there, the towel held out behind him like wings.

'*Are* you gay?' I asked. I was serious this time.

He thought, wrapped the towel around his waist, sat on his bed. 'Madelaine told me *you'd* fucked men.'

'Ah.'

'Well?'

I thought. It was no secret anyway. 'Just the once,' I said. 'It was a couple of years ago.'

'Why only the once?'

'I dunno. It was with this friend. It got awkward.'

'So tell me.'

'The details aren't important.'

'Of course they are.'

I lay back on the bed, stared at the ceiling. There was no reason not to tell him. *He* was stuck with *me*, too. I said, 'I didn't know he was gay at first. Then he told me, and wanted to know if I was interested. I didn't think I was. We kissed one night, when we were drunk. But that was about it for a while.'

'And then?'

'Then another night we'd been drinking all day at his place. He'd gone to bed and I was sitting on the floor with a cask of wine. And it hit me. I wanted to fuck him.'

It was still a strange memory. It'd come from nowhere, a desperate blast. I'd sat there on the floor, glass in hand, shaking with it. Not knowing what to do. It'd never happened before. Suddenly I wanted a prick. Someone *else's* prick, clashing with mine. Both of them erect. Like swords, duelling. It was ridiculous. And compelling. It wouldn't go away.

'So what'd you do?'

'I got up, went to his room and woke him. He said okay and I climbed in.'

'And was it good?'

'I dunno. We were both very drunk. Not that good maybe.'

It *was* good, for me at least. Not so much for him. We rolled around and kissed. He had a lean, hairless body and

I could feel his prick aginst mine. I broke off kissing, went down for it. It was small and half erect and I wanted it, more than I'd ever wanted a piece of anyone's body before. I wanted to *swallow* it. So I sucked and pumped, but it grew no larger, no harder. Maybe he was too drunk, maybe I was just no better with penises than clitorises. After a while I gave up and he started on me, first with his mouth, then with his hands. *He* knew what he was doing. I writhed about the bed and came into his fingers, loving it.

'Anal sex?' Wayne asked.

'No.'

'And it was just that once?'

'I woke up next day and I was horrified. I got out of there. I couldn't face him for days. And certainly not for sex.'

Wayne shrugged. 'I wouldn't worry. Most gays are used to that sort of stuff from straight men.'

'He was disgusted.'

And he had a right to be. I should've had more style. It was nothing to panic about. It was just *sex*. I wasn't even sure of what I felt about men anymore. I hadn't met one since that I was remotely attracted to, but I still had visions. Pricks. Strong bodies, pitted against each other. I masturbated over them sometimes, instead of women. I didn't know what it meant. I didn't think I could ever do it again.

'So what about you?' I asked Wayne.

'You worried are you, about the two of us alone for the next six months?'

'Just curious.'

'Well God knows, there won't be any *other* sex happening. Not at a lighthouse. But no. Not really. I prefer women.'

'You've slept with men though.'

'Sure. Often enough. More than you anyway. You haven't fucked anyone much, have you?'

It was that obvious, then. 'No.'

'That's what Madelaine said. She said you're too tense about it. Male or female. You should just relax. Enjoy it.'

I didn't want to hear this. I had problems, I knew that. Hang-ups about everything.

We switched the lights off, went to bed. I lay there. It was hot. Sleep wouldn't come. Orange light filtered through the windows from the street. The sound of cars. The ceiling fan. I thought about things. About Wayne. About his ease with men, women, fucking. Why didn't I have it?

I thought about his body, red and white, like the American flag. There was no appeal there. I imagined it fucking—fucking Madelaine. In her huge bed, both of them drunk, naked, laughing. Madelaine short and round and big-breasted. They looked appalling together. I thought about her and me. I remembered her hands, her legs, her cunt. How they'd felt. How they'd smelled. Had I enjoyed it at all? Had she? I didn't know. And no matter how I pictured it, Wayne was still there. Ugly and thin. Fucking her better than I ever had.

NINE

Next day it was three hours of final tedium on the road, then it was all over. Darwin. We sailed down a long strip of industrial sites and takeaway joints, glorying at it. Capital of the Northern Territory and bombing target for the World War Two Japanese airforce. Population variable, depending on the weather. We cruised the main streets, inspecting things. Neither of us possessed much knowledge about the place, other than that it had mostly vanished in 1974. If we'd expected any signs of the cyclone to remain, there weren't any. Still, we'd arrived, and that was something.

The town itself seemed green and open. There were lots of thick, leafy trees and loudly flowering plants. Maybe they were orchids. We were in the tropics now, after all. Eventually we found the tourist section. It was a street full of backpacker dorms and cheap motels. We booked a twenty dollar room. Two beds, no TV, communal showers. Cash was low. Wayne went off and made his phone call in the foyer. I lay on the bed and waited. It was hot and it was humid, and it felt good not to be moving. Wayne came back.

'He wants to see us this afternoon,' he said, 'Three o'clock.'

'What's his name?'

'Terry Gallagher.'

'And what is he exactly?'

'Some boss in the Conservation Commission. They look after all the national parks up here, and the weather station's in a national park. He said he thought we were getting here a week ago.'

'You said it was this week.'

'That's what I thought.'

'Did you *know*?'

'What does it matter?'

'Jesus, Wayne.'

It was a promising start.

For lunch we wandered into the centre of town. There was a mall. Just off that we found a Kentucky Fried. I indulged. Wayne watched me eat. He was in a McDonald's mood. We asked the Kentucky Fried girl where we might find one. She said that Darwin had no McDonald's. Wayne and I looked at each other. There was nothing to say. Wayne ordered nuggets.

We walked around some more. It was a frontier town alright. Tourists were everywhere. The mall thronged with tanned young bodies, money-belts around their waists. There were European accents, Asian accents. Travel agents offering tours of Kakadu and the Kimberly. Cut-price air fares to Bali. And this was in the off-season.

We went down to the beach. There was no surf. Nor was there anyone swimming. Warning signs mentioned marine stingers, sharks, and crocodiles. It was hard to take the crocodile threat all that seriously, even if the Territory was famous for them. In a swamp, in a creek, certainly—but a city beach? Perhaps that was why tourists like us died so often. It didn't matter. We weren't there to look at the beach. It was the ocean we wanted.

We looked out across it, north and west. There were huge white rain clouds piled on the horizon. I'd forgotten exactly which body of water it was. Perhaps the Timor Sea. Or the Arafura. Either way we weren't looking east and it wasn't the Pacific, and that was the important thing. We'd travelled somewhere. There was a feel about Darwin. In the air. It was a weight, a heat and humidity that was nothing like Brisbane. Coming down from Asia. The breath of the monsoon.

On the other hand it wasn't southern Chile, or the remotest Russian Tiaga, or the upper reaches of the Zaire River. Australia was only so big, and we were still in it. We got sick of looking at the ocean and the clouds. We went back to the hostel. At two-thirty we drove out to the offices of the Northern Territory Conservation Commission, to see about our jobs.

Wayne's connection, Terry Gallagher, turned out to be the Managing Director of the entire Commission. We were ushered into his office at about three-thirty, after sitting in the waiting room, staring at framed photographs of Territory scenery. Terry was a big, solid, balding man. He was dressed in shorts, shirt, long socks and a tie. He was drinking a can of Victoria Bitter beer. 'Sorry,' he said, indicating the beer, 'I was just having a coffee break.'

I took that as a positive sign. We sat down, he sat down. 'So you finally made it,' he said to Wayne.

Wayne nodded, didn't speak. He was looking uncomfortable. His hand was on his chin, fingers playing with his lip.

'How's your father?'

'Alright.'

'Yeah, he sounded fine when we cooked this thing up.

Like I said though, you were supposed to be here a week ago.'

'I didn't realise.'

'Mmm.' He looked at me. 'And who are you exactly?'

'Gordon Buchanan. Wayne said he needed someone to work with him. At the weather station.'

'Oh. It's only a one-man job though, you know that don't you?'

'No.' I looked at Wayne. 'At least *I* didn't.'

Wayne looked back. 'Well, neither did I.'

We sat there. Terry sipped on his beer.

'Of course,' he said, 'The two of you can go out there if you want. Split the work. It's supposed to be a bitch to do alone anyway. But there's only the one pay cheque.'

I looked at Wayne again. He showed no signs of adding anything. I said, 'How much money is it?'

'You'd have to ask the Bureau of Meteorology. They pay you. We just send you over. It's a bit of a grey area, just who's in charge of the whole thing. It's their weather station, you see, but it's in our park.' He got up and called someone from an outer office. A young man came in, wearing a brown ranger uniform.

Terry pointed to Wayne and I. 'Tom, these are the guys going across to Cape Don. Can we organise them a flight?'

'Sure. When?'

Terry meditated a moment. Then he picked up the phone and dialled. He talked for a while, wrote some things down, then hung up. He turned to Wayne. 'That was the Met. Bureau. They want to see you tomorrow. Give you the training for the weather station. So I suppose you can go the day after.'

Wayne nodded. Sat. Said nothing.

I gave up on him. I said, 'Ah . . . where exactly are we going?'

'Hasn't anyone told you?'

'Only that it's a lighthouse somewhere.'

'Jesus. Well, you're going to Cape Don. It's a few hundred ks northeast of here, on the tip of the Cobourg Peninsula.' He turned to a map that hung on the wall behind him. It showed the Northern Territory. He pointed to a small knob of land on the very tip of the state. 'There. The lighthouse marks the channel between the mainland and Melville Island.'

'And what else is there, exactly?'

'Not much. There's no road to it or anything, but there's an airstrip nearby. The lighthouse is there of course. And the weather station. A few old houses that used to belong to the lighthouse keepers, one of which'll be yours. We have a couple of rangers stationed there. Some boats. A two-way radio—there's no phone. That's about it.'

He paused. Sighed.

'To tell the truth the whole thing's fucked up. The Met. Bureau's pissed off because they have no say in who gets sent over there, and so are the traditional owners. I don't suppose you know. The park is called the Gurig National Park. It takes up the whole Cobourg Peninsula. We manage it in partnership with the Aboriginal owners. Half of it, with their permission, is open to very limited tourism. The other half, the half where you're going, isn't. They don't mind us having a ranger or two there, but they're not so keen on you weather observers.'

Wayne laughed. 'They haven't even met us yet.'

'What I mean,' Terry said evenly, 'is that they've been making noises about getting their own people to run the weather station. So they're not too pleased that we gave it to you without asking them first. But that was a favour to your father. I don't suppose you've ever worked with Aborigines?'

Wayne shook his head. I shook mine.

'Well, it's too late now. Tom, get the flight organised for Wednesday. Is there anything else we have to tell them?'

Tom said, 'You'll have to open an account at the Nightcliff supermarket. We have a deal there. Supplies get flown out to Cape Don once a week, on Fridays. You radio your weekly order to the supermarket, then they pack it up and get it to the plane. Take shitloads of insect repellent. The settlement is right up by the mangroves, and the sandflies will eat you alive. Have you got a cheque account, or credit cards?'

Again, we shook our heads.

'Better sort something out then. The supermarket usually wants monthly payments, and you can hardly get cash out there.' He smiled at us, a little pitying. 'And most important of all, don't forget to take alarm clocks.'

'Alarm clocks?'

'You'll see. And take wind-up ones, not electric. There's power out there, but the generators aren't the most reliable. That's about all I can think of.'

'Thanks Tom,' said Terry, 'Get on to that flight.'

'Sure.' He asked our names, we told him, and he was gone. There was a pause. Terry finished off his beer.

'You an artist too?' he asked me.

'No.' Another pause. 'I'm a writer.'

'I see. A writer. Novels?'

'I'm trying.'

'Uh-huh.' He was through with me. 'Wayne, we thought we might get you to paint some portraits while you're over there.'

Wayne sat up. 'I don't do many portraits.'

'Really? Your father says you do excellent portraits. We thought we might get a series from you. Some of the traditional owners. The elders. Allan Price for one—he's the tribal spokesman and chairman of the park board. A few others. We'd pay you of course.'

'Well . . . I'll think about it.'

'Have a look out there. It's beautiful country. I'll get a message to you after you've had a couple of weeks to settle in. You've won an award for portrait painting, I hear from your father.'

'I didn't exactly win.'

'Of roadworkers, wasn't it? Commissioned by the Queensland Department of Transport?'

'No, they held a competition. They're having some sort of Bicentennial exhibition, at Expo. They picked four on a shortlist. I'm one of them.'

'Well, as I say, see how you go. But there're plenty of things to paint on Cobourg.'

'Uh . . . I don't do many landscapes either.'

Terry nodded vaguely. We waited. Tom came back. 'Wednesday,' he said, 'Two o'clock. Be at the Northwing office at the airport. I also rang the Nightcliff supermarket and told them to expect you.'

'That's that then,' said Terry, standing up. We stood up too. He handed us the paper he'd written on. 'Remember, be at the Met. Bureau tomorrow morning. Ten o'clock. That's the address. And don't fuck around over at Cape Don either. Things are touchy enough without you two making it worse.'

'We won't,' said Wayne.

And we were back in the waiting room.

We headed for the hostel.

'You didn't tell me you were on a shortlist,' I said.

'I don't even like doing portraits. I just did it to keep Mum pacified.'

We drove in silence.

Finally I said, 'So who opens a cheque account for the supermarket? You or me?'

'What do you need to open a cheque account?'

'I don't know. Some ID, I suppose.'

'I don't have any.'

'Okay. It's me then.'

Wayne lit a cigarette. Dangled a hand out the window. I watched him. I was angry. I said, 'Did you really not know it was only a one-man job?'

'No one ever said exactly. But I wasn't gonna come up here alone. Why, don't you want it now?'

'I don't really have any choice, do I.'

'I suppose not.'

'You could've at least done some of the talking in there. Terry is *your* father's friend, not mine.'

He blew out the smoke. 'I thought I'd leave the questions to you. I'm never any good at that sort of thing. You are though.'

I looked at him.

It wasn't a compliment.

I caught the bank just before closing, and got the cheque account organised. I didn't even know from where or when the money would arrive to fill it. Or how much it would be. Only half of the cash would be mine anyway. A one-man job, a one-man wage.

The bank told me to come back on Wednesday morning for the chequebook. I walked out into the heavy Darwin afternoon. That was enough official organisation for the day. It was time for a drink. I went back to the hostel. In the lobby I found a copy of the *Northern Territory Times*. I took it up to the room. There were only two nights of civilisation left to us.

We went through the entertainment pages. Two pubs showed signs of life. One of them, out in the suburbs, had

'Bikini Girl Jelly Wrestling'. The other, in the city centre, had 'The Joe Francis Band, Live From Sydney.' For a Monday evening, it was about as good as anything Brisbane might offer. Which wasn't bad, seeing Darwin was about one-twentieth the size. We chose the Joe Francis Band, simply because it was within walking distance, and went back out to the streets.

We found the pub, the Victoria Hotel, in the town mall. We went upstairs. It was early yet, and the place was mostly empty. We ordered our beers, sat at a table. Band equipment was set up on a low stage, down one end. There was a chicken-wire barrier stretched across in front of the stage. I thought about the barrier and what it meant and what I wanted. It seemed we'd come to the right place.

TEN

Despite the hangovers, we made our ten o'clock appointment with the Bureau of Meteorology. The Bureau's administration building was in the city centre, but we'd been told to go to their weather station out at the airport, for practical training. A security officer directed us to a long, low shack not far from one of the runways. We parked, went inside, and gave our names.

A young man came out to meet us. He had a thin, pale face and long black hair. He was eating a carrot sandwich. Brown bread, the carrot grated.

'You're the Cape Don boys.'

'That's right,' I said. Somehow it had been decided, I would be the speaker for the two of us. It wasn't a question of dominant personalities. Dealing with these sorts of authorities was a responsibility neither of us really wanted. Wayne obviously wanted it least. So it had fallen to me.

'Ever done any weather work before?' the man asked.

'No.'

He shook his head. 'Well, at least this time they gave us a whole day to train you. Usually it's just a couple of hours.'

He finished up his sandwich and shook our hands, told us his name was Lawrence. He wasn't happy with the situation, but he didn't seem to hold it against us personally. First he gave us a tour of the building. None of it meant much to me. There were rooms of radar screens, charting rooms, computer terminals, all the things you might've expected in a weather centre. Lawrence didn't bother explaining how it all worked.

'You won't be using anything like this at Cape Don,' he said. He took us to the lunch room, sat us down, and explained. 'Out there you'll have only certain instruments. Your job will be to read those instruments once every three hours, make various calculations, and encode the results in a field-book. You also have to radio the information back to us here in Darwin. Each reading and reporting session is called an observation. It should take about ten minutes, once you're used to it. Your reading times are 9 a.m., midday, 3 p.m., 6 p.m., 9 p.m., 3 a.m, and 6 a.m.. We let you have midnight off.'

Wayne looked pained. 'We do weather that early in the morning? What if we sleep in?'

'Don't. You can't miss observations. We rely on *regular* information from our weather stations. Besides, you only get paid per observation. So if you skip one you skip the money for it too.'

I said, 'What does the money come to, per week?'

'If you get every observation, about four hundred and fifty.'

Four hundred and fifty. Divided by two, and taking away tax, I was worse off than I'd been at the bottle shop. Financially it was a disaster then. On the other hand, it sounded like only an hour or two's work each day. Nor would we pay any rent. Keeping that in mind, the money didn't seem so bad. I wouldn't starve on it, and I wouldn't run out of alcohol. And anyway, writing was supposed to be the whole point here, not wage-earning.

Lawrence found a blank field-book and showed it to us. It was a wide-leafed journal, the pages divided into columns and boxes. He gathered up a few pens and manuals. Then he led us outside to show us the routine.

First, we went to a small box on a short pole about twenty metres from the shack. 'This,' said Lawrence, 'Is the thermometer screen.'

He opened the ventilated door. There were four large thermometers inside. Two upright, two on their sides. One of the upright thermometers had its bottom wrapped in cloth, and the cloth was dipped in water. It was, Lawrence explained, the Wet Bulb Thermometer. The other was the Dry Bulb Thermometer. By comparing the readings of the two, humidity could be calculated. The two thermometers on their sides were the Minimum and Maximum Thermometers. They recorded minimum and maximum temperatures. The Wet and Dry were read every three hours, the Minimum and Maximum only twice a day. We read them all, and recorded the information in the appropriate place in the field-book.

Next to the box was a rain gauge. That was straightforward. We opened it, looked in, saw that there had been no rain in the last three hours, wrote so in the field-book. If it *had* been raining, then we were supposed to record what type of rain it had been. Showers. Storms. Sleet. Heavy or light. Lawrence opened one of the manuals, showed us a long list of official precipitation types from which to choose.

From there we went back to the shack. Inside there was a large, highly accurate barometer. Lawrence taught us how to read it, and how to calculate the real air pressure by taking into account temperature and height above sea level. Then he showed us a barograph. It recorded the rise and fall of barometric pressure over a weekly period. The paper had to be replaced every seven days, and the used sheet stuck in the back of the field-book.

From there it was over to the read-out for the wind meter. Pressing one button gave you the current wind strength. Pressing another gave you the maximum wind gust over a specified number of hours, a third gave you the average wind strength over the same period. It also told wind direction.

'So what was the story with Cyclone Tracy?' I asked, 'What was the maximum gust?'

'217 ks. That wasn't the maximum though, that was just when the meter blew away.'

We went back outside again.

'Now this is the only tricky part,' he said, looking up. 'The clouds.'

We looked up. There were clouds up there alright. Big fluffy ones coming in from the ocean. I remembered from my school days that the big fluffy ones were called cumulonimbus.

'There're four things you have to tell us about the clouds,' Lawrence went on, 'How high they are. What type they are. How much of the sky they cover. And which way they're going.'

We kept looking up. How *high* they were?

'For the height, we divide them into three levels. Low, middle and high. Low level is anything below eight or nine thousand feet. Middle is nine thousand up to twenty thousand feet. High is twenty thousand feet and upwards.'

I said, 'How do you tell?'

'Practice is the best thing. Knowing the type of cloud helps too.' He opened another manual. There were several pages of colour photographs of clouds, each photo accompanied by a name. 'All you really have to do is match what you see to one of the pictures, and you've got the name.'

We tried it out. Sure enough, the big fluffy ones were cumulonimbus. Code name Cb. Cb3 for smaller ones, Cb9 for the massive storm types. We selected Cb3. It seemed simple enough.

'See,' said Lawrence, 'It says here that Cb3 is almost always low level. And looking at them you can *tell* they're low level. I'd say about five or six thousand feet. And there are certain types of cloud that are usually mid level, and high level too. You'll get to know them. See that sheet of thin cloud, way up beyond the Cb3? That's clearly high-level cirrus. A little wispy, so it's this type. Ci4, not Ci1 or Ci2. You can tell it's high because you can't see it moving, like the Cb3s are. Too far away. But you have to watch the middle-level stuff. Ac5 can look just like Ci2. Cs5 is a dead ringer for As1 and even Cs9. And something like St6 can fuck you right up. Height is everything. You see what I mean?'

He was pointing at dozens of different pictures. They all looked the same. Wayne and I exchanged a glance. We had no idea what he meant. We nodded.

'Fine. The next thing is direction. Work out where north is, then line the clouds up against something tall and still—like a light pole—and watch.'

We did so. The Cb3s were coming, we decided, from the north-east. The Ci2, no matter how long we watched, didn't seem to be moving at all.

'Go with gut instinct,' Lawrence said, 'Don't stare for hours, just take a quick glance up and go with whatever direction comes to mind. You'll always be right. The human eye can do amazing things if the brain isn't overruling it.'

He was gazing up keenly, waiting. A weather evangelist. Wayne and I threw our human eyes skywards and went with our gut instincts. Mine said south-west. Wayne's said south-west. We turned to Lawrence.

He blinked. 'Well, you'll get it eventually. The last thing is to decide how much cloud of each level there is in the sky. We divide the sky into eighths. The Cb3 for instance is taking about half the sky maybe, so that's four-eighths. The stratus seems to be almost over the whole sky, so we'll say seven-eighths. Okay?'

My mind was going numb.

'How are we supposed to do this at night?'

'If there's a moon it's quite easy. One thing though, at night the thin, high level stratus can be almost invisible. You have to look for things like blurred stars, or rings around the moon.'

The explanations went on. I was barely listening. They were only clouds. At one point, four grey military jets screamed down the runway next to us and blasted sky-wards. There were more taxiing about in the distance. It appeared that this part of the airport was an RAAF base. Lawrence peered after the jets as they vanished in the clouds.

'F-111s,' he said. 'You'll get to know those fuckers pretty well, believe me.'

'Why?'

'You'll see.'

Then it was back inside the shack again. We sat down at a desk, and Lawrence showed us a decoding sheet. All the figures we'd written in the journal now had to be coded. There were also calculations to be made, using the air pressure, and various thermometer readings. In the end we had a list of letters and numbers, about thirty digits long. 'This is what you read over the radio,' Lawrence said, 'And back here we punch it straight into the computer. Then at the end of each month you send in the field-book, so we have a written record as well. And that's all there is to it.'

It wasn't though.

We went through the entire observation and recording process again. Wayne and I were doing it on our own this time, Lawrence looking on. Wayne had trouble. He wrote in the wrong columns, read the instruments back to front, took the maximum wind gust for the average. Together we took almost forty minutes to reach the encoded list. The clouds were our biggest problem. They'd changed since our last look. We stumbled around, glancing up quickly, going for the gut reaction. Height. Type. Eighths. Direction. It was hopeless.

Lawrence did his best to remain calm. He took us off for lunch at a takeaway near the airport. 'We'll have one more run this afternoon, then I'll have done all I can. But practise it, huh. Please.'

'We will.'

'I'll also have to get your names and bank accounts. Pay is monthly. We add up all the observations you've done and work out what you're owed. It's a sliding scale. The night observations are worth more than the day ones, for obvious reasons.'

He went on with various details, then it was back to the airport. The afternoon test run was a huge success, just under half an hour. It was three o'clock by that stage. Lawrence ushered us into one of the computer rooms. A man was sitting at a keyboard, listening to a speaker and typing in what he heard. There were distant, crackly voices coming over the speaker, reading out letters and numbers.

'That's the three o'clock 'sked'—scheduled call,' said Lawrence, 'We've got about a dozen weather stations out there, and they all report in at the same intervals. Listen.'

We listened. Voices came and went, some male, some female. It was a faraway and desolate sound.

'One of those, of course,' said Lawrence, 'Is Cape Don.'

We walked out to the car. We were now fully trained and accredited Weather Observation Officers. As titles went it was the biggest I'd ever had. Lawrence came out with us. He'd grown a little strained towards the end of the day, now he seemed quite cheerful. 'Seen much of Darwin yet?'

'We only got in yesterday. We spent last night at a pub in the mall. The Victoria.'

'Ah, the Vic. Used to be a good one, but it's a bit of a tourist trap now. If you stick around you'll find better ones. When are you leaving?'

'Tomorrow.'

'Maybe when you get back then. Believe me, Darwin grows on you. In the meantime, if you have any problems over there, just radio in.'

'Thanks.'

'You'll have fun. Cape Don is a beautiful place. We get over there ourselves sometimes, to do maintenance on the station. Great fishing. Which house are they putting you in?'

'We don't know yet.'

He laughed. 'I can guess. Take some cleaning gear. But seriously, make sure you do the weather properly over there. Don't miss any observations, and fill out *everything* in the field-book. Cape Don's been a real pain for us lately. The last few people they've had out there have been useless. To tell the truth, we didn't want you two for this job. We had our own people lined up. I hear Allan Price did too. You know who he is? The old Aboriginal spokesman?'

I said that we did.

'You might find you aren't all that welcome,' he smiled, 'When you get over there.'

ELEVEN

Wednesday, our last few hours in Darwin. We'd done nothing with the previous night. Just sat in the room, reading, staring at the walls. We were committed now, and we were tense.

In the morning I picked up my new cheque book from the bank. Then we found our way to the Nightcliff supermarket. We were sent to the office, where we mentioned the name of the Conservation Commission and were thus granted an account. Then it was time to shop. We pushed the trolley up and down, wondering what to take to the lighthouse. Insect repellent was one certainty, four bottles, tropical strength.

Food was another. Steaks, mince, pasta, vegetables, bread, sauces, herbs and so on. Enough for ten days. The way we figured it, we wouldn't be ordering any more food in until the following Friday. Then there were the toiletries, some first aid gear, batteries, cleaning liquids. Everywhere we looked there seemed to be something we'd need. The trolley filled. We found some cheap wind-up alarm clocks, took two of them. We bought envelopes, steel wool, pain-killers. A carton of Winfield Blues for Wayne. Then we were in the alcohol section. We looked at all the cartons of beer, the bottles of spirits.

'Can we even take alcohol?' I said, 'Some of these Aboriginal places are supposed to be dry.'

'No one told us we couldn't.'

We loaded a second trolley. Two cartons of Fourex cans. A bottle of bourbon. A four-litre cask of claret. It didn't seem so much, when we considered those ten days. We added another carton. Then we pushed both the trolleys down to the checkout and watched while the stuff was tallied up. It came to over two hundred and seventy dollars.

'On credit,' I said, and explained who we were. The staff seemed used to it. We waited while they packed it all in boxes and then wrapped the boxes in tape to survive the flight. We carted the stuff out and jammed it in the car. Even the front seat was full by now. We contemplated it all. For a couple of vagabond, wandering souls, we had an enormous amount of essential equipment. We squeezed ourselves in and drove to the airport.

The Northwing terminal was a small shed in a large car park. There was an office in the shed and a woman behind the desk. We told her who we were and she checked a timetable, then told us the plane would be along any minute.

I said, 'Is there any problem with me leaving my car in the car park for the next six months?'

'Six months! Won't your battery go flat?'

'I guess so. I don't see how I can avoid it.'

She thought. 'You could leave the keys here if you want. I could drive it home every once in a while. Keep the battery charged.'

'That's very nice of you.'

'Well, actually, it'd be handy for me too sometimes. My husband and I share the one car.'

I gave her the keys. We went outside to wait.

'Are you crazy,' Wayne said, 'Giving her your car?'

'She had an honest face. Besides, she won't treat it any worse than I would.'

Still, I was surprised at myself. I didn't even like loaning the car to friends, yet alone strangers. Maybe it was the Darwin air, or the sense of occasion. It didn't seem the time or the place to be suspicious of people. We were jumping off into the unknown and who knew when or if we'd be back.

I looked out over the tarmac. There were plenty of planes parked there, big and small. Presently one taxied our way. It was a little single-engine Cessna, blue and white, with the word Northwing painted on the nose. It looked old. I'd been hoping for a twin-engine. I'd never flown before, and two sounded more encouraging than one, as far as engines went.

The plane pulled up and the pilot climbed out. He wore mirrored sunglasses.

'Cape Don?' he said to us.

'Uh-huh.'

'Where's your stuff?'

I cocked my thumb towards the car.

He looked. 'Jesus Christ.'

We looked too. It was ludicrous.

'Maybe you should get a bigger plane,' Wayne suggested.

The pilot wasn't amused. 'Whatever doesn't fit, doesn't go.'

We unloaded the car, carrying each box or item over to the pilot. He stacked them in the various compartments. The plane turned out to be a four-seater and there was a surprising amount of space. Our things disappeared.

Finally all that was left were four large boxes and Wayne's two easels. There was nowhere to put them. The pilot dove in and after some grunting and heaving, pulled one of the rear seats out. He dumped it on the ground. The boxes and the easels took its place.

'How long you guys staying over there?'

'Six months.'

He looked at his plane. 'Might just be long enough to get all this unpacked. Well, hop on in.'

Hop on in. Looking at it, all laden down, the Cessna and it's single engine looked tiny. The single engine in particular. But then again a single engine could pull a semitrailer, a boat, even a train. What was three people and half a ton of artistic lifestyle in comparison?

I looked at Wayne. 'You flown before?'

'Sure.'

'Then I'm taking the front seat.'

He shrugged, nodded.

We got in. The pilot showed us how to buckle-up. Then he talked on the radio briefly and we were moving. Across the tarmac, around some corners, then onto the runway. I looked along the strip. I thought about landings and take-offs—the danger times, when all the deaths occurred. I wondered if this was fear. Was I going to be afraid of flying? Maybe it was like seasickness, you could never know until it happened to you. I'd never been to sea either.

The pilot upped the revs, then released the brakes. We moved down the runway, picking up speed. I watched the dashboard. Nothing went red. Then suddenly the nose pointed up and we were airborne. I experienced a moment of total terror. I laughed, cut it off abruptly. The fear faded. I looked out the window. So this was flying.

We were climbing steeply. The runway vanished and we were over the swamps that bordered the airport. Then it was houses. People mowing the back lawns. Some goats in a paddock. Then it was the ocean, shimmering and blue. I was impressed, and a little unsure. I'd always imagined that planes carved their way through the air as steadily as a car on the road. I hadn't expected the light, skittish sensation. The way the little craft bounced and slid about in the air.

We kept climbing. The ocean unrolled below us, points of land jutting out. I turned and looked at Wayne. He was gazing out with his usual indifference. Whatever was going to crack it, it wasn't flying. I turned forward again. We were nearly up to the clouds now. They were small, white and fluffy. Cumulus no doubt, Cu2.

We levelled off just above them. I checked the altimeter. It said five thousand feet. I took note of that for future reference. I was a Weather Observation Officer now, and if these clouds were at five thousand feet today, chances were they always would be.

Time passed. Twenty minutes. Forty. The novelty of flight wore off. I searched the ocean below for ships. Nothing. I became bored. I watched the pilot. He looked maybe fifty. Worn. Also bored.

I raised my voice above the engine. 'You done this trip before?'

The mirrored sunglasses glanced my way. 'Often enough.'

'So what's Cape Don like?'

He thought. 'Got a good airstrip.'

I nodded. It was a pilot's perspective on life.

He looked at me again. 'You don't know a thing about it, do you?'

'No.'

'I'll say this then. I don't fly many people *in* to Cape Don, but I seem to fly a *lot* out.'

I thought about that. Thought of nothing else to say.

More time passed. Eventually, I could see the coastline of a large island down to our left. On our right the mainland had appeared again. It curved out in a point towards the island, leaving a wide channel in between. Finally the pilot leaned over. 'That's Melville Island on the left. And to the right . . . can you see it?'

I squinted. The mainland appeared heavily forested. Near the tip of the point there was a small, upright sliver amidst the trees. We were headed directly for it, and losing height. The lighthouse. Eight days since Brisbane and there it was. It wasn't what I was expecting. It wasn't white. It was brown. Thin as a spike. Nor was it set on the coast, on some high, rocky point. There *was* no high, rocky point. The land seemed low and unbroken, and there was no beach, only mangroves. The lighthouse itself was positioned well back from the water, in a small, bare clearing.

The plane banked and we circled the area. I stared down. I saw houses, their roofs of silver corrugated iron. Sheds and paths. A four-wheel drive. A human figure emerged from one of the houses, and looked up. Then we levelled off and headed inland. The bush widened out, stretched to the horizons. There were no other houses or roads or fences or anything in sight. Nothing but a red slash of bare earth up ahead. The airstrip.

The pilot got us in line. It seemed a short, scraggy space. I tensed. The trees rose, very fast. It was worse than taking off. We dipped suddenly, hit the dirt, bounced, hit again, and then we were on the ground. I relaxed. We slowed and swung round, taxied back through the dust. There was a track there, leading off into the bush. We stopped near it. The pilot checked various things on the dash, then killed the engine. Silence fell.

'Well boys,' he said, 'Here you are.'

TWELVE

We climbed out. I walked away from the plane. The air was hot, humid and still. A windsock hung limply on its pole. Otherwise there was nothing to see but the bush lining the strip. Tall eucalypts, leaves of drab green and red. A crow called in the distance, stopped. Cape Don, the Cobourg Peninsula.

I looked around. Wayne was staring off, smoking a cigarette. The pilot was already unloading our gear. 'The ranger should be here in a minute or two,' he said. 'That loop I did around the lighthouse, it was to let him know we were about to land.'

We helped with the unloading. After a time I could hear the sound of a car engine. A Toyota four-wheel drive emerged from the little track and parked itself next to the plane. A man got out, removed a cigarette from his mouth, looked at us.

'G'day,' he said.

He was maybe forty or fifty years old. He didn't look like a ranger. He was wearing a ranger shirt, but it was ragged, faded almost to white. A round belly showed through the buttons, hung over the rim of his shorts. He had long wispy hair, and was wearing thongs.

'G'day,' I replied.

'So which one is the artist?'

'I am,' said Wayne.

The ranger offered his hand. 'Vince.'

'I'm Wayne. And that's Gordon.'

Vince looked at me. 'I was told they were sending me an artist and his French girlfriend. You're no French girlfriend.'

I said, *'Pardon moi.'*

The stare continued. 'Must've been someone's idea of a joke.' He turned to the pilot. 'Any mail?'

'No one gave me any.'

Vince nodded. He took out a pouch of tobacco and began rolling a new cigarette. He looked at our pile of luggage.

I said, 'We didn't really know what to bring.'

'You got insect repellent?'

'Yes.'

'You'll survive then.'

We loaded up the Toyota. When it was finished we waited and watched while the pilot got his plane going again. He taxied off to the far end of the strip, then turned and roared back down. He lifted, rose, cleared the trees, then curved away to the west. We watched the plane until it disappeared. Vince stubbed out his latest cigarette. It was his fourth or fifth since we'd met. 'Let's go,' he said.

I rode in the front, Wayne rode in the back. Vince drove without speaking. He had a tight, closed face, sunburnt and unshaven. The cabin smelt of tobacco and petrol. I watched out the window. The track wound its way through the bush, rising and falling slightly. A few times I caught the faint tang of salt air. The ocean was near, but the trees and scrub were too dense to see far on either side.

Vince broke the silence. 'Exciting flight?' he asked.

'No. Not really.'

'Least you finally got here.'

'Are we late?'

'I was told you'd be here a month ago. That's when the last weather observer left.'

'Who's been doing the weather observations?'

'Me.'

'Are you the only person here?'

'Until now.' He glanced over. 'What're you? Another artist?'

'I'm supposed to be writing.'

He nodded, lips clamped around a butt. 'A writer.'

After a few more minutes we drove up a long, gentle slope. At the top the bush fell away and we were in the clearing. It was a rough circle, partly gravel, partly clumps of long brown grass. On the far side was the lighthouse. It looked no better from the ground than it had from the air. It was graceless, a tube of unpainted concrete. At other points around the circle were three houses, some sheds, and a few palm trees.

'I'd give you a tour,' said Vince, 'But this is it. There's the airstrip, there's here, and there's the road in between. There's a little bay too, back a bit, where we keep the boats. But that's all.'

We bumped across to the furthest house and pulled up in front. We climbed out.

'This is where you'll be living.' He pointed at the other two houses. 'That one over there's mine. And the other one belongs to Russel and Eve. That's the Aboriginal ranger and his wife, but they won't be around for a while.'

I looked at our house. It was old, with thick stone walls.

A low verandah ran around it. Parts of the verandah were in ruins, the floor gone, the gutters hanging askew from the roof. The other two houses were in much better condition. Freshly painted, fully intact.

'It's a bit of a mess compared to the others,' Vince said, watching us, 'But come on through.'

We explored. It must have been, at one stage, a beautiful place. It had large, airy rooms and high ceilings. French windows opened from every room, out to the verandah. Vince gave us some of its history. It had been built, along with the lighthouse, in 1916. The light had needed three keepers in those days, hence three houses for the men and their families. Later it was semiautomated and only needed one. Then, in 1983, it was fully automated and the last keeper was retired. Apparently by then the houses were in serious decline. When the Conservation Commission took control of the area it was decided to refurbish two of them. The third, however—ours—was considered too far gone to bother.

I could see why. The house was built on a slope, dropping away from front to back, so that the back verandah should've been seven or eight feet off the ground. There hardly *was* a back verandah. The stairs had disappeared completely, and most of the floorboards had collapsed as well. Small bushes and vines were growing up through the naked support beams. All that was left was a space about ten feet square, immediately outside the kitchen door.

Inside, the place was filthy. The kitchen was black with grease and soot. It smelled as if someone had been cooking in there with kerosene. The laundry and the bathroom were thick with spider webs and dust. The bottom of the bathtub was layered with rotting oranges. The huge dining room wasn't too bad, but it was devoid of any furniture except one small table and the rusting hulks of three refrigerators.

As for the bedrooms, there were four of them, opening off a long central hallway. Two of them were completely empty. Another was crowded with a jumble of blackened bed frames and old mattresses. The last was being used as a storeroom. It was stacked with cans of paint, insecticides and various other noxious items. There was also some fishing gear, a couple of scuba tanks, a compressor, even a spear gun.

Everywhere the paint was faded and peeling. Much of the woodwork was rotten, both in the floors and the ceiling, and most of the glass was smashed. The lighting consisted of naked and loosely attached fluorescent tubes. The only luxury items visible were ceiling fans, one in each room, two in the dining room. All of them were switched on, revolving on low speed, squeaking and scraping.

'Don't ever turn the fans off,' Vince said, 'They've been on for years. In this air they'd rust solid in a few weeks if they stopped. And you need them. The wind helps keep the sandflies off at night. Without them you'd get eaten alive.'

We emerged onto the front verandah again, stood there for a moment. I wasn't sure what to say. This was our *house*?

Vince cleared his throat. 'I suppose I should've cleaned it up a little before you came. No one's used it in years. I switched one of the fridges on for you though.'

'Thanks. A lot.'

He shrugged one shoulder. 'Let's get your stuff in.'

It was around four-thirty by the time we were unloaded. Vince mentioned that, as we should know, there was a weather observation due at six p.m. His plan was to do the next few observations himself, until we were settled in. He also thought it might be a good idea if we watched him do a couple first. So if we wanted we could meet him at the weather shack at five forty-five. He pointed out the shack, a small building near the foot of the lighthouse. With that, he got in the Toyota and drove back to his own place.

We watched him go. Then we wandered through our house again. Despite all the grime, there was still a gaunt beauty about it. Space was the thing. The rooms were built to a colonial scale. We found ourselves on the back verandah, looking out. There was a view of the ocean, pale blue, maybe a mile off. The whole settlement seemed to be built on a low plateau, slightly higher than the surrounding country. It rose in a tilt from east to west, and our house was near the higher edge. Not far from the back verandah the land dropped away again to the scrub, and beyond that were glimpses of mangroves along the shore.

It wasn't an inspiring view, but it was the only one the house offered. I paced out those floorboards that seemed safe. 'I suppose there's room for one or two chairs here.'

'What chairs?' said Wayne.

We went back inside and talked about rooms. Of the two usable bedrooms, Wayne took the smaller, I took the larger. We wrestled some bed frames out of the junkheap, and some mattresses. Wayne scored a double bed, I took a single. I put it in the centre of the floor, under the ceiling fan. It made the room look even bigger and emptier. Artistic austerity.

The next thing was to unload all the perishable food into the working fridge. We wrestled the other two hulks into a corner, out of the way. Then it was the kitchen and the bathroom. The mess was profound. Some emergency cleaning was necessary, even for the likes of us.

We found an old scrubbing brush, a worn broom and a bucket in the laundry. We set to. Going through the drawers we found a few pieces of cutlery, some plates and bowls, and one small saucepan. The stove was gas, and it was working. We wondered about the source of the gas, then discovered a large cylinder in the growth under the back verandah. There was no hot water system. We unpacked one of our own saucepans and boiled some water to help with the scrubbing.

By five-thirty the kitchen seemed a little better, and the oranges were gone from the bathtub. The sun had disappeared behind a bank of clouds in the west. Inside, the rooms were growing dark. It was a ghost house. I flicked a light switch. The hard fluorescent light took all the dim space and made it appear shabby and small. And still very dirty. Neither of us had any real dedication to cleaning. Even if we did, there were days of work waiting there.

'It'll do won't it,' said Wayne.

I agreed.

We made our way out to the front steps, sat down. Wayne lit a cigarette. There were one hundred and eighty days to go. We considered our new world.

The clearing was maybe two-hundred metres across. The lower half of the plateau was fringed by trees, the upper half ended in low cliffs. The three houses, the lighthouse and the weather shack were all linked by bitumen paths. The paths were bordered by white stones. Here and there along them were small streetlights. The effect was almost quaint, the stones and the streetlights. A hint of something old. Stylish.

It wasn't stylish anymore. It was dusty and bare. The paths had faded away in places, or were overrun by gravel tracks for larger vehicles. The garden beds were just dirt and weeds. The new prefabricated sheds clashed with the older buildings. And there was junk everywhere.

We sat. The air was still and heavy. Wayne's cigarette smoke hung in slow curls. The low throb of an engine came from inside one of the sheds. I assumed it was the generator. There was no sea breeze, no taste of sea air, no sound of surf or seagulls. It didn't feel like we were anywhere near the ocean. It felt like we were on some back lot scrub property. One that was going broke.

'Think you might wanna paint any of this?' I asked Wayne.

'No. Feel inspired to write?'

'Not yet.'

THIRTEEN

We sat there until quarter to six, then walked along the bitumen path to the weather shack. There was no sign of Vince. We looked in. The shack was a single room. There was a desk with a two-way radio on it, and a pile of weather field-books. A chart of cloud types hung on the wall. There was also the read-out for the wind metre, the barometer and the barograph. Everything was dusty. Spider webs crowded in the corners. A steady crackling came from radio, interspersed with thin wailings and pipings of interference.

A door slammed. We turned. Vince was coming out of his house. He had a can of beer in his hand, Victoria Bitter. He was followed by a small, fat, hairy dog. It bounded along the path, tongue lolling. When it saw Wayne and I it dashed across, barking.

'Shut up,' said Vince.

The dog desisted. It wandered off along the path, giving out half barks at nothing.

'His name's Kevin,' Vince said, 'He's not mine. He was here when I arrived. The last ranger owned him.'

'I didn't think dogs were allowed in national parks,' I said.

'They're not. How's the house?'

'We could use some furniture.'

'I'll see what I can find. You guys have been trained for this weather stuff haven't you?'

'We had a day in Darwin.'

'Shit, you know more about it than I do. I had to teach myself.'

We followed him into the shack and watched him go through the routine. It was all very much as we'd been taught. The thermometers, the gauges, the barometer, the clouds. Vince seemed to know perfectly well what he was doing. By a couple of minutes to six he had all the encoding done. We waited for the call to come through on the radio.

'You two used a radio before?'

'No.'

'It's simple enough. Just remember to say 'Over' at the end of every statement.'

At six o'clock a clear female voice broke through the static. She announced that it was the Darwin operator calling all weather stations on behalf of the Met. Bureau. She gave a call sign and we could faintly hear one of the other weather stations responding. The Darwin transmitter would be the strong one, of course, while the outlying stations would be weaker. The distant weather observer began reading out the numbers.

Vince was swinging the microphone back and forth, bored. 'We're usually one of the last ones called. You don't really need to have the encoding ready until about five past the hour.'

We listened to the voices. Vince explained a little about the radio. 'You'll have trouble getting through at night, at 9 p.m. and 3 a.m. especially. Too much static for some reason. The operator might ask you to try a different channel, but it doesn't help much. If you can't get through, just leave it. You can report the night-time observations the next morning, when the air's clear again.'

The radio said 'Darwin calling Victor Lima Nine Charlie Uniform Cape Don, do you copy, over.'

Vince raised the mike. 'This is Victor Lima Nine Charlie Uniform Cape Don, I copy, over.'

'Go ahead Cape Don, over.'

Vince read out the numbers, repeating every set of digits twice for clarity. At the end he said 'Over' and dumped the mike on the desk. 'That's it. And don't worry, our call sign is written there on the wall, in case you can't remember it.'

I nodded. It all seemed clear. 'When do you want us to take over?'

He thought. 'Well, officially each weather day starts at the 9 a.m., so I'll go through until then.'

We wandered out into the evening. The streetlights were on and the fading light was taking some of the harsher edges from the scene. Still, it was just a few houses amongst the scrub in the middle of nowhere.

'How long have you been here?' I asked.

'Five months so far. It was only supposed to be temporary. The last guy stationed here had a breakdown and left without giving any notice. They flew me up as a replacement.' He stared off into the distance. 'Now they tell me they want me here for two years.'

'Jesus.'

He shrugged. 'Listen, you two doing anything for dinner tonight?'

We shook our heads.

'How about coming over to my place then. I'll bang up a roast. A welcome to Cape Don meal.'

'Okay.'

'Give me twenty minutes or so. You brought drinks with you didn't you?'

'We did.'

'See you later then.'

He made off towards his house. Kevin bounded across to join him, got tangled between his feet. Vince swore at the dog wearily, kicked it inside.

Vince's house was the same design as ours, but in vastly better condition. No rotting floors or holes in the walls, and fresh paint everywhere. And it was furnished. There were comfortable chairs and couches in the living area, a dining table, polished floors, even a hot water system. There were also three spare bedrooms, with proper beds in them. I wondered about that, and about where all the previous weather observers had lived. Obviously not in the house Wayne and I had been given. No one had lived *there* for years.

I didn't ask. It was Vince's house and indeed Vince's ranger station, he could send us where he liked. We all sat in the living room, under the ceiling fans. It was still hot. The dog squatted on the rug and panted steadily. We drank beer. Wayne and I were in the lounge chairs, Vince was on a stool, at a desk. There was an old typewriter on the desk, stacks of paper, and several empty bottles of port. Otherwise there was a large bookshelf, full of books and magazines, and a stereo. We sat there in awkward silence.

'No TV?' I asked Vince.

He gave a smile. 'Can't pick anything up out here. You can barely even get radio.'

'Oh.'

No relief there then. The walls were adorned with maps and posters. I noticed one of them was a chart of different types of aircraft, shown in silhouette.

'Why the planes?'

'I'm supposed to keep an eye on the coastline, on behalf of customs. Report any suspicious-looking planes or boats. Smugglers. Boat people. Whatever.'

'Have you ever seen any?'

'No. But then I haven't been able to get away from the house and do any real patrols lately. There were your bloody weather reports, for one thing.'

'Where do you patrol?'

'In theory, up and down the coast. By boat. I'm supposed to have access to one big forty-foot cruiser and two small runabouts. There's supposed to be *three* rangers here as well. Instead it's just me, the cruiser's been in Darwin for months, for repairs, and there's only the one little dinghy down at the bay. I wouldn't trust that too far either.'

'You're the only ranger in the whole park?'

'Of course not. For a start, Russel would be here normally. And over the other side of the Peninsula, where the tourists go, there're rangers everywhere. That's Black Point, the park headquarters. But it's a couple of hours away by boat. And I wouldn't try it in that dinghy unless I had to.'

'There're no roads at all?'

'No. Cape Don's virtually an island. We're cut off from the mainland by a belt of swamps and creeks.' He got up and pointed this out on a large-scale map of the peninsula. 'The only settlement between us and Black Point is Araru. Here. It's an Aboriginal outstation. That's where Russel and Eve are. They're spending a week or so with Russel's father, Allan Price. You know who he is?'

'The tribal spokesman.'

'Uh-huh. But there wouldn't be more than a dozen people over at Araru. The Gurig Aborigines only number eighty or ninety all up. In four clans. They move about the place, but most of them usually live at Black Point. They like to keep an eye on the tourists. They only allow about twenty in at a time.'

He gave us a rough rundown on how the park worked. It had been set-up in 1981. It included all of the Cobourg Peninsula and the waters surrounding it. Before that the peninsula had been under various government authorities and private companies. No one white had ever found much use for the place. Even so, the Aboriginal owners had been hemmed into an increasingly small part of the peninsula, and eventually transported en masse over to Croker, an island away to the east. They returned in 1981, and were now partners with the Conservation Commission in running the park.

It was an experiment. It was a national park, which meant the usual restrictions on visitors concerning the treatment of flora and fauna. But the Gurig people themselves had full rights to pursue their traditional lifestyle. That included the hunting and harvesting of all animal and plant species in the park, native or introduced. They also controlled access. To the park in general, and in particular to any sites they considered sensitive or sacred.

The place was also a game reserve. The introduced species included feral pigs, buffalo, Timor ponies and banteng cattle. The banteng were particularly important. They were on the international big-game hunting lists, and Cobourg was one of the last places on earth that they were still plentiful in the wild. Thus many of the tourists were hunters. Apart from entry fees, they had to pay the Gurig people as safari guides, as well as paying bounties on anything they killed. Up to a thousand dollars a head. It was the park's prime cash industry.

But that all happened over on the east side of the

peninsula, forty or fifty ks away. Our side was off limits to tourism, without express permission from Allan Price.

I said, 'We were told he wasn't too keen on us coming.'

'I wouldn't know. I haven't seen him for a few weeks. He doesn't visit here all that often. They used to all live over here, years ago, back when the rest of the peninsula was out of their control. There's a bunch of old shacks down in the bush. The government used your house as a school then. They had a white teacher who lived there, and she had maybe ten Aboriginal kids as students. It didn't last long.'

He went off to the kitchen. Wayne and I sat. There was a classical piece on the stereo. From my brief inspection of Vince's music collection, classical was all he possessed. He came out bearing plates. We sat down to eat. There was roast beef, thick gravy, roast potatoes, carrots and beans. We ate and drank while the orchestra played.

I nodded towards Vince's desk, the typewriter and all the paper. 'So what do you type?'

'Letters.'

'Who do you you write to?'

He shrugged. 'The editor. The Conservation Commission. Friends down south. University libraries. My old lecturers. My son.'

'You haven't always been a ranger?'

'No.'

It turned out Vince had worked in various jobs up until about thirty, then ended up at university. This was in Tasmania. He studied anthropology. He'd ventured into South Australia, working on Aboriginal languages. Then into the Northern Territory. He lost interest in the academic side, dropped out, and joined the Conservation Commission. Since then he'd worked in various national parks in the south of the Territory, and with various Aboriginal clans. He still communicated with the university though. I gathered he was something of an expert.

He'd also married while at university, and had a son. The wife, however, hadn't shared his liking for desert life, and eventually they were divorced. And then, after ten years in the outback, he'd suddenly been sent to Cape Don. The Commission hadn't asked or explained, they'd just ordered.

'They're bright boys there in administration,' he said, 'Everything I know is desert-related. And they send me here. Cape Don. A tropical and maritime park. Boats. Mangroves. Crocodiles. I know fuck-all about any of it.'

'Can you get out?'

'There's only one thing I *do* know about Cape Don. Once your here, it's very, very hard to get away again. You might wanna remember that over the next six months.'

'We'll be alright,' Wayne said, 'We've got things to do.'

'You mean the writing and painting?'

'Uh-huh. That's the whole reason we're here.'

Vince lit up a cigarette, pulled on his beer. 'I met a lot of people who called themselves painters and writers, back in the desert. They were always breaking down, getting lost, annoying the shit out of everyone.' He watched his cigarette smoke rise. 'They said the same sort of thing.'

After dinner we dumped our plates in the sink, returned to the couches. Vince went back to his stool. He was on scotch and water now. I'd noticed a box of scotch in the kitchen, along with several bottles of port and cartons of beer. He drank steadily. His position on the stool was upright and stiff. Bitter, somehow. He played classical composer after classical composer, the volume increasing. Our attempts at conversation slowed. At ten to nine we all trooped out for the evening weather observation.

It was fully dark now, and the lighthouse was

illuminated. It had twin beams, each pointing in opposite directions, and it revolved quickly. The air was so clear the beams were only faintly visible. Above the light were the stars, soft and slightly dimmed. There was no moon. Otherwise there were only the streetlights, a glow from the generator shed, and a great surround of darkness.

We watched Vince go through the readings. He had a torch for checking the thermometers in their box. It was 28.6 degrees. We discussed clouds. Possibly there was a very high, thin layer of cirrus up there. Vince decided there was, and put it at five-eighths. Inside the shack, the static on the radio had got worse, but at nine the call from Darwin came through, and Vince managed to make himself understood in return.

We went back to drinking and the music. Wayne and I were still on beer. Vince had switched to port. He sat on his stool with his eyes closed, swayed slightly, listening. The talk had stopped altogether. I stared at the ceiling, let the alcohol and the orchestra meet in my head. In the background was the zip and splutter of insects frying in the bug-zapper on the verandah. Finally Wayne and I looked at each other. It was time to go on home.

We thanked Vince for dinner. He nodded, not moving from his stool, his eyes closed. We made our way out, followed the white stones back towards our house. Strains of music followed us. Just on the fringe of the light, near our house, there were four wallabies, feeding on the grass. They were large and fat. At our approach they started and bounded off, back into the dark. I could hear them thumping through the scrub.

'I think I'll roll a joint,' Wayne said.

We climbed up the front steps, switched on some lights. It was depressing. After the comfort of Vince's house, our place looked filthy and bare. As welcoming as a train station. I could hear the buzz of the fluorescent tubes. Wayne went to his room to roll the joint, I settled on the back verandah. The darkness was more complete out there, away from the streetlights. There was only the pale beam of the lighthouse, sweeping overhead. And the stars, brighter now. I listened for the ocean. Still nothing. Maybe there was no surf at all in this part of the world.

Wayne brought the joint out and we smoked it, sitting on the safe ten-foot square, dangling our legs over the edge. Then we went to our rooms. On the way I peered out the front door. The wallabies were back, silently grazing. Something about them was sinister. Round, grey shapes, lumping their way across the grass. Maybe I was a little stoned. Homesick. Wallabies were utterly harmless.

I went into my great, empty bedroom. In the tropical night it managed to look cold. I threw some sheets on my single bed, imbibed various asthma drugs, climbed in. The mattress was lumpy, but bearable. I wrapped the sheet around me, grew hot. I threw the sheet off, felt the ceiling fan cool the sweat. I considered masturbating. It'd been six days, since Dalby. An unusually long time. All those shared rooms with Wayne. Somehow the desire wasn't there. I lay, wide awake, listening to the fan, to the low pulse of the generator.

A screen door somewhere in the house banged softly. A breeze, not from the ceiling fan, stirred through the room. I thought about the schoolteacher who'd been posted here. I wondered which room she'd been in. This one? How had she felt, alone here every night, listening. I thought about ghosts in the hallway, about all the people who had lived here before me. Aboriginal kids, running up to school. Their parents, away in the scrub. The lighthouse-keepers and their wives and children. In this room, thirty, forty, seventy years ago, when the house was new and fine and beautiful.

All gone. I found I had an erection. I used it, wiped it off with a handkerchief, and waited for sleep.

FOURTEEN

Next morning I tried out the shower. The tub was big and deep, but the water came out low-pressured and lukewarm. There'd be no joy there.

At twenty to nine we ventured over to the weather shack for our first official observation. Wayne had shown no desire to do it, so I was taking the first one. From there we'd alternate. Wayne would do the twelve, I'd do the three, Wayne the six, me the nine and so on. As there was no midnight observation it would be a two-day rotation. With at least a six-hour gap between readings, and nine every second night, hopefully sleep wouldn't be a problem.

Vince was at the shack, red-eyed and ill, to supervise one last time. I set to with the field-book. It was an overcast morning, with low patches of dense grey cloud. We decided it was stratocumulus, type 5. I managed the encoding in good time, then dealt with the radio. Compared with Vince's easy radio drawl I sounded nervous and awkward, tripping over all the numbers.

When I was finished Vince took over on the radio. He

waited until a channel was clear, then put a call through to the Darwin operator. He wanted to place his order with the Nightcliff supermarket for the Friday deliveries.

'It's a little late,' he told us, 'Normally they like the order by Wednesday at the latest. Thought I'd wait though, see if there was anything you guys forgot to bring. Is there?'

We ordered a broom, a new scrubbing brush, and another carton of beer. When the call was finished we strolled out into the day.

'So what are you gonna do?' I asked Vince, 'Now that you're free.'

'Sleep.'

He shuffled off, his black thongs slapping. Wayne and I moved back towards our house, wondering what to do with ourselves. Now that we had arrived and had settled and the job had started, we weren't sure what came next. We ambled round the compound, checking out the details. There wasn't much we hadn't seen already. A water tank on a tower. And old plough, half-buried in the dirt. A collection of fuel drums. More small sheds. One of them was a garage for a second four-wheel drive. Its hood was up and parts of the engine missing. There were spider webs in the cabin.

In another shed we found machinery, drums, netting, a smashed wardrobe, broken furniture in general. We dug around and came across some old kitchen chairs, three of them. We took them back to our house, arranged them around the small table in the dining room. Seating. Even so, the room still looked absurdly empty. It was a big space, stretching from one side of the house to the other, with wide double doors at either end, opening onto the verandah.

It had also been, as Vince said, a schoolroom. At one end, tacked on the wall, were three cardboard cut-out clocks. They were flyblown and curled and very old. The first of them was red and set at eight o'clock. The second was orange and set at midday. The last was green and set at four. The first had the words 'We start school at—' written on it. The second said 'We have lunch at—'. The third, 'We go home at—.' Eight till four, then. They had a long school day.

At the other end of the room were some lines painted on the wall, under writing that said 'How high am I?' Next to the lines were names. Nola. Dulcie. Judith. Enid. Veronica. Trenton. Robert. And Daniel. Eight students. The highest was no more than four feet, and each name appeared only once. Maybe the school had only lasted one year.

There was only one thing left to do.

'The lighthouse?' I said to Wayne.

'The lighthouse.'

We went out. There it was, brown against the grey sky. It still looked ugly. Near the base were several tilted panels—solar cells. They fed into a small shed which was fenced off and securely locked. No doubt it held the batteries for the light. The door to the lighthouse itself was bolted, but there was no padlock on the bolt. We slipped it back, opened the iron door, and went inside.

More disillusionment. The steps weren't spiral. They went back and forth like ordinary stairs. The room at the base was cramped and contained nothing but some boxes and a large coil of rope. We climbed up. I didn't count the stairs. At the top was another iron door, about half normal size. We opened it and climbed through. We were on a balcony that circled the tower. A few feet above us was another, smaller balcony that circled the actual light. A ladder led up to it. We didn't bother. We were high enough.

We looked out. Waited. Looked out some more. Somehow it wasn't satisfying. The ocean was there, but it seemed empty and flat. The coastline too was featureless, receding in either direction, endless mangrove and reefs. Otherwise there was only the bush, stretching away into the low hills. There was nothing for the eye to fix on, nothing that gave any real sense of perspective or place. And why else did you climb things, if not for perspective?

We climbed down. It was hot and we were sweating. The day waited to be filled.

We set about arranging the house for our private pursuits. My prime concern was a desk. There was nothing suitable anywhere. I dug through the junk shed again and found two more chairs with missing seats. I took them to my room, along with one of the doors from the broken wardrobe. I set the chairs about four feet apart, then lay the door across the backrests. The door had a full-length mirror on it, so I had the mirror facing upwards as the writing surface. I unpacked all the paper and ink and pens, arranged them on the desk. I sat down to test the feel of it, leaned on my elbows, stared at my reflection. Ten or twenty seconds passed. A mirror? For writing? Jesus.

I got up and found Wayne. He was making his choice about a studio. There were only the two spare bedrooms available—the one with all the old beds, and the one which was the chemical dump. The former was by far the bigger of the two, but also the darkest. The chemical dump, Wayne claimed, had the superior light.

So we began rearranging the bottles and cans, moving some of them in with the old beds. In the end we'd cleared half the room, which gave Wayne space enough for his two easels. We also uncovered a workbench on which he arranged his equipment. We stood admiring it all for a minute. It looked no more like a studio than my wardrobe door looked like a desk. Nor did it seem any more likely that Wayne was about to start painting than I was about to start writing.

Midday came along and with it Wayne's first observation. I tagged along for moral support. Wayne muddled his way through. The clouds were still low and heavy, the temperature an even 32 degrees, the wind very slight from the north-east. When it came to the radio, Wayne sounded even worse than I did. He got the call sign wrong, forgot to say 'Over', or to repeat each sequence of numbers. The operator sighed over the air and corrected him. Finally he was finished.

Outside again we were met by Kevin. He didn't bother barking. He panted at us. The heat and the humidity must have been lethal for him. It wasn't the place for a long-haired dog. Wayne squatted down and scratched his head.

'Hello Kevin,' he said.

We headed back towards the house. Kevin followed, trotting along the path. I assumed that Vince must still be asleep. The dog was in search of company. We sat on the front steps. Kevin dumped himself between Wayne's legs. It was obvious who he liked out of the two of us. Wayne kept scratching him. It was mutual.

'Look at all these ticks,' said Wayne, 'He's crawling with them.' He was digging around in Kevin's hair. I looked. There were fat black ticks all along the dog's spine. Dozens. Wayne tugged at them with his fingers. One came out. It squirmed between his fingers, pincers clutching. It was huge. Wayne put it on the step, crushed it with his thumb. The tick burst. Blood oozed onto the wood.

Wayne held Kevin down, got started on the others.

After my three o'clock observation we put two chairs on the back verandah and sat there. We opened some beer. Stared out. Bush. Ocean. Low clouds. Out to sea there even appeared to be rain. Precipitation. We talked about dinner.

'Can you cook?' I asked Wayne.

'Nothing special. What about you?'

'Spaghetti. Steak and chips.'

'Right.'

'You *have* lived away from home before haven't you?'

'Sure. I'm not big on cooking though.'

'I suppose I could make steak and chips then, tonight.'

'Fine with me.'

'Whoever doesn't cook has to wash-up.'

'You don't really think we're gonna wash-up every night?'

'No.'

We sipped on our beers.

'Did you notice a washing machine over at Vince's place?'
Wayne asked after a while.

I thought. 'No, I didn't.'

It was suddenly very quiet. It took me a moment to
notice what it was—the generator had stopped. And with
it all the ceiling fans in the house. The silence was dense.
Then there was the soft swish of wind in the trees. Bird
calls. A moment later the generator started up again. The
ceiling fans followed. The sounds of nature faded away.

We drank, stared out. Towards dusk the air began to fill
with small, black sandflies. They were swarming up from
the mangroves down below. Hordes of them. We'd noticed
this the previous evening, but inside, under the ceiling
fans, they hadn't been so bad. Now they were unbearable.
We slapped and scratched, then brought out the insect
repellent. I slathered it over my legs, arms and face.
Tropical strength. It seemed to work.

We went on sitting.

Wayne had the six o'clock observation, so at five-forty he
headed off alone. I began work on the dinner. Steak and
chips and peas. I went through our implements. One battered frypan, three pots. The gifts of my mother. It seemed
sufficient. All I needed now was music.

I went to my room, got my stereo. It was smaller and

older than Wayne's, but it functioned. I set it up and switched it on. The radio dial was mostly static except for one ABC station that was reading market prices. It sounded distant and irrelevant. I made a decision not to listen to the radio for the next six months. I'd ignore the world. No news broadcasts, no newspapers either. If we were supposed to be isolated, then we may as well be serious about it. It seemed a good decision. I found a tape, slotted it in, switched it on.

I cooked. I carved a couple of potatoes into chips. The steaks went into the pan. The peas into the pot. It all bubbled away. Wayne came back, got himself another beer from the fridge.

'How'd the weather go?' I asked.

'Fine. That operator in Darwin sounds like a very strong woman.'

'The operator?'

'Tough. You can hear it in her voice.'

'How do you like your steak?'

'Rare.'

Dinner was served on the table in the schoolroom. We moved our two chairs in from the verandah and sat there under the fluorescent lighting. Naked floorboards extended off to either end of the room. On the table there were two knives and forks. A bottle of tomato sauce. Salt and pepper. It was a dining room for working men.

I didn't feel like a working man. The steak was dry and the chips were soggy and the weather barely qualified as a job. After we'd finished, Wayne cleared the plates away and actually began washing-up. I took my beer and wandered out onto the front verandah. I looked across the compound to Vince's house. It was brightly lit, but there was no sign of him. I pictured him on his stool, upright, glass in hand. Did he expect us to return the dinner invitation? Did he expect any contact with us at all?

I remained on the front steps for a while, but there was nothing to see. I went back through the house, took the chairs to the back verandah and sat. Nothing there either. Wayne finished with the washing-up and joined me. We looked out at the blackness. Time passed slowly. Life without television.

In the end I resorted to the bourbon, and Wayne got himself stoned. We drank and smoked and talked from time to time. At eight-forty I took my glass of bourbon, and the torch, and stepped out for the nine p.m. observation.

I was drunk by this stage. I peered at all the meters and gauges, then staggered around gazing for the clouds. The sky was utterly black, so I wrote down eight-eighths of heavy cover. I began the encoding and finished it at four minutes to nine. I sat there waiting. The radio buzzed and sang. The fan swirled. I put my head behind my hands and stared at the ceiling.

I studied the spider webs in the corners. They were wispy, dirty things. I realised that the spiders in them were redbacks. Big, fat ones. I counted seven, just doing a quick sweep. I grew alarmed. I looked under the chair and under the desk. There were webs, but no spiders visible. I would have to be careful.

I also noticed, under the desk, several piles of old magazines. I pulled them out. They were mainly *People* and *Post*. I checked the dates. They were all over six months old. I flicked through a *People*, checking out the naked women. Breasts everywhere, some of them bigger than weather balloons. I dumped the pile. There were over a hundred issues there. They'd keep.

At nine the operator was on the air. I listened as she went through the list, picking up the names of the other weather stations. I heard Meningrida. Jabiru. Murgenella. The names meant nothing. I'd need a map. Wayne was right though, the operator sounded very much in control. A million square kilometres of air space, and it was all her territory. For most of the stations she greeted the weather observers by name. A matriarch. I imagined her as large, hard-bitten, dragging on a cigarette. Then the call Victor Lima Nine Charlie Uniform Cape Don came through. I answered and was heard. I read out my list of numbers, then I made my way back to the house. I was free until six a.m.

Wayne was still on the back verandah.

'We're gonna have to get some better chairs,' he said, 'These are terrible.'

'Indeed.'

'What games did you bring?'

'Scrabble and cards.'

He thought, shook his head. 'I'm not that bored yet.'

'How long do you think it'll take?'

We sat there until about eleven, drinking slowly, then called it quits. I went to my room and sat at the desk. I looked down at myself in the mirror. I got up and went through the pile of books I'd brought. Nothing looked interesting. I undressed, switched off the light and lay on the bed. The house was already growing familiar. I didn't think of ghosts or past residents. I switched the light on. I found the alarm clock and set it. Five-forty a.m.

FIFTEEN

The days passed. We settled into the three-hourly routine of the weather. It looked like being an easy enough life. The only chores were the early morning observations. Whoever had the 3 a.m. could easily stay awake for it, but the 6 and the 9 needed the alarm clocks. The ones we'd bought were the old-fashioned style—wind-up, with big bells on the top. It was an ugly sound to wake to, but that was the nature of timekeeping.

The weather itself varied. The first couple of days were mostly fine and hot. Then on Friday morning there were storms—huge Cb9s that rolled in off the sea with thunder and lightning and heavy rain. Thirty-three millimetres. It was loud on the iron roof. Water streamed through the gaps in the verandah ceiling. The ground sweated and steamed after the rain had passed, and within an hour everything was dry again. It was, we assumed, typical wet season weather. There was a old weather book in the shack with annual details on Cape Don conditions. The average March rainfall, it said, was just over 300 mm. That was fine with me. I liked rain.

Friday afternoon, after the morning storms were gone, the supply plane arrived. It did the low circle of the compound to identify itself, then flew off towards the airstrip. Vince picked up Wayne and I, and the three of us drove down along the track. The plane was waiting at the strip. It was the same one that had flown us over, with the same pilot. The cabin was jammed with grocery boxes. We were just the first on a long delivery run. We unloaded our boxes. The pilot gave Vince a small sack of mail and Conservation Commission correspondence. Vince handed over a wad of his letters, to be mailed back in Darwin. Then we drove home.

Vince kept mostly to his house. He didn't seem to do anything or go anywhere. The weather was our job now, and the lighthouse didn't need him. Exactly what his duties towards the national park itself were, I didn't know. What *did* a ranger do in a park that was Aboriginal land, and in which no visitors were allowed? We saw Kevin from time to time, and caught snatches of classical music on the breeze, but that was all.

Wayne spent a few hours in his studio, playing around with the easels and putting some canvas on a frame, but he did no painting. I sat at my desk several times. I loaded ink into the pen, wrote a few words with it. It was curious, seeing my handwriting on paper again. I missed the computer keyboard. I thought about writing novels. I'd done it before, after all. This would be my third attempt. Still, I couldn't seem to remember how it was done. Anyway, it felt too early to start. It would take a week or two. To get the feel of the place.

I wandered around the compound. There was nothing to see, nowhere to go. There was nothing to get the feel *of*. Only the bush. I walked off into it, looking around. In a few minutes the lighthouse was out of sight. I was enveloped by dense trees and ferns and long grass. Swamps glistened. It had a dark, disturbing feel to it. Hot. Still. And I wasn't a bushwalker, I wasn't aware of what to look for, be wary of. If I walked half an hour deeper in I'd probably never get out again. 'City boy starves within three hundred yards of own house.' I walked back to the compound.

On Sunday afternoon Vince came over and asked us if we wanted a look at the coast by boat. We said yes, as long as we were back in time for the next observation. We drove a short way down the track and took the one and only turn. It led down to a small bay. 'Keep an eye out for crocs,' Vince said, as we climbed out.

'Are you kidding?' I asked.

'Probably not.'

It was another overcast day. The water was grey and calm. The bay itself was roughly circular, opening northwards to the ocean. There was a narrow beach of sand where the track ended, but otherwise the bay was bound by mangroves and mudflats.

'You'd be unlucky to strike one on the beach,' Vince went on, 'But it is their territory.'

I took a long careful look. On the far side of the bay was the mouth of a creek. It wound its way back into the mangroves. It seemed very dark in there, a black tangle of branches and mud. No crocodiles though. We walked down towards the water's edge. There was one boat, pulled up above the high tide line. It was an aluminium dinghy with an outboard motor. Back up on the beach there were fuel drums and other equipment. Vince pumped petrol into a smaller can, fuelled-up the outboard.

'Is this going to be a patrol?' I asked.

'Sort of.'

'What are you looking for?'

'Anything.'

We shoved the boat into the water. Wayne and I climbed in and Vince pushed us off. We drifted a few yards. The boat had a central console with a wheel and a throttle on it. Vince hit the starter button. The engine whined and turned. I noticed lifejackets piled in the stern. Should we be wearing them? I looked down. The water was very clear, the bottom of rippled sand. The outboard wasn't starting.

We waited. Vince gave up on the button, played around with the outboard itself. He tried again. It turned over, but it didn't sound healthy and didn't start. We bobbed gently up and down, going nowhere.

'Fuck,' said Vince.

'What's wrong with it?'

'How should I know? I don't know anything about boats.'

He jumped out. The water was only knee-deep. He pulled the boat back to shore, and together we dragged it up the sand. Vince examined the outboard.

'It's stuffed,' he said, eventually.

'Can you fix it?'

'Maybe.'

We helped him disconnect it and load it into the back of the Toyota. Then we drove back towards the lighthouse. Vince smoked silently, staring through the windscreen.

I said, 'What else are you supposed to do here? If you don't have a boat, I mean.'

'Who knows. There'd be a management plan for the place *somewhere*, but I haven't seen it.'

We got back, unloaded the outboard into the workshed. Wayne and I returned to our house. There was nothing more to wait for, I decided. Assuming the boat wasn't going anywhere for a while, we'd seen all of the Cobourg Peninsula that we were likely to see.

But we waited anyway. We drank. Something about the atmosphere encouraged alcohol consumption. It was the heat, the fact that the beer seemed to sweat straight out of you, leaving you untouched, permanently thirsty. The hangovers weren't severe, and the hayfever and asthma were behaving themselves.

There was something, too, about the back verandah. We sat there for hours during the night, propped up on the kitchen chairs, listening to tapes, slotting can after can into the styrofoam coolers. We talked every now and then, but a lot of it was just sitting, looking at the stars. The rain came and went. At times there was lightning far out to sea. Wayne rolled joints. We watched the lighthouse beam sweep overhead.

Every afternoon around four the power went off briefly, came on again. I finally worked out it was Vince changing over the generators. He showed me around the generator shed. There were three of them, large diesels, set in the concrete floor. One of them was in pieces. Another, according to Vince, was in bad need of an overhaul. Only the third was reliable. Vince had been on the radio to Darwin several times, demanding new parts. He'd been waiting for months. As it was, he ran the two functioning generators on twenty-four hour shifts and hoped for the best. It was, he said, typical of everything at Cape Don.

We saw more of Kevin. He wandered into our house every now and then. Sniffed around. Lay at Wayne's feet. Departed. Wayne pulled ticks from his back. Vince eventually told him not to bother. New ticks replaced the old ones, and the new ones bothered the dog more. Kevin himself did what he could. The ticks were in the grass, so whenever he crossed the compound he stuck carefully to the paths. He didn't move fast, and even then he was only active in the evenings. Throughout the day he stayed under the ceiling fans and suffered. There was no suggestion that his real owner might ever return and collect him.

We learned from the dog. Night was the time for move-
ment.

Finally Vince donated two of his lounge chairs to our
cause. He said he didn't use them himself anyway. He
warned that we would have to return them though, if any
official visitors arrived. His house was the ranger station,
and the chairs were station furniture. We asked if the
chance of visitors was likely. He said he doubted it. We set
the chairs on the back verandah, and began to pass our
evening sessions in comfort.

SIXTEEN

Twenty to six, Friday morning, our seventeenth day. I hit the button on the clock and stopped the alarm. The room was dim, the air cool under the ceiling fan. The French windows were open. I looked out, saw it was raining. I got up, pulled on shorts and shirt, went out into the hall. The house was quiet, the rain whispering. Unwashed plates sat on the table. I pissed in the toilet, slipped my thongs on, flapped down the hall again, out the front door.

A grey world. Somewhere, perhaps, the sun was up. It occurred to me that a weather observer should know what time the sun rose and set. The phases of the moon. The tides. I would never be a true professional. I walked across the compound, raising my face to the rain. The sound of the generator was muted. Mists drifted below in the bush. I had the place to myself. Only two other people anywhere in the region, and both of them sleeping.

I went through the weather. Temperature at 25.9 degrees, rainfall 28 mls in the last three hours. I worked through the encoding, then sat awaiting the call from

126

Darwin. It was all standard stuff by now. I flicked through a *People* magazine, stared out the door. The static on the radio was heavy. At six the operator came through, but she couldn't hear me in return. I was instructed to switch to another channel and did so. It didn't help, I was talking to no one. The operator gave up on me and called the next station. I began writing a note to tell Wayne that he'd have to call in the 6 a.m. details when he got through at nine.

I finally realised that there was nothing written in the 3 a.m. slot. The 3 a.m. was Wayne's that morning. He hadn't done it. It meant I had to correct some of my figures. For one thing, 28 mls had fallen in the last nine hours, not the last three. It was a bad one to skip, the 3 a.m. Not only because it left a long gap between the 9 p.m. and the 6 a.m., but because it paid the most. Fifteen dollars, compared to seven-fifty for a mid-afternoon slot.

It was our first missed observation. One in over two weeks though, the Bureau could hardly complain. I stood in the doorway and watched the morning. I was no longer tired. That was the problem. You had to be up for only twenty minutes to do the weather, but it was long enough for the body to forget about going back to sleep. I walked through the rain to the house.

I made toast. I sat on the verandah and watched the water drip from the roof. I felt good. Maybe it was true what some people said. Mornings weren't so bad. Around eight I went back to bed and read. At twenty to nine I was still awake. I heard Wayne's alarm start ringing. It clicked off. I waited. The minutes passed. His door didn't open. Eventually I rose and knocked on his door.

'Wayne? You getting up?'

There were muffled sounds from inside. Then the door opened and he poked his head out, bleary-eyed.

'What?'

'The 9 a.m. observation. You've only got about five minutes left.'

He grunted, shuffled back inside. He came out dressed, then headed off towards the weather shack. I sat on the front steps. The rain had stopped. The day's heat was building, steam drifting across the ground. After about fifteen minutes Wayne came back.

I said, 'How'd it go?'

He still looked mostly asleep. His face and his arms were spotted, livid with sandfly bites. He didn't have the skin for mangrove country. 'It was fine.'

'What happened to the 3 a.m.?'

'I dunno.'

'Did you set your alarm?'

'I didn't get up, that's all. I was pretty stoned when I went to bed.'

'You've gotta get up Wayne.'

'It doesn't matter if we miss just one.'

'No, but what about the nine? You would've missed that too if I hadn't been awake.'

'Alright, I'll make sure I get up next time.'

'We only get paid for the ones we do.'

'I know. Don't panic.'

He banged through the screen door and was gone. I sat there. The screen door banged open. 'If you were so worried about it,' Wayne said, 'Why didn't you just do the nine yourself?'

'Because it's not *mine*. It's not my job to make sure you do yours.'

'Okay, so if I miss one then I don't get paid for it. It's my loss.'

'It's not just the money. They won't like it in Darwin if we start missing them every day.'

'They won't care.'

'Yes they will.'

'Well what d'you care? We're not making a career out of this.'

He was gone. I was glad. I had no reply to the question. Why *did* I care? It was only a job. It wasn't the real reason we were there. In six months we'd be gone and it'd make no difference whether we'd done it well or not.

Wayne came out again. 'You know, you could've just made up the stuff for the 3 a.m. We can never reach Darwin on the radio then anyway—how are they to know if we actually got up for it or not? We could sleep right through the three *and* the six.'

I looked at him. 'We are not going to do it that way.'

'Jesus, why are you so fucking responsible all of a sudden?'

'Because *one* of us has to be.'

He thought, went to say something, went away.

I sat. That'd fixed him.

Then I thought.

It'd fixed me, too.

SEVENTEEN

It rained off and on for the next few days. Wayne and I were confined to the house. It was a big house though, and we managed to avoid each other. I sat at the desk long enough to write some letters. Otherwise I lay on the bed and read. I could hear Wayne in his studio, his stereo on high volume. As far as I knew, he hadn't started painting. We didn't mention the observations again, and Wayne didn't miss any.

We received some news. It was Tuesday. I had the midday shift. The Darwin operator came on air, but instead of the usual routine she first relayed a message from the Met. Bureau to all coastal weather stations. It was an announcement that a tropical low in the Arafura Sea had developed into a tropical cyclone. It was named Matthew. It was 400 ks north of Cape Wessel, and heading south-west at 10 ks an hour. A high wind warning was current for the coast of Arnhem Land and the Cobourg Peninsula. I considered this. There were no high winds being recorded on our wind meter, and only a few patches of rain. I had no idea where Cape Wessel was.

After I'd reported our weather I went over to Vince's house and informed him of the situation. We consulted the map. Cape Wessel was five hundred ks east of us. That put us roughly in the cyclone's path. We went back out to the weather shack and studied the barograph. The air pressure was currently around 1004 mb, and on a slight downward bent. Maximum wind gust for the day so far, 12 kph.

Vince decided that for the time being nothing need be done. If it seemed that Matthew was going to come close, he'd see about getting the place ready. We'd wait on the weather reports.

'In the meantime,' he said, 'I'd better radio Russel and Eve and the others over at Araru. They're a bit closer to it than we are. They might wanna know.'

We watched the barometer overnight. It rose and fell in the usual daily cycle, but the overall trend was slowly downwards. The radio reported that Matthew was maintaining speed and direction. I grew excited. I'd never been caught in a cyclone before. I thought about things I'd heard. Howling winds, torrential rains. The deceptive stillness of the eye, passing over. Would we still be expected to make weather reports in the middle of a cyclone? In winds 200, 250 ks an hour? I pictured myself battling across to the weather shack at 3 a.m.—the sky convulsing, rain stinging in my eyes—to scream a last report down the airwaves to Darwin.

And by late next day things were looking encouraging. The sky was overcast and a steady, light rain was falling, draping the ocean with grey. Maximum gust was up to around 30 kph. In the evening Vince dropped over to discuss the situation. He'd spent the day cleaning up around the compound. Stacking away petrol drums, bits of junk, anything that might become airborne debris should the cyclone hit.

'If it does,' he said, 'You guys will have to move over to my house.'

'Why?'

'You think this house is safe?'

'It's made of stone.'

'The walls are, but I wouldn't trust the roof, or what's left of the verandahs, if a real wind got up. I'd take over the weather too.'

'You mean do our observations?'

He nodded seriously. 'This is a Conservation Commission station, and I'm in charge of it. You guys are my responsibility. I don't want the two of you blundering around in a cyclone.'

I thought about that. 'What about you?'

'I'd rig up a safety line from my house to the weather shack. I'd be alright.'

'A line. You're kidding.'

'You've got no idea what those winds can do, do you?'

'You've been in a cyclone?'

'I was in Darwin for Tracy.'

'Shit.'

He nodded. 'Shit indeed.'

'So what was it like?'

He scratched his ear. 'Actually . . . I spent the night in a pub.'

We looked at him.

He shrugged. 'I was just having a few drinks there, you know, for Christmas Eve. The police dropped in and said it looked like the thing'd hit that night, told everyone to stay put for the time being. Who was gonna argue? The owner kept the bar open, so we sat there all night. It was a solid place, big thick walls and a good reinforced roof, so we hardly knew what was going on outside. The power went, and some of the windows got smashed, and there was lots of noise, but nothing you wouldn't expect. No one went outside. It was too dark to see anything anyway. It wasn't until daylight that we realised what had happened. We staggered out half-pissed, and the town wasn't there anymore.'

I thought about the pictures in the papers and on TV, the wreckage, the deaths and injuries, the mass evacuations . . .

'Did you stay?' I asked, 'Afterwards?'

He nodded. 'Joined one of the clean-up crews. Even found one of the bodies.' He paused. 'That was a few days later though.'

That night the Bureau had a special message for Cape Don. Due to the proximity of the cyclone, we were to go on emergency footing. Instead of the three-hourly reports we were now to do an observation every hour, midnight included. We did as they asked. It was more money for one thing, and we weren't doing anything else. It was no time for painting or writing.

The rain continued most of the night and the barometer kept edging downwards. At 3 a.m. it was 996. Maximum gust by the next morning was 50 kph. According to the bulletins, Matthew was just under 200 ks to the north-east.

Next day, not long after the midday report, Vince arrived at our front steps. He was driving the Toyota. 'I've just been on the radio again to Araru,' he said, 'Russel and Eve are on their way back by boat. I'm off to meet them. Wanna come?'

We climbed in. The rain, for the time being, was holding off. The clouds were still dense though, and low, streaming across the sky. We rattled out of the compound and down into the bush. It was dim down there, the wind tossing the trees, smacking large drops of moisture down onto the windscreen. Water pooled on the tracks, gleamed in freshly flooded swamps.

We didn't take the turn to the bay. Vince explained that normally Russel and Eve would dock there, but not today. They were wary about the present weather, so they were making the trip as short as possible. There was another small inlet on the far side of the airstrip. It would save them maybe twenty minutes at sea if we met them there.

We reached the strip and drove directly across it. There was another small track, barely more than two wheel ruts, winding through the trees. Vince paused and slipped the Toyota into four-wheel drive. We bumped and slewed along. The undergrowth was thick, and the ground alternated between loose sand and red mud.

I said, 'Why didn't they stay at Araru, if the weather's that bad?'

'Russel thought he should be here, just in case. It's his job, after all. They'll make it across. They're an experienced lot with boats, the Gurig. They're mainly a sea people y'know. They might hunt inland, but they always live near the coast.'

'What sort of boat do they have?'

'Just a dinghy, same as mine.'

We made slow progress through the bush for another fifteen minutes or so. Then we emerged onto a tiny beach. It ran down into mangroves on either side. It was situated at the mouth of what appeared to be a rapidly-flowing channel, maybe fifty-yards across. Beyond it was the wide grey ocean, capped with white. The wind was much stronger here, wilder, whistling in my ears. Low waves were being driven deep into the mangroves. The black branches surged up and down, awash with foam.

'This is as far east as you can go,' Vince half-yelled, head turned away from the wind, 'This creek flows from the swamp that cuts us off from the rest of the Peninsula.'

'How long does it take to get here from Araru?' I shouted back.

'About an hour. In good weather.'

We all stood on the beach, hands in pockets, leaning into the wind. We stared out to sea. The land curved out to a point, then there was nothing. Only mist and shadow. I could almost sense the cyclone out there now, a greater darkness beyond the horizon. From time to time a stronger gust would flick up spray from the sea, stinging our eyes and forcing us back on our heels.

At length, a black dot appeared. It was a small boat, hugging the coastline. As it closed in I could see it was an aluminium dinghy with an outboard motor. It was making heavy going in the swell, chopping awkwardly from crest to crest. Five people were in it, all Aboriginal. Standing upright, riding the waves.

Vince peered at the boat, nodded. 'I thought he might be with them.'

'Who?'

'Allan Price. You two wait here. If he wants to meet you, I'll call you down.'

Wayne and I waited at the top of the beach. Vince went down to the water's edge. His thin hair was streaming in the wind, and his thongs sank in the sand. The boat swung into the smoother waters of the channel. There were four men and one woman. They stared up at Wayne and I, then at Vince as the boat neared the shore. Two of them jumped out and pulled the boat in. The other two men and the woman then stepped out and walked over to Vince.

I assumed the woman was Eve. She looked quite young, with a thin, frowning face. She hung back, carrying a cardboard box of gear. The two men were older. One seemed about thirty, tall, with swept-back, greyish hair. He was wearing a ranger shirt. Russel, then. He nodded to Vince, waited. The other man was smaller, and much older. No shirt. There was white hair on his chest, a straggly beard of it on his face. His expression was severe, stern. Russel's father, Allan Price. He shook Vince's hand, and the two of them turned to the ocean, conferring.

The rest of us waited. I felt conspicuous, standing there on the sand. The two men at the boat kept glancing up at Wayne and I. The looks weren't friendly. I remembered we were two city boys, white, with only a few weeks in the place, and no one had wanted us there anyway. We waited. The skies blew. The mangroves writhed. Whatever Vince and the old man were saying, no one else there could hear it above the wind and the sea.

Finally they were finished. They shook hands again. The old man gave one long, dark look up to Wayne and I. Then he spoke a word to Russel, and walked back to the boat. The other two pushed off, jumped on board. In moments they were motoring out of the channel again, all three standing straight, riding the swell with ease. Vince and the other two came up the beach.

'Gordon and Wayne,' Vince yelled, 'This is Russel and Eve.'

They nodded at us, saying nothing. We nodded back. We all stood there. Eve shifted her box, stared away. A sheet of rain was coming in off the ocean, wind-driven. The boat had already vanished.

Vince gave up trying to light a cigarette. He looked at Russel. 'Rough crossing?'

'Not so bad.'

Vince indicated the darkness in the northern sky. 'Your old man call up this cyclone?'

Russel followed his glance out to sea, gave a short smile. 'Not this one.'

EIGHTEEN

Dusk came early. The air was heavy with cloud and rain. In the weather shack the barometer was down to 986 and dropping fast. Vince and Russel had spent the afternoon on final preparations, now they made for their houses, battened them down. We entered the long night of the cyclone.

Wayne and I sat in our house. The wind was regularly gusting over seventy now, blasting the rain in under our verandah. A sheet of iron somewhere up on the roof was giving out ominous screeches. The screen doors around the house banged open and shut. After dark the reception from Darwin started to go. The last report we heard was at nine p.m. Matthew was 80 ks north-east and holding steady on course. Winds at the centre were reported to be between 160 and 200 kph.

We kept up the hourly observations, even though it was impossible to radio them in. It seemed unlikely that we'd be sleeping much anyway. Vince dropped in. If the winds got up over 100 kph at any stage, he wanted us over in his

house. We agreed, but reluctantly. We didn't like the idea
of placing ourselves under Vince's control. It felt good out
there on our own back verandah, staring into the wind and
darkness. We wanted to go it alone. We were out of beer,
but we had a cask of wine, and were drinking steadily.

In the meantime there was a degree of boredom in the
waiting. The back verandah was too wet for lengthy periods
of sitting, so we spent most of the time in the long, empty
dining room. The ceiling fans were still on. Away from the
wind and rain, it was as warm as ever. Wayne was sketch-
ing on a pad, I was reading. We kept the stereo down low.
It seemed important to listen to the sounds from outside.
Or for the long groan of the roof giving way.

'What about Scrabble,' I asked.

Wayne threw down the pad. 'Okay.'

I went through the luggage and found the Scrabble set.
It was old, the box squashed flat. The board was there
though, and there seemed to be plenty of letters. We set it
up on the table.

'Ever played this?' I asked.

'I don't think so. Have you?'

'Only a couple of times, years ago.'

'Are there rules?'

We found them on the back of the lid, read through them.
There were details I'd forgotten. No capitalised words, and
a fifty-point bonus for using all seven letters at once. There
were rules, too, about consulting the dictionary. I went to
my room and got the only dictionary I'd brought with me.
It was a relic from my school days. An *Oxford Concise*. For
an alleged writer, I wasn't planning to use much of a
vocabulary.

We played a game. The house shook and rattled. Rain
came and went in loud rushes. Wayne had to leave midway
through for the 11 p.m. observation. There was no point in

bothering with the umbrella, so he came back wet, towelled off. He reported eight-eighths cloud cover, and a barometer reading of 980. Precipitation was nineteen mls in the hour and the maximum wind gust an even eighty. He also won the Scrabble. Our scores were both around the one-sixty, one-seventy mark. Neither of us had scored any seven-letter words. I had a feeling it was possible to play considerably better.

We started another game.

At 1.50 a.m., it was my turn for the observation. I'd made a comeback in the Scrabble stakes and was up two games to one. Highest score two-forty, one seven-letter word. Wayne had gone back to his drawing. I ventured out into the night, torch in hand.

It was wild and lonely out there. All the streetlights were on, and the three houses were brightly lit, but everything was blurred with wind and rain. The trees visible on the fringes of the compound were dim, frenzied shapes. Beyond them was total void—no stars or moon, only a great, whistling darkness.

I turned my face away from the rain, made it to the shack. From the doorway I looked back at the houses. I assumed that Vince, and Russel and Eve, were all still awake, but there was no sign of any of them. Both houses were fitted with modern storm-shutters on the verandahs, and these were down. I turned back inside.

It was dry and still in the little room. The redbacks sat fatly in their webs, undisturbed. The radio was a mass of static. The first thing I did was check the wind meter. Maximum gust, 91 kph. What would 180 be like? 220? Then it was to the barometer. I peered at it, blinking drops of water out of my eyes. 976. Four points in three hours. That was about as fast as a barometer could drop. That was plummeting.

I got through the rest of the weather, then set off for the house. Halfway across the wind rose, roared, blasted me sideways. Somewhere ahead there was a sharp bang and the world went abruptly black. The houses, the street-lights, everything disappeared. For a moment the night and the cyclone had me. I reeled, stuck my arms out, hit the ground. I lay there, staring up, wide-eyed, lost in noise. The lighthouse beam—still turning, the only light remaining—was veering across the sky. The fucking thing was *falling*.

The gust eased. The lighthouse wasn't falling. It was some sort of illusion in the wind and darkness. I lay there for a moment, feeling solid earth. Then I got to my hands and knees. I switched on the torch and cast the light around, illuminating wet grass and driving rain. I wasn't sure what to do. I was soaked, muddy. Maybe this was it, the beginning of the end. A light appeared. It was Vince, with another torch. I stood up carefully, waited for him.

'That was a strong one,' he shouted.

'What happened to the lights?'

'Probably the generator.'

We went over to the generator shed. Its door was loose, slamming in the wind. We went in. The generators were silent, but there was no sign of any damage. Russel appeared. He and Vince peered around the shed, but found no reason for the breakdown.

'It was the dodgy one,' Vince said finally, 'Maybe it just packed it in?'

I told him about the bang I'd heard. We decided it may have been nothing more than the door giving way. Perhaps there'd been some obscure vacuum effect that made the engine stall. There was nothing for it but to fuel-up the third generator and see if it started. It did. The lights came back on. We went out and examined the night.

Wind and rain and tumult. Wayne came out of our house. He reported that the last gust had taken several sheets of roofing from the back verandah. He sounded shaken, yelling over the wind. I thought about what it might've been like, in a suddenly dark house, hearing metal rip away. We all went back to the wind meter. Maximum gust, 130 kph.

'That's it,' Vince said, 'You're coming over to my place.'

We didn't argue.

For the next four hours we sat in Vince's living room. There were none of the creaks and groans of our own house, and the storm outside sounded more remote. Vince also had some beer left, so we drank it. He remained at his desk, on his stool, sipping port and listening. I was tired now. The cyclone showed no signs of either intensifying or easing. Vince let Wayne and I continue the observations, but they gave no certain indications. The barometer was stable, the big gusts hovering around 100, 110.

By 6 a.m., though, they'd fallen back into the 80s. There was a grey light outside. Everything in the compound still seemed to be in its place, even the roof of our house. The rain remained heavy, driving across the clearing. Streams of water cascaded down the track into the bush. By 8 a.m. the winds had eased dramatically. Maximum gust in the hour was only in the 60s. At 9 a.m we could hear Darwin again. The announcement was that Matthew was now eighty kilometres west, north-west of Cape Don, and heading directly west at fifteen ks an hour. It had curved in, toyed with us, now it was swinging away.

'That's that then,' I said.

Vince shrugged. 'Cyclones do turn around y'know. Everyone thought Tracy was gone, then it just came back.'

It was true, I knew, but it didn't seem likely. It was Melville Island's worry now. Wayne and I went back to our house. I inspected the damage on the back verandah. The new hole in the roof was down the far end, where the floor was already missing. It wouldn't affect us. I looked out. The sea was still grey and tumbled, and the horizon black, but somehow, in the pale morning light, it was not impressive.

It was over, I decided. I yawned, turned for bed.

NINETEEN

The cyclone didn't return. It sailed on westwards and expired in the Indian Ocean. At Cape Don the rain stopped, the winds vanished and the sky cleared. The Bureau took Wayne and I off our emergency footing. It was back to the routine.

Over the next week or so the weather remained hot and dry. There were no more thunderstorms or showers. The humidity dropped steadily. We knew what it meant. The monsoon had changed. The wet season was over, we were into the dry. For the next five months we'd have meteorological stability. No rain, no clouds, no wild variations in temperature or air pressure. Just endless blue skies and warm, still nights.

And dull times for weather observers. The observations still had to be done, of course, but whatever challenge that job might've ever had, it was gone. The reports were the same every day. There was only one thing new. In the mornings we'd all be thrown out of bed by a series of sharp, booming explosions, followed by a dwindling roar. It was the RAAF and their F-111s. Now that the weather was fine, their training runs took them out over Cape Don. For amusement they liked to drop down low and go supersonic or subsonic just over the lighthouse.

The tourist season.

Wayne started on a painting. I looked in from time to time, examined the canvas. I didn't know what to make of it. Art was a mystery. I saw dark colours, blacks and browns and ochrous reds. Abstract human figures. Swirls. It was ugly and beautiful, but I had no idea what his motivations were, what he was saying. I played it cool. Said nothing.

But it was a sign. It was time to get started myself. I sat down at the mirror and thought about writing. I already had the ideas. I'd had them for months. Still, knowing where to begin was the problem. I tried planning chapters, narrative. I gave up. Planning was an odious thing. I was a *writer*, not an economist. I went with the spirit, leapt into it. Things got confused. I didn't know what I was doing. After two or three days I stopped.

I wasn't concerned. There was plenty of time. Instead I started writing letters. Leo. Madelaine. Other old friends. I described the lighthouse and the compound at length. I described Vince. Russel and Eve. The Scrabble games Wayne and I were playing. The letters ran twenty, thirty, forty pages. They were good stuff, I still had it. Writing *letters* was no problem at all.

Otherwise I read books, sat on the back verandah, drank, and watched the world. Cape Don was familiar enough now, the compound and the bush and the distant ocean. It was slow and quiet. Vince was in his house, Eve and Russel were in theirs, and Wayne and I were in ours. We were all only a hundred yards apart, but no one went visiting much.

Vince and Russel did stray into view from time to time, working around the place. Neither of them seemed very busy. They mowed the grass. They fiddled around under the hood of the second four-wheel drive, or with the generators. Minor things. I couldn't see any *ranger* work being done. There were no patrols. The outboard motor hadn't been fixed, and they were still waiting for the cruiser to come back from Darwin.

I wondered a little about Russel. I hadn't spoken to him since the cyclone. All I knew about him was that he'd been at Cape Don far longer than Vince. Years. His whole life, in fact. It was *his* land, after all. Cape Don, the whole Peninsula. Vince told me that the Commission had a scheme to get the traditional owners active as rangers to help run the park. To date, Russel was the only one who'd joined.

And Kevin didn't like him. I noticed that whenever Russel went near Vince's house, the dog went beserk. Barking, yapping, snarling. Even in the middle of the day, when normally Kevin couldn't be roused to do anything. Russel didn't seem to care. He laughed at the dog, kicked it, ignored it. I mentioned it all to Vince one afternoon, in the generator shed.

'It's not just Russel Kevin hates,' Vince said, 'It's anyone black.'

'Why?'

'Russel reckons he was trained that way. You know, put in a bag, beat up, then shown someone who's Aboriginal. That sort of shit.'

'By who?'

'I dunno.'

'But isn't he owned by the ranger who was here before you?'

'Yep.'

I thought about that. I said, 'Would a *ranger* train a dog that way?'

'No idea.'

'Do you know this guy?'

Vince glanced up from the generators. 'Look, I don't know anything about it. I've never met him. All they told me was that he went crazy and left.'

I didn't press it. Vince seemed to have his own burdens. Boredom mainly. There was never more than an hour or so's employment for him each day, otherwise he just sat in his living room. And drank. A visit would almost invariably find him drinking. He'd be perched on his stool, typing or just staring at the page, classical music blaring, a cigarette smouldering in the ashtray. Lights would be on in his house till two, three, four in the morning.

Every fourth night or so the generators would fail. I'd be woken by the sudden silence. Without the ceiling fan it was too hot to sleep. I'd wander outside with the torch and stand by the generator shed, waiting for Vince. The generators were his special curse. Sometimes he wouldn't arrive, so I'd go over and hammer and yell at his door. Eventually he'd come stumbling out, red-eyed and half-wild, redolent of alcohol.

But no matter what happened, there remained a polite distance between us all. No one ever entered anyone else's house without knocking first, and waiting to be asked in. Even Russel and Vince, though they worked together and seemed on perfectly friendly terms. I'd watch Vince go over to Russel's house, knock on the door, then wait at the bottom of the steps for Russel to come out. Russel himself had nothing to do with Wayne and me. And Eve hardly ever left their house. I came across her only once out in the open. I said 'Hello Eve.' She gave me a sharp look and hurried off. I felt like I'd said something obscene.

Maybe I had. Maybe that was the way of small communities. There was a strict etiquette to be observed. Privacy.

Finally Russel and Eve packed up their gear and headed back to Araru. A boat came over for them. Why they had stayed so long at the lighthouse wasn't clear. Why they were going back to Araru wasn't clear either. It was down to the three of us again.

Vince stayed in his house and drank. Wayne and I drank too. Friday nights were the heavy sessions, after the supply plane dropped off fresh supplies. Saturday night as well. There was a certain amount of danger to it, being drunk out on the back verandah. Wayne fell through one of the holes. He was striding about, stoned, drink in hand. There was a crack and he vanished. I got up, looked down. He was sprawled in the bushes, looking around, a little stunned.

'You fell through,' I said.

'Shit. Is that what it was.'

Our weekly order was three cartons of beer, a bottle of bourbon and two four-litre casks of wine. We'd try to stretch it over the week, but usually by Wednesday we were down to the dregs. Thursday nights were dry. We began ordering VB instead of Fourex. They tasted about the same, but VB was the Territory drink. The green can seemed appropriate in the tropics in a way that the golden Fourex can just didn't.

The days passed. Wayne missed another 3 a.m. observation, and then a 6 a.m. We squabbled about it, but got nowhere. Wayne had no concern for the job at all anymore. Nor could I think of any serious reason why he should. He had the painting now. And I still had the writing. I stared into the mirror on my desk. I started chapters, threw them away.

Mail started arriving from Brisbane. Life there seemed much the same as ever. People were forming relationships, breaking-up, getting bored. Still, excitement was in the air.

The town was gearing up for the opening day of Expo. Everyone knew it would be the biggest party the planet had ever seen. Brisbane finally exploding onto the international stage, eclipsing Melbourne, eclipsing Sydney. Taking its place among the great cities of the world. New York, London, Paris.

Back at Cape Don, the radio operator had begun calling Wayne and I by our first names.

TWENTY

One morning Vince came over and announced that Cape
Don would be receiving visitors. A group of the Conservation Commission hierarchy was making a tour of the park,
and would be overnighting at the lighthouse. Our friend
Terry Gallagher, the Commission boss, would be among
them. So Vince wanted his chairs back.

'And you might wanna clean this place up a little,' he
said, 'In case anyone looks in.'

We thought about it. He was right, the house was a mess.
The dining room was slowly filling up with a clutter of
empty grocery boxes, beer cartons, stubbies, magazines,
overflowing ashtrays. We stacked some of it into corners. I
left the kitchen to Wayne. Serious washing-up was done
only once every three or four days, and it was his turn.

The dignitaries arrived the next day. A large twin-engine
plane did the circuit of the lighthouse and Vince went off
to greet it. He was cleanly shaven. He was also wearing a
complete ranger uniform, washed and ironed. Shoes. It was
unnerving. After he'd gone Wayne and I sat on the front

steps to wait. Something about Vince's tone the day before had suggested a hope that we might stay decently out of sight while his guests were around. We were determined to at least be visible.

The Toyota returned, parked outside Vince's house and discharged five visitors. Three men, one of them a pilot, and two women. None of them were in ranger uniform. I recognised Terry Gallagher but the others were strangers— middle-aged, office types. It was close to lunch time, and Vince had set-up a table and chairs for a barbecue under a tree next to his house. He and the women went over and sat down.

The three men made straight for the lighthouse, disappeared inside. They emerged on the very top balcony, yelling and laughing, boys on top of the biggest phallic symbol for miles around. They called down to the women. The women ignored them. They were relaxing in the shade, beers in their hands. Vince sat with them, stiff on the edge of his chair, not drinking. He looked uncomfortable and very sober.

When the men came down Terry broke away and walked over to Wayne and me. We exchanged greetings, discussed how the job was going, commented upon the cyclone. Had it been rough? No, we answered, not so rough. Then Terry asked if he could see some of Wayne's paintings. There were still, he said, those portraits to be discussed.

We all went into the studio. It was familiar enough now to both Wayne and me. We'd forgotten that half the room was stacked with chemicals. And that Wayne had splattered paint all over the floor and walls. Vince had said this was no problem, as the house would be demolished sooner or later anyway, but it didn't look good.

Then there were the paintings themselves. Whatever was going on in Wayne's mind, it was getting blacker. He'd cast huge dark slashes across the painted canvases—purples, greys, deep browns, black. Bits of paper and torn out text were stuck here and there. Photos from *People*. It was ugly and chaotic and I was quite impressed. Terry wasn't.

'What happened to the portraits?' he said, after a pause.

'I only do portraits by commission.'

'Mmmm. Well this isn't really what I had in mind.'

'No.'

'I was thinking of things I could hang in the office.'

'Right.'

'You can sell this stuff?'

'I dunno.'

We all stood there, nodding to ourselves for a while. Then Terry excused himself. He had to get back to the barbecue. There was no more mention of portrait painting. Wayne watched him go.

'Looks like I got out of *that* one.'

Later that afternoon I was sitting in the dining room when a man appeared. It was one of the guests. He hadn't knocked or announced himself. He nodded at me, carried on. He had a clipboard and was looking around the house, noting down information. He looked in the bathroom, the back verandah, the bedrooms. He spent some time in the kitchen. Wayne hadn't cleaned-up yet. The man came out, scribbling on the clipboard, went off down the hall. I forgot about him.

Later still, Vince dropped over with important news. He'd been asked to accompany the other guests on the rest of the tour of the Peninsula. There was to be a general meeting over at Black Point for Commission staff. He'd be gone for three or four days. That meant Wayne and I would be in charge. Vince was a little dubious about this, but there wasn't any choice, seeing Russel was away.

'It's the generators I'm worried about,' he said, 'You guys know anything about engines?'

'Gordon's the farm boy,' Wayne said.

Vince looked at me. 'Well?'

'Well yes, I was raised on a farm, but I don't know anything about engines.'

'You'll do.'

We went over to the shed and talked about the generators and what I might expect from them. There were still only two in working order. I noticed that they were Perkins diesels. My father's tractors ran on Perkins diesels, and I had, in fact, done a *little* work on them. Vince was impressed. I was qualified after all. We talked about life on the farm. Then he showed me the four o'clock change-over routine. It was simple enough—five minutes of servicing and fuelling and playing around with the mains switches. Anyone could've done it.

We went outside. The generators were covered. Otherwise all Wayne and I had to do was meet the supply plane when it arrived, and make sure Kevin got fed. So much for the duties of a park ranger.

Vince said, 'Have you noticed the guy walking around with the clipboard?'

'Yeah. Who is he?'

'He's inspecting all the equipment and accommodation around the place. He showed me his notes. About you two. Among other things, he reckons that you've effectively vandalised your house, and that your domestic habits are disgusting.'

'Really?'

Vince nodded, rolling a cigarette. There was a certain ease between us now. We were two men of the Territory, and we'd shared a discussion on machinery.

'He thinks I should do something about it.'

'And?'

'Oh I might've.' He sniffed. 'If the guy wasn't such a prize dickhead.'

Next morning I drove them all out to the airstrip. The plane was still there. They all piled in. Vince hung back.

'Right,' he said, 'Don't fuck-up while I'm gone.'

'We won't.'

'We? I mean *you*. You're in charge.'

'Okay.'

Vince got in the plane. I waited until they were airborne. Then I drove back to the lighthouse. Wayne and I were alone.

TWENTY-ONE

Cape Don, population two men and a dog. It made no real difference. Wayne spent the afternoon painting in his studio. I wrote letters in my bedroom. Kevin slept in the shade of our verandah. At four I changed the generators over. There were no problems.

In the evening we gathered for dinner and Scrabble. We played Scrabble most nights now, at least one game. After my initial loss the tally was 17 to 1 in my favour. Wayne didn't seem to be grasping the more advanced tactics and strategies. Myself, I was clocking-up at least one seven-letter word per game, and averaging around 250 to 300 points. There was, I felt, still some way to go. What did a Scrabble champion average? What was the record for one seven-letter word? What was the highest overall score ever? I was keen to learn.

But we had no alcohol and the night was slow. The next day was a Friday, grocery day. Around midday I was sitting on the verandah, waiting for the plane. Wayne came out.

'I'm going exploring,' he said.

'Where?'

'Eve and Russel's. I wanna see what sort of stuff they've got.'

'You're going in their house?'

'They're not here. They won't know.'

'But you can't just go in.'

'Why not?'

'Wayne, you just can't.'

'You coming?'

'*No.*'

I watched him go. He went up the front steps of their house and disappeared inside. I waited. The man was a fool. It was indecent. Going into Russel and Eve's uninvited was like breaking and entering. They'd shown no desire to have us in there, no desire to have *anyone* in there. I thought about Russel suddenly arriving and finding Wayne. I thought about accusations, violence. Allan Price being informed. Banishment.

Even worse, I was curious. What *was* in that house? It wasn't something I normally concerned myself with, other people's possessions. But there wasn't much to think about or see around the lighthouse. The interior of Russel and Eve's house was the only place strictly off-limits, the only mystery. Time passed. Wayne didn't emerge. I had the midday observation. I went off, did it, came back. Still no Wayne. Fuck him then. I went to my room. It was another two hours before I heard him clump up our front steps. He went into his studio.

I lay there on the bed. Now I was genuinely angry. Bad enough he'd broken an unwritten law, he could at least have told me what he'd found. I debated with myself for a few minutes. I shouldn't care. The information was soiled, obtained by foul means. It was no use. I got up, went to the studio. Wayne looked up at me, all innocent.

'Well?' I said.

'They've got a TV.'

'Shit.'

This changed everything. A *television*.

I said, 'I thought you couldn't pick anything up around here.'

'You probably can't. It's connected to a video. They've got a stack of movies over there. I watched one.'

'Jesus. What was it?'

'*Pale Rider*. It's a Clint Eastwood western. That's all they've got, westerns and martial arts movies. It wasn't very good.'

'And what's the rest of the house like?'

'Their bedroom's nice. They've got a great big bed with a mosquito net canopy.'

'You went into their *bedroom*?'

'I just had a look.'

It didn't matter. Videos. Why hadn't Vince thought of that? Why hadn't we? I went back outside, looked across at Russel and Eve's house. This was cruel. A television, movies, so close. I wrestled with temptation. Did privacy really matter? I had no interest in the martial arts films, but westerns, they weren't so bad. I walked down the stairs. I could at least go and see what titles they had, there was no harm in that . . .

There was a noise in the air. I looked up and saw the supply plane coming in on its loop. It was a white cross in the sky, the hand of God, a sign. Stay away from the video, it said.

I did what I was told. I walked over to the Toyota, drove out to the strip.

It was a happy time. Fresh food. Letters. Three full cartons of beer, the bourbon, and the wine. Wayne and I settled into the night's indulgence. It was always the same. Whatever petty arguments we'd had through the week, they vanished with the first drink on Friday night. Alcohol solved everything. Indeed, the arguments only ever came on Wednesdays or Thursdays, when the alcohol was gone.

We drank. It was a fine night on the back verandah, cloudless, the sky alive with stars. Beer after beer went down. Dinner came and went. The 9 p.m. observation came and went. We had nothing more to do for six hours. Cape Don was all ours, we were Lords. Wayne rolled a couple of joints and we switched to bourbon. The world fell away as it always did. Details became imprecise, concepts vaster. A need for action seized me.

'We have to do something,' I said.

'Like what.'

'Let's go for a drive.'

Wayne looked at me. 'I thought the vehicle was for national park use only. Or if we had an emergency.'

'I think we qualify for both.'

We stumbled out to the Toyota. We looked up at the lighthouse, the beam sweeping eternally, and discussed the idea of climbing it. A drive seemed better. There was nothing to see up there anyway. We got in. I was behind the wheel. In Brisbane I never drove this drunk. It wasn't so much that I respected the danger of it, it was because I valued my licence.

This was Cape Don, however. I gunned the engine and took off, fishtailing. We roared down the hill. Wayne had brought the bourbon and coke and the glasses. He poured me a drink. I guzzled it down and weaved my way along the track. Trees flashed by on either side.

I kept the speed up. On one corner we swung wide and careened through the scrub. The Toyota was fitted with a large bullbar. Bushes and small trees vanished beneath it. Power. We were immune. I swung off the road again deliberately. We thumped and crashed through the greenery, dodging the large trees. It was wonderful. This was what we needed. We'd been sitting still far too long.

Then we hit the airfield. Now it was time for the serious driving. I cruised out onto the strip. We were down one end. How long was it? Five hundred metres? A thousand? The important question was to what speed could I get the Toyota before we hit the end of it. I flattened the accelerator, worked through the gears. Wayne was out the window, yelling something into the wind. Red gravel streamed away under the headlights. Through a hundred, up to one hundred and ten, one twenty, one thirty.

'I can see the end,' Wayne cried.

I looked ahead. Trees showed up in the dim lengths of the headlights. The end of the strip. Was I on high beam or low? How much room did I have? The speedometer was still climbing. One forty-five. Not so fast in Grand Prix terms, but in an old Toyota on a lonely, drunken night on an airstrip, fast enough. I slammed down on the brakes, locked them instantly. Wayne was thrown against the dash. The Toyota skidded in a long, straight path. We stopped a good fifty yards short of the trees. Red dust billowed past us. Wayne threw himself back.

'My turn.'

We swapped over. I took charge of pouring the drinks. Wayne U-turned and we were gunning down the strip again.

'I got to one forty-five,' I said, 'And stopped within fifty yards of the trees.'

Wayne was hunched over the wheel. 'I can beat it.'

We roared along. I hung out the window, let the dry air rip at my face. There were things, possibly, to think about. A crash. Death. Injury. None of them mattered. The trees loomed. Wayne screamed 'One fifty!' and hit the brakes.

Again, the long, perfectly straight slide. A ton or so of metal out of control. The slightest swerve either way and the Toyota, high set and top heavy, would be cartwheeling. We stopped. We were closer, it seemed, to the trees than last time.

'My turn,' I said.

We kept at it for what seemed like hours. We couldn't beat one fifty and we didn't hit the trees. Eventually we got bored with straight up and down speed. We reverted to fishtailing and circling and doing figure eights. The fine gravel of the airstrip was perfect. Neither of us had ever done anything like it before. We were possessed, we were country yokels. The Toyota leaned and tilted and two wheels were intermittently airborne, but we didn't roll. It had nothing to do with skill. Only with luck, and with the fact that over a short distance the Toyota was anything but fast.

Finally we packed it in. The bourbon was long gone and we couldn't think of anything else to put the vehicle through. We headed home. Wayne was at the wheel. He followed my example, curling off the track to destroy saplings and bushes and anything else that the bullbar could crush. Back at the compound he executed one long last slide that brought the Toyota up against the front steps of our house. There was a slight bump of contact, then he cut the engine. We piled out, staggered inside and got ourselves fresh beers. We hit the back verandah.

We stopped. There was a vision there, out on the ocean. A blaze of lights. It was close in, dazzling and huge, like a floating circus. It took us some time to realise what it was—a cruise ship, passing along the coast. It was beautiful, a visitation from the Gods. People were out there, only a mile away. Dancing and drinking and fucking, hundreds of them, thousands. I could hear music, I was sure of it. Laughter.

Wayne and I sat there. Our night was suddenly worthless. We watched the ship, loathing it, envying it. Finally it disappeared around the headland. We started on the beer again. It wasn't the same.

I was on the three a.m. observation. At two forty-five I headed over to the shack. I was in a sour mood. Fuck the cruise ship. What sort of arseholes went on cruises anyway. I picked up the mike, hit the call button and yelled 'Cape Don calling. Barometric pressure, 966. Cloud cover total. Maximum wind gust, 350. We're on lifelines here. The house is gone. The ranger is gone. It's a fucking *cyclone!*'

There was only static, as always. I took the pen, the field-book and the torch, and headed out into the night.

TWENTY-TWO

I woke up worried. It was twelve-thirty. I'd missed the 9
a.m. observation. It wasn't the observation I was worried
about. Once the worst of the hangover had been dealt with,
I examined the Toyota. There were branches and leaves
caught in the bullbar, and in the grill. I pulled them out.
There was also a sizeable dint at the bottom of the bar. I
tried to remember. Had it been there before? And if it was
new would Vince notice? Damage to national park property.
Would he care?

I began wondering about other damage we might've
done—to the bush alongside the track. I had dim memories
of the Toyota barging through the scrub, unstoppable. I got
in and drove slowly down the hill. I came across a clear
set of tracks, verging into the trees. There were saplings
snapped in half, flattened ferns, tyre marks in the undergrowth. The carnage was repeated all the way out to the
airstrip, on both sides of the road. Damage to national park
property, damage to the national park itself.

Then I saw the strip. All up and down the red gravel

expanse there were stark, white skid marks. Some of them, maybe, were made by the planes when they landed—not the circular ones though, or the figure eights, or the dozens of long, straight slashes at either end. Vince would fly in and he'd look down at the strip and he'd see. He'd know.

I drove home and sat on the back verandah. The deck was littered with beer cans and cigarette butts. There were the plates from our dinner, swarming with ants. Underneath the verandah there was already a pile of older cans and bottles. We'd let them drop through the holes rather than clean them away. I felt tired and disgusted. The man with the clipboard was right, we were living like pigs.

A little later I heard Wayne get up and start clattering around the house. I waited for him to come out on the verandah. He didn't. Instead I heard the Toyota starting. By the time I got out front it was disappearing down the hill. Where would he be going? To review effects of the night, as I had? It didn't seem likely. I might be concerned, but I doubted Wayne would be.

Eventually it was time for my 3 p.m. observation. I went over and examined the field-book. Wayne hadn't made the 6 a.m. or the midday. We had a twelve-hour gap in the weather. Darwin, along with everyone else, would not be pleased.

Wayne wasn't back by evening. I did his 6 p.m. observation and waited. Still no Wayne, even by seven. I sat on the back verandah and sipped on beer. What if he never came back? What if he'd been eaten by crocodiles? Then there were footsteps on the front stairs. There'd been no sound of the Toyota pulling up. Wayne came out to the verandah. He was red-faced and panting.

'Where have you been?' I said, 'Where's the car?'

He gulped for air. 'I crashed it.'

Jesus Christ. 'What?!'

'It's not that bad. It's just in a swamp. It's bogged.'

'What the fuck did you do to it?'

'Hang on, I'm exhausted. Give me a minute.' He went off, got some water, flopped into a chair. 'I've been walking for hours.'

'Wayne, *where* is the car?'

'Miles away. Out at the inlet, you know, where we met Russel and Eve during the cyclone.'

'What the hell were you doing out there?'

'Nothing. I just thought I'd go for a drive. You went for one this morning, so why couldn't I?'

'But out there?'

'It's nice.'

'*Nice*? What happened?'

'I'd almost made it. I could see the beach. Then I sort of went off the road.'

'Off the road?'

'Uh-huh. Down an embankment. I hit a tree. In a swamp. A mangrove swamp.'

'My God.'

'There really isn't much damage.'

'Were you in four-wheel drive?'

'I forgot. I wondered why the thing was sliding around so much.'

'Well did you at least *try* four-wheel drive to get out?'

'Yeah. I'm not stupid. But the wheels just spun. It's really muddy. Then it was getting dark. I wasn't gonna hang around in the mangroves at night. There'd be crocs everywhere. So I started walking home. It nearly killed me. I had no water, nothing.'

'So it's just sitting there, in the swamp.'

'Hey, you don't know what it's like out there at night. It's pitch-black, and there's all these noises. I didn't know whether it was crocs or pigs or buffalo or what. I had to run the last mile or two.'

I watched him swill down the water. I had no sympathy for him. This was all we needed.

I said, 'Well what're we supposed to do now?'

'I dunno. But I was thinking about it on the way back. How high does the tide come up over there?'

The tide.

Jesus fucking Christ.

Something had to be done. Fast. The first thing I thought of was the other vehicle, out in the shed. I went and looked at it. Its hood was up and the engine was still in pieces. There was nothing else but the ride-on mower they used around the compound. It might make it as far as the airstrip, but no further. It could hardly free the Toyota, in any case.

I went back to Wayne.

'We'll have to walk back there. Maybe the two of us can get it out.'

'Tonight? You're kidding.'

'We have to. What if it floods.'

'Maybe it won't. Anyway, it can't float away. It's stuck on the tree. We can get it tomorrow. I need a beer.'

I watched him go to the fridge. He was incredible. I reined my temper in, thought. He was right, of course. There was no real point in going over there that night. We'd be fucking around in the dark, in the mud, maybe even in water. And there might really be crocodiles. The morning would have to do. Vince was due back in two days. That gave us just tomorrow to sort the mess out.

I brooded over the details. Wayne took his beer and went off to the studio. His stereo boomed out. Obviously *he* wasn't worried. Life with Wayne. It was getting to me. I'd never considered myself a tense person, but he was driving me there.

I went to bed around midnight. I was up again by eight-thirty. At nine I was sitting on the front steps with a few bottles of water for the walk. Wayne was over doing the observation. As soon as he was finished, we'd be off. I wasn't sure what the two of us could do with the Toyota that Wayne hadn't already done, but there might be something he'd missed. Maybe there was some wood around we could put under the wheels. Maybe he hadn't tried reverse.

Then there was a high drone coming from the east, and moments later the twin-engine Commission plane was doing the circle of the compound. I watched it, appalled. They were a day early. It flew off towards the airstrip. There was nothing I could do but watch it go. Vince would be left waiting there. Sooner or later he'd realise we weren't coming to get him and he'd start walking.

Wayne came across from the weather shack.

'Was that the plane?' he asked.

'Yep.'

'Shit.'

'We better start walking.'

'Why? We can't get to the car now.'

'We can at least meet Vince halfway. Then the three of us can turn around and go back for the Toyota.'

'Oh . . . '

'And *you* can tell him what happened.'

We set off. It was another warm, bright, perfect day. The bush was green and alive. I was in no mood to enjoy it. I was looking at all the damage again. We'd been left alone not even three days. In that time we'd levelled half the native forest, torn up the airstrip and lost the Toyota in a swamp. So much for proving ourselves trustworthy.

We met Vince somewhere around the halfway point. He

was still in his full ranger uniform, sweat gathered at the armpits, breathing hard. He was no fitter than Wayne or I, and a lot older.

'Where's the transport?' he said.

Wayne explained. At least the shit would fall on his head, not mine. Vince listened. He wasn't happy. He turned to me.

'Why'd you let him go? I told you that vehicle was only for park business.'

'*Me?* I didn't know what he was doing.'

He pointed at Wayne, kept his eyes on me. 'I already had a fair idea what sort of idiot *he* is, but you, Gordon, you were supposed to watch things.'

I didn't reply. This wasn't at all fair.

'Anything else I should know about?' he asked.

'No.'

He shook his head. 'Well, let's get back to the house.'

'Shouldn't we keep going to the Toyota. While we're here?'

'Fuck that. I'm not gonna walk over there in this heat.'

He started off. We trailed along behind him. If he'd noticed the slashes on the airstrip, or the tracks trampling the bush, he didn't mention them. That was something at least. Maybe things weren't as bad as I'd thought. What, after all, were a few skid marks and some bent foliage? And we might've lost the Toyota, but we hadn't burnt a house down or anything. Cape Don was still there. The generators were running fine, and we'd fed the dog.

We got back to the compound, went with Vince into his house. One of the smaller bedrooms had been converted into an office, and there was another two-way radio on the desk. It was smaller than the one in the weather shack. Vince informed us that it was for purely local use—for calling Black Point, or Araru, on park business. This time he called up Araru. After he'd given their call sign a few times a heavy, Aboriginal voice answered. Vince asked for Russel, waited.

'Russel'll take care of it,' he said to us. 'Him and a few of the boys can boat over to the inlet a lot easier than we can walk there. Five or six of them should be enough to get the Toyota out. Then Russel can drive it back here.'

'That's that then?'

'Not quite. If I ever leave you two here again you only use that vehicle to pick up passengers at the airstrip, nothing else.'

'Uh-huh.'

'Keep off the fucking airstrip, and keep on the track. God knows what the others thought when they saw what you'd done to the runway. This is a *national park*, for Christ's sake.'

'Sorry.'

'It's my own fault. I should never've left you two here alone. Russel should've been around. I should have another assistant ranger. I should have a boat. Fuck, I shouldn't even *be* here . . . '

Then Russel was on the air. Wayne and I left Vince to it and crawled home.

TWENTY-THREE

The Toyota returned mid-afternoon the next day. And with it Russel, Eve, and about another dozen people. Men, women, kids, all jammed in. I was sitting on the steps as they came laughing and hooting up the hill. They unloaded themselves into Eve and Russel's house, then Russel drove the Toyota across to Vince's. The two of them inspected it. I couldn't see any obvious damage, but they spent some time studying the front wheels. I decided not to join them. I went back into my room to read.

A while later I heard Kevin barking on our verandah. Wayne and I went out. Russel and Vince were there at the foot of the steps, with four other Aboriginal men. Kevin was doing his best to block their way.

'I think you owe these guys a few beers,' Vince said, 'Seeing they cleaned-up your mess.'

'I suppose we do. Kevin, shut up.'

Kevin backed off and they all tramped onto the verandah. I went inside, got our last carton, brought it out. We all settled down, squatting on the floor. The beers passed around amidst mutters and laughs. Wayne opened a pack of Winfield Blues, and they did they rounds too.

'Is the car alright?' Wayne asked Vince.

'The body is. But when you put it in four-wheel drive, I don't suppose you locked the hubs on the front wheels?'

'Uh . . . no. I didn't know you had to.'

'And I suppose you spun the shit out of the wheels trying to get free?'

'Sort of.'

'That's that then, the bearings are fucked.'

'Is that bad?' I asked.

'Just be grateful I'm not gonna make you pay for it. It'd cost you more than a few drinks.'

Even so, we were being punished. Our precious beer supply was dwindling fast. The four men introduced themselves. Con. Davie. Long Bob. Jerry. They smoked and drank. Mostly they spoke in Gurig, sometimes in English. They asked our names and where we were from and what we were doing there. Wayne they were particularly amused by. They made remarks about the Toyota.

'She was pretty easy to get out.'

'Just a push, eh.'

'How'd you get stuck there anyway?'

'Bloke'd have to know nuthin', get stuck in a place like that.'

Wayne smoked, looked at the floor, endured it. One of them turned to me. His name was Long Bob. He was very tall, his narrow face half-hidden behind a frosted-grey beard. 'You from Brisbane, right?'

'That's right.'

'Government's there, eh?'

'Uh . . . the Queensland Government, yes.'

'No, that federal mob. Australian Government.'

'That's in Canberra.'

'Canberra? Where the hell's that?'

'Down south.'

He gave me a sideways look. 'That Malcom Fraser then? He still Prime Minister?'

'Uh . . . no, not for a while. It's Bob Hawke now.'

'Shit eh? Bob Hawke!'

He started laughing. They all did. Even Vince. I sat there, no idea what was going on. After a while Long Bob leaned over, poked my leg.

'Hey. S'alright mate. Bit of a joke.'

'Oh.'

'Just seein' if you knew.'

'Oh.'

They forgot about me again. I pulled on my beer. I felt stupid. Slow. After an hour the beer was all gone. Everyone said thanks, then they rose and wandered out into the sun. Vince went back to his house. The rest of the men went with Russel to his. The women and kids were already settled there on the front verandah. The men joined them. After a while I could see a cask or two of wine being passed around the group. I could see Eve too. She was laughing and talking, playing with the children. There was nothing silent about her now.

I retired out the back, looked at the sea. All Wayne and I had left now was the red wine. I drank a glass, slathered myself with insect repellent as evening fell. It was the usual routine, but the mood was different. Yells and shouts drifted across from Russel and Eve's house. Other people were around, a lot of them. People who sounded happy and relaxed and utterly at home. Wayne and I, hiding away in disgrace in our house, we were something else.

The crowd stayed for several days. Mostly they seemed to hang around Russel's house. Sometimes they'd wander down to the bay and come back with fish, or crabs. Once even, the skinned remains of a wallaby. It was their right, after all, to hunt wherever and whatever they liked. From what I understood though, none of the bigger game had ever worked its way through the swamps and creeks to reach the land around Cape Don. So there were no buffalo, and no banteng.

Generally they left Wayne and I alone. A few of the kids appeared in our hallway, shrieked when we saw them, ran out again. Only one of the adults bothered with us. His name was Con. He seemed about our age, short and solid, verging on fat. He dropped in one night while we were playing Scrabble, wanting to borrow a few cigarettes. Wayne handed some over. We offered him a drink. He sat down and stayed about an hour. He asked us more about ourselves, about the painting and writing, about what we thought of Cobourg.

'I'm not Gurig y'know,' he said, 'I'm Tiwi. From Melville Island. Just visiting.'

It seemed he mostly hung around in Darwin. He'd been in prison a few times, for drunk and disorderly, and assault. That's why he was in Cobourg at the moment. He was lying low from the law over some incident at a Darwin hotel. The police might've found him on Melville, but they'd never bother looking in Cobourg. He had cousins among the Gurig people, so they didn't mind having him.

'You boys don't have anything to smoke do you?'

'Other than tobacco?'

'Yeah. Gunja, y'know.'

Wayne brought it out, and he and Con smoked a joint.

'Be careful with this stuff,' Con said, 'That Allan Price finds out you got this here, you'll be out. He doesn't even like the grog much, but gunja, you're gone.'

'Does he ever come over here?'

'Dunno. He doesn't like me, I keep out of his way.'

'You lot gonna be around for a while?'

'Nah. Better over at Araru, or Black Point. Not even any fucking women around here. None that want me anyhow.'

Everyone finally packed up. Con came to say goodbye. Wayne gave him a pack of Winfield Blue. We had plenty to spare. Wayne ordered ten packs every week, but smoked less than one a day. The surplus was growing.

Con climbed into the Toyota with the others, then Russel drove them back to their boat. Russel and Eve were staying on at the lighthouse. Once the crowd was gone the mood of the place faded back to normal. The weather was serene, dry and unchanging. The generator thumped along twenty-four hours a day. Kevin snuffled up and down our stairs, slept on Wayne's bed. Wayne himself painted or didn't paint in his studio. I ran up win after win on the Scrabble board, sat at the desk from time to time, stared into the mirror, and wrote absolutely nothing.

TWENTY-FOUR

Vince finally got sick of waiting for his cruiser to come back from Darwin. For *anything*—his generator parts, his outboard motor parts—to come from Darwin. Cape Don was falling apart and the radio calls were getting him nowhere. He decided he'd go to Darwin himself. He booked passage on the supply plane and flew out. There were no worries about leaving Wayne and me on our own. Russel was there this time, to watch over us.

There was nothing to watch. For the next few days all was quiet. Wayne and I barely left our house. I was feeling a little low. The writing wasn't happening and time was beginning to weigh heavily. I walked from room to room. I read books, wrote letters. None of it seemed enough. We saw no sign of Russel or Eve. Then one afternoon I heard yells and screams from their house. I went out, looked over. They seemed to be having an argument.

A door slammed. Russel came running out, then Eve. They were both half naked. Russel in shorts, Eve in a bra and pants. Eve had a fishing spear. She was trying to stab

Russel with it. He was avoiding her lunges with ease, laughing at her. Eve was screaming. I couldn't pick up the words. Kevin ran out and joined in, barking. Wayne emerged from his studio.

We watched. For all her anger, Eve was handling the situation with a certain dignity. She gave up trying to stab Russel. She stomped back to her front steps and sat there, spear at the ready. He wasn't getting back in. Russel himself watched her for a time, then pulled some tobacco out of his back pocket, began rolling. He sat down under a tree. Kevin stopped barking, stood between them. Stalemate. We all waited.

'Look at her,' Wayne marvelled, 'She's beautiful. She was gonna kill him.'

'I think if she *really* wanted to kill him, she would've. She was taking it easy with that spear.'

But we were staring at her. We couldn't help ourselves. It was her naked back, her shoulders, her long legs, cradling the spear. She was breathing fast, radiating fury. We'd never seen Eve in anything but her long floral dresses.

'Imagine it,' Wayne said, 'The two of them over there, in that bed, under that mosquito net. Jesus. All that anger.'

'I'd rather not think about it.'

It was too late. It was there.

'How often are you wanking these days,' Wayne asked, staring at Eve and the spear.

'Once a day I suppose.'

'Twice for me. So you think we should do something about it?'

'Sorry?'

'Maybe we should fuck.'

'Very funny.'

'Who said I was joking?'

I said nothing.

'C'mon,' said Wayne, 'I know you're bored.'

'No.'

He laughed. 'Relax Gordon, I *am* joking.'

Eve looked across, saw us. She stood up, faced us, hands on hips. We couldn't meet her eyes. Or her body. We retreated inside.

I roamed the house. I was restless. Sex. It had me. I didn't want it. It was pointless. More than pointless, there at the lighthouse. With Wayne. I went to my room. There was a pile of *People* magazines there. I'd been working my way through the collection. There were perhaps two hundred of them around Cape Don, in the weather shack and the sheds, some of them years old. The ranger who was there before Vince must have owned them. The one that had gone mad, stir-crazy. The magazines couldn't have helped.

It was all those breasts, endless pages of them, at least a dozen different pairs per issue. And the adds for X-rated videos. The pictures of mud wrestling, jelly wrestling. The candid snaps that men had sent in of their wives or girlfriends, in lingerie, wet T-shirts, naked. A magazine for the Territory. For lonely men in remote areas.

I lay on the bed, flicked through. It was no use. The breasts were all huge, some of them verging on the fantastic. And the poses, and the colours, none of it was real. I threw the magazines away. I thought about Eve. I thought about mosquito netting. It was hot, sweaty. I had my clothes off, I was stretched on the mattress, my prick in my hand.

I tried for a vision. This was the room for it. Huge and dim, the fan turning slowly over the single iron-framed bed. French windows open, a rectangle of light. Tropical heat. Slow heat, for slow fucking. Mosquito nets hazing everything with white.

I began pumping. It was Eve, riding me. Her bra tight

and high, her teeth gritted in anger, grinding. The anger was important. I didn't know why. Something needed to be purged, desecrated. I needed the emotion. Eve faded away. She became another woman, one I'd slept with, just once, one of the disasters. Rolling breasts, her head down, her thick lips parted, frustrated, swearing at me. Because I was failing. Useless. She became yet another woman, someone I'd loved and hungered after for years, pointlessly. A slim pale body and a stern face, a cunt that was impossibly cool and smooth. Distant. Someone I couldn't even hope to touch.

It wasn't enough. Rejection wasn't enough. It took cruelty, pain. My arms arching back, strapped to the bed frame. Ropes burning my skin, a gag. And then it was a man, faceless, lithe, the two of us straining, strength against strength. Fucking me. Beating me down. Then Eve again, naked now, crouched on me, nipples on my chest, head next to mine, gasping, hating me, softer and faster and harder . . .

I came. The vision was gone. There was no vision, only splinters. I didn't know what they meant, what I wanted. I wiped my penis down, lay there in a dusty, empty room. I felt bleak and hopeless. Nothing was solved, nothing released.

I got dressed, went out onto the verandah. I looked around the compound. Eve and Russel were gone. I was glad. I felt like I'd been masturbating in their faces. I went back inside. The door to Wayne's room was closed. I wondered what he was up to. If he was having better luck than me.

I needed distractions. From the boredom, from the frustration, from everything. Cape Don itself offered nothing. There was only one choice.

I took a fresh packet of Winfield Blue from Wayne's supply.

It was a grave, beautiful, thing, the unopened pack. Perfect in shape, colour and promise. The graphic designers and advertising consultants had done their job. I took it out onto the front verandah and sat on the steps. I unwrapped the plastic, opened the flip lid, inhaled the smell. Dark. Rich. Twenty-five tightly packed cigarettes. I pulled one out, held it, considered what I was about to do.

There were things of which to be aware. Lung cancer, emphysema, clogged arteries, lopped-off limbs. There was foul breath and yellowed fingers. There was the expense, the ash on the carpet, the pinhead burns in the shirts. And then there was the asthma.

It didn't work. The horrors were all years away, and none of them seemed to compare with what I needed now. Satisfaction. Of any sort.

I looked at the long, slim tube. It would not, I knew, taste anything even close to good. But I was ready for that. Enjoyment would come later. Addiction, too, would come in time, once it'd been earned. All I wanted, for now, was tolerance. Lungs that would take what I gave them.

I slipped the cigarette between my lips, lit it, inhaled. There was smoke and the hot tang of ash. I got it halfway along my throat, then coughed it out. The body was resisting. I could afford to be patient. I could work my way down the airways. I let the taste recede, took another puff.

I got through maybe two-thirds before I was gagging. I stubbed it out on the floor. I felt sick, but overall it didn't seem too bad for a first serious attempt. Eight-year olds and ten-year olds were probably mastering the art with greater speed, but then kids learnt everything quickly. I was a late starter. I closed the pack, stared out at the compound. Dust, sun, dead grass. I felt sicker now.

And still not satisfied.

TWENTY-FIVE

Vince came home. He'd got nowhere with the bureaucracy in Darwin. Budgets were being revised, money was short. They couldn't promise he'd get his cruiser, or his engine parts. Vince was of the opinion that they could all go and fuck themselves. He packed his uniform away, went back to his drinking.

I decided something had to be done about the writing. There were no more excuses. We'd been at the lighthouse nearly three months now. Wayne had been painting from the first few weeks, it was time I followed the example. I still had almost two and a half thousand sheets of blank paper. Nor had I used more than a couple of my one hundred ink cartridges. People were expecting a novel when I got home. I'd *told* people to expect one.

The problem was horror novels. I'd already written one and started a few others and it was all years ago. Somehow the idea had lost its appeal. Why did I want to write horror novels? What was horrifying anyway? Most of the horror writers I'd read were terrible. My own horror novels were terrible.

I began toying with other ideas. I had a recurrent image of a room packed with fat, naked men, all with long, sleek penises. It was nothing sexual. They'd move and sway around the room, the men and the penises. I decided that the men were angels, and that they knew things about the world. How it began, how it would end. And they were closeted in a bar in some small north Queensland hotel. They might even be canecutters. Drinking. Swearing. Filling in eternity. Waiting for something.

The other image was of a woman, obsessed with sewage. Waste products. She accessed the treatment plants at night, sniffed the effluent, studied it, read things in it. Divined the future from the remnants of the past. In the meantime she worked as a nurse in Townsville. There she read the future in blood. Pus. Saliva. Semen. Bodily secretions of any kind. She too was just passing the time. She too knew things about the world, and sooner or later she'd be linking up with the canecutting angels in their bar.

I wrote a few paragraphs. I began thinking about Christian sects and cults. I'd studied them at university. Jehovah's Witnesses. Seventh-Day Adventists. Mormons. They'd fit in there somewhere too. You could never go wrong with religion.

It lasted three or four days and maybe forty pages, then I threw it all away. It was dreadful. Why was I bothering? Even if I *could* pull it off, there were already thousands of slick, offbeat novels out there. After three or four they all seemed the same. I needed another plan. Maybe a western. Or a detective story. But there were millions of them too. I moved around the house, thinking desperately. Maybe it wasn't going to work. Maybe in six months I wasn't going to write *anything*.

I went and stood in the doorway of Wayne's studio. I was

smoking a cigarette, slowly and carefully. Wayne was sitting on the floor, staring at a canvas. He looked up at me.

'How many you up to now?' he asked.

'Three or four a day.'

'Enjoying them?'

'No.'

He nodded. I assumed he understood. It wasn't a question of pleasure. I had no craving for nicotine yet. It was necessary, that was all.

I said, 'I can't do it. I can't write anything.'

'Really?'

'Really.'

'That's tough.'

'At least you're painting.'

'This? This is shit'

I looked at it. Maybe it was. I didn't know. It was easy for Wayne, he could afford to be critical. At least he was doing what he'd said he would.

I said, 'How many do you need for an exhibition?

'More than this.'

'You gonna make it?'

'I dunno.' He stretched back on the floor, stared at the ceiling. 'I've been sitting here, looking at these things . . . I'm bored. I wanna go home.'

'You can't go home without an exhibition.'

'You can't go home without a novel.'

It was true. We were trapped. I looked around at all the canvasses. It was alarming suddenly. I had no idea what any of them were. Wayne had been in that little room for weeks on end and he'd been thinking about *something*, but I couldn't see it. I'd been living with him all that time and I still couldn't see it. He was in his own world. He was an alien.

It was a cold feeling. What was I doing there with him?

I wandered back across the verandah, sat down on the stairs. I stared at my feet. Three months to go, three months. I needed a novel.

Nothing came. My brain was rotting. Too long without use. I hadn't showered in days, or shaved. Or changed my clothes—hand-washing them in the sink wasn't worth the bother. Cape Don didn't demand personal hygiene. It didn't demand anything.

I looked up. Vince was walking across the compound. It was close to four p.m., time to switch over the generators. He looked half asleep, flapping along in his thongs, gut hanging over his shorts. He stared at the ground. Maybe he'd just woken up. Cape Don didn't make many demands on *his* time either.

Vince entered the shed. The generator died. I sat in the warm, still silence. Wayne came out of his studio.

'Fuck art,' he said.

He headed for his bedroom, shut the door. I heard him flop onto his bed.

All of us, we were sliding into decline.

TWENTY-SIX

Vince received some news from his ex-wife. Their son was on school holidays and wanted to visit the lighthouse. He was ten years old. I didn't know how things stood between Vince and his ex-wife, or what the custody arrangement was, but it was clear Vince hadn't seen his son for some time. Certainly not since being posted to Cape Don.

The news had an effect. Vince eased up on the drinking. His eyes lost some of their red glaze. He cleaned out his house. Pieces of his uniform began reappearing. More importantly, he put in another order for parts for the outboard motor. This time the order was with a private firm at his own expense, not through the Commission. He wanted the stuff fast. He planned, he said, to take his son fishing.

The boy arrived on the Friday supply plane. I drove out with Vince. He was looking as good as he ever would, shaved and clean and fully dressed.

'Looking forward to seeing him?' I asked.

'What d'you think? It's probably the only chance I'll get all year.'

But he sounded nervous. I thought about that. The kid might have expectations. His father was a national park ranger, in command of his own station on the remote and wild northern coast. It sounded impressive, the job of a man who was steadfast and capable. Vince had a lot to live up to.

So did Cape Don. I'd long ceased to think of the place as a functioning ranger station, or as anything at all. It existed, and for some reason we were all stuck there. That was it.

We hit the strip, climbed out. The boy was waiting by the plane. He was sandy-haired and freckle-faced. There was even a family resemblance. He was a young Vince, before the years and the sun and the alcohol had done their work. Vince blushed and grinned and put out his hand.

'G'day Danny.'

'G'day Dad.'

They both seemed embarrassed. Perhaps I shouldn't have been there. What did I know about divorce and separation and absent fathers. They deserved some privacy.

'Danny, this is Gordon. He runs the weather station.'

'G'day Danny.'

'Hi.'

I began loading the grocery boxes. There was also a special package—the outboard motor parts. Vince was chatting with the pilot, all false joviality. Danny stacked his own gear into the Toyota. He was looking around, up and down the strip. I tried to remember my first impressions of the place. Even in the middle of the wet season it had seemed drab and dusty. Now, well into the dry, it really *was* drab and dusty. What was Vince going to do with him for a whole week?

I sat in the back for the drive home, let Danny up front. Vince asked him about the flight over, about the rest of the family, about school. Danny gave ten-year old answers. Alright. Okay. Nothing much. We drove up the hill and there it was. Cape Don. Three houses. Cement lighthouse. Sheds.

'You keen to do some fishing Danny?'

'Sure Dad.'

Even with the new parts it was another three days before Vince got the outboard going. In the meantime he and Danny drove around the place in the Toyota—I didn't know to where, or for what. Maybe Vince had been saving up some work for himself, to impress. They also went on a bushwalk. They loaded up with water and sandwiches and headed off into the scrub. I watched them go. Bushwalking. It was something I hadn't really considered, not since we'd first arrived.

According to the maps there was nothing to see out there anyway, not in the country around Cape Don. No gorges or caves or waterfalls. No Aboriginal paintings, no spectacular views, no landmarks of any kind. Just endless scrub, swamp and mangrove. Even the Cobourg people themselves didn't bother with it much. They stuck to the coast, or the better land eastwards. But at least Vince and Danny didn't get lost. Vince was a ranger, after all.

And on the fourth day of Danny's visit work was finally completed on the outboard motor. Vince attached it to the dinghy, gave it a test-run in the bay. Then, that afternoon, he and Danny loaded up and went fishing. Deep sea, Vince said, out on the reefs.

I saw them off, went back to my own life.

They weren't back by five. I changed over the generators seeing Vince wasn't there to do it. Evening fell. Wayne and

I ate dinner and played Scrabble. It was over seventy wins to one now, in my favour. I was getting two seven-letter words per game, and scores averaging anywhere between three or four hundred. Wayne seemed to be losing interest. He was still wallowing in the one fifties, two hundreds. After the game I went out and checked the compound for the Toyota. It wasn't there. It was fully dark and Vince and Danny were still out fishing?

It seemed unlikely. They were probably pulling the boat up on the sand at that very moment, then they'd be driving home. Or maybe they were looking at stars, or examining the night's bush life. There were lots of things a ranger could do at night. It was nothing to worry about. I went back inside and read for an hour, came out again. Still no Toyota.

It seemed strange. I hadn't noticed Vince and Danny packing any torches or lamps. I went back inside again. Then it was getting towards nine. There was still no sign of them. The bay was only a five-minute walk away. I wondered if I should go down and check.

I waited until ten. I went into Wayne's studio, asked him what he thought.

'They'll be alright,' said Wayne, 'Vince is a master bushman isn't he?'

'They're at sea, not on land.'

'There's nothing *you* can do.'

'I thought I might walk down to the bay, have a look.'

'Don't forget the torch.'

'You wanna come?'

'I've been out there once at night. Never again.'

I took the torch and went outside. I stood in the compound for a moment. Then I went over to Russel and Eve's house. It was the first time I'd ever called on them directly, the first time I'd even looked through their front door.

There was a long, empty hall. And silence. The lights were all on, the ceiling fans spun. I knocked on the screen door. 'Russel? Eve?'

After a moment, Eve came out of one of the doors. She looked rumpled and sleepy and bothered. I hadn't even seen her for a few weeks, since their fight. Sexual fantasies aside.

'Yeah?' she said.

'Is Russel there?'

'He's asleep.'

'Oh.' A pause. 'Could you wake him up?'

She rolled her eyes, went back into the room. Russel came out, yawning, already rolling a cigarette.

'Yeah?'

I explained about Vince and Danny. I asked him if they'd told him they'd be late.

He shrugged. 'Nuh.'

'Should we go down and have a look?'

'You'll be right alone, eh?'

'Oh. Okay.'

I was on my own. I began walking down the hill, waving the torch in front of me. It was ridiculous. No one else was worried. I was getting paranoid, too much time on my hands. They'd probably run me down on their way home. Laugh at me. There'd be some obvious explanation.

I stomped along the track. On either side was the deep, still, blackness of the bush. Sounds came out of it. Knocks. Thumps. A scattering of leaves. Animal sounds. Some of them sounded large. I thought about Wayne, running back from the bogged Toyota. At least I had a torch. I knew there was nothing out there likely to cause me harm, but fear was an old and spiritual thing. Reason had nothing to do with it.

I came to the turn for the bay, headed down it. The bush

faded away to mangroves. Now, indeed, there *were* reasons to be wary. I was alone at night in the mangroves, in crocodile territory. It was everything I'd been warned against. People got eaten this way. I flicked the torch all around, saw nothing but branches and mud. I came to the beach. The Toyota was there. That was all. No boat, no Vince or Danny. I sat on the hood. I played the torch out into the bay. It was low tide. Mud and puddles. Nothing.

I sat there. The sky was overcast and it was very dark. A faint, damp breeze drifted in from the sea. It felt cool. Almost cold. The mangroves waited behind me. Silent.

I didn't like it. I walked back to the compound and knocked again on Russel's door. He came out.

'They're not there. The boat's not there.'

'Yeah?'

'What should we do?'

He thought. 'Weather's alright. Might just be on a beach somewhere. Campin' out.'

'They would've told us.'

'Maybe. Better wait till mornin.'

He wandered back down his hall. I stood there. We weren't going to do anything. I walked back to the house. Wayne was still in his studio. I explained the situation to him.

'Shit,' he said, 'They've overturned. They've been eaten by sharks.'

'Russel doesn't think so.'

'How does he know?'

'He doesn't.'

Wayne gave up his painting. We had a few drinks out on the verandah, pondering the mysteries of the sea. I stayed awake, waiting for my 3 a.m. observation.

They didn't come back.

TWENTY-SEVEN

Next morning was cool and grey. Russel came over to the house, got me, and together we walked down to the bay. Birds called. Wallabies bounded out of our way. Russel ambled along, smoking. If he was worried about Vince and Danny, he didn't show it. Even so, I didn't expect that we'd find them. They were lost. Gone. Floating now out somewhere in the Arafura Sea, fish nibbling at their feet.

We got to the beach. The Toyota was still there. The tide was up. Small waves tumbled and splashed on the beach. And floating a hundred yards or so out on the bay, bobbing up and down, was the boat. Vince and Danny were in it, bent over the sides, paddling with their hands. They saw us. Stopped.

'What'ya doin'?' Russel called across.

Vince looked tired and angry. 'Out of fucking petrol.'

Russel laughed. He nodded towards the fuel drums on the beach. 'Swim in. Plenty of petrol here.'

'No fucking way.' Vince pointed along the beach. In the mud leading into the mangroves there were tracks. Two sets of them, each one a central furrow with claw prints on either side. Russel considered them.

'Couple of big fellas eh?'

Vince nodded grimly. 'They're bloody everywhere down here.'

Crocodiles. I'd been there last night, right there, in the dark, and so had two *crocodiles*. My life had been in danger. Maybe it still was. The tracks went from the water up into the mangroves, but there were none going down again. I backed away a little.

Russel shook his head, smiled. He went to the petrol drum and filled a small can. Then he peeled off his shirt and waded into the sea. No crocs emerged from the mangroves. When the water was deep enough, Russel dived in, surfaced, flicked the water out of his hair. He whooped It was a morning dip. He was enjoying it. Vince stood in the bow, staring at him. Danny watched too, with wide, sleepy eyes.

I kept an eye on the crocodile tracks. I supposed the chance of an attack was, in reality, fairly slight. I supposed that Vince probably knew that too. Still, no parent wanted to risk getting eaten in front of their own child. I could understand why Vince was staying in the boat.

Russel swam the last fifty yards, reached them. Vince helped him on board. They refuelled, played around with the engine a little, finally got it started. They motored in, Vince standing stiffly at the wheel.

'As for you,' he said to me, once they were all ashore, 'What're you, deaf?'

'Why?'

'Russel says it was you down here with the torch last night. Danny and I were over the other side of the bay, yelling our guts out. Didn't you hear?'

'No.' I was, in fact, partially deaf in one ear, but Vince

didn't seem in the mood to hear that. 'What, were you just floating around over there?'

Russel laughed. 'They weren't floatin'.'

Vince glowered. 'We were stuck in the mud. I ran aground.'

He got the story out. It was a sad one. The evening before he and Danny had kept fishing until around sunset, then headed in. The problem was the tide was going out. The tides were sizeable around Cobourg, over three metres, and the bay was shallow. Vince wasn't too sure of his way. They'd run aground and stuck fast.

This had happened about half a mile across the bay, near the mouth. They were forced to spend the night in the middle of a mudflat. The boat was within walking distance of the shore, but they'd heard crocs slopping around in the mud. They'd stayed on board. It wasn't much fun. They had no torches and no food. And some of the crocodiles sounded close.

'And you couldn't hear us, so we were stuck there.'

'What was I supposed to do even if I had?'

'Well . . . shit, at least you would've known where we were.'

'And how did you run out of petrol?'

'That. That was the fucking *outboard's* fault. The tide came in again about two a.m., but when we went to start the engine there was no petrol in it. There must be a leak somewhere. God knows, I filled the fucking thing up before we left.'

So all they'd been able to do was ride the tide and wait for dawn. When it was light enough to see the beach, they'd started paddling towards it. It was very, very slow. Swimming would've been easier, but then there were the crocodiles.

Russel thought it was all hilarious. I felt for Vince

though. It wasn't the fishing trip he'd promised Danny. Getting caught by tides, sitting in the mud, bobbing about without an engine, none of it was good. None of it was professional. It sounded like something Wayne or I might've done. And then to have Russel just swim out like that, not giving a shit about the crocodiles . . . mockery was the last thing Vince needed.

He went back to examining the outboard motor. He couldn't find the leak. Russel helped him disconnect the whole thing, load it in the Toyota. Danny had already climbed in the back seat, bored and sleepy and waiting.

'So did you catch any fish?' I asked him.

He didn't look at me. 'No.'

It was a stony drive home. We unloaded outside the work-shed, carried the engine in.

'I'm going to bed, Dad,' Danny said.

'Okay.' Vince mustered a grin. 'You'd need it after last night. But at least you've got something you can tell your mates about, back at school, hey.'

'Yeah. I guess so.' Danny shuffled off.

Vince watched him go, his face getting hard. 'Sure. He can tell 'em how his father, a fucking park ranger, can't even take him on a fishing trip without stuffing it up.'

'Kids don't think like that,' I said.

'How would you know?'

We stood there.

'So,' I said, 'What'll you do with the outboard now?'

'Junk the piece of shit.'

I wandered home. The drama was over. There was no drama. Only a mild incompetence. Even so, Vince was being too hard on himself. He didn't know the waters around Cape Don yet, the tides. How could he? He was a desert man. We all knew that. It was the Commission's fault. They were the ones who'd put him in charge of a maritime park, in charge of an ocean. No training. No experience. Vince could just explain all that to Danny, if he thought it mattered so much. And Danny would understand.

I got to my room, lay on the bed, thought about sleep. After a while I heard a loud banging from the workshed. Swearing. It was Vince. He was still angry, still taking it out on himself. I remembered, then, that it was Danny's once a year visit to an absentee father. And that if there was one thing Vince wouldn't want to give him, it was more excuses.

TWENTY-EIGHT

Danny departed on the next supply plane. Once he was gone Vince retreated into his house, to his desk and his stool. The ranger in him was through. He'd made his attempt at parenting. It was back to the alcohol and the classics. For the following week we heard the composers blasting till three, four each morning. We watched the empty bottles and cartons pile up outside his back door. At times I'd see him in the afternoon on his way to change the generators. Wild-haired and red-eyed, stumbling along in the dust.

There was nothing we could do for him. We were in our own limbo, stagnating under the dry season's sun. Wayne wasn't painting much, I wasn't writing at all. I slept and read and smoked. The smoking was my only form of progress. I'd mastered over ten cigarettes a day, and I was enjoying them a little now. I'd acquired some style. My only worry was the asthma. I kept waiting for the attack, the deathgrip, but it never came.

Instead I developed a boil. It was on the back of my knee.

I'd never had a boil before. At first I had no idea what it was. It grew over several days, until the knee became stiff and painful. I waited for the head to develop. Did you pop boils? Lance them? And what caused them anyway? Poor diet? Lack of fresh fruit and vegetables? Certainly our diet was monotonous. Like the rest of our lives.

Even Friday nights weren't what they had been. All the alcohol and marijuana couldn't hide the fact that Wayne and I were growing increasingly sick of each other. We argued over minor things. Books. Music. Movies. The fact that Wayne was missing more and more observations. The fact that Wayne didn't wash-up when it was his turn. The fact that I did all the accounting and banking, organised the payments to the Nightcliff supermarket, dealt with Vince or Russel when necessary, while Wayne did nothing.

I was tired of being the responsible one. It was fine for Wayne to be off in his own world, wherever it was, but what if I hadn't been there to arrange the mundane details for him? I brooded, watched him drift vacantly about the house. What was he thinking about all the time? Apart from his art, did he have any idea about anything at all?

Finally it was a Saturday night. We were on the back verandah. It'd been a long evening, drunken and testy. The boil made sitting down uncomfortable. It was big now, with a sharp, red head, but so far I'd done nothing to it.

I got up to go to the kitchen. I'd had enough of conversation with Wayne. And I was hungry.

'I'm gonna make some chips,' I said, 'You want some?'

'Chips? Deep-fried chips?'

'Yes.'

'Are you making anything else?'

'No.'

'Just chips?'

'*Yes*. Do you want any?'

'No.'

'Fine.'

I boiled the oil and sliced up some potatoes. What was wrong with making chips? There wasn't a takeaway for two hundred miles, what else was I going to do? I threw the potatoes in, watched them fry. In ten minutes they were ready. I spread them on a plate, got the salt and a fresh beer, went back out on the verandah.

Wayne started picking at the plate. I tolerated it for a time. Then he grabbed a huge handful. He didn't ask. He just grabbed a great huge handful and began stuffing them in his mouth.

I put the plate down, looked at him. 'You said you didn't want any.'

'So?'

'I would've made enough for both of us if you'd said you wanted some, but you said you didn't.'

'I changed my mind.'

'Fine. Have the fucking lot then.'

'What's wrong with you?'

'Why don't you ever do anything around here? Why's it always have to be me?'

'You want me to make the chips from now on?'

'*No.* I just wish you'd . . . I dunno, be a bit aware for a change. I don't wanna be in charge all the time.'

'As if you'd ever let me be in charge.'

'Bullshit.'

'Gordon, you're a control *freak*. Even if I wanted to do all the organising you wouldn't let me.'

'You'd fuck it up, that's why.'

'See? What am I supposed to do?'

I took my beer and stormed-off to my room. He was insufferable. A *control freak?* That was low. I sat at my desk and lit up a cigarette. They were good for everything, cigarettes. Peace. Anger. I sucked in big furious drags, started coughing. I retched and burped, stubbed out the cigarette, sat there.

Arguments about french fries.

We were losing it.

Finally, in the shower, I took the boil between two fingers, gritted my teeth and squeezed. It was exquisite pain. The head popped, blood and pus gushed out. I kept squeezing, marvelling at it all. The mound of tight red skin subsided. I felt pleased with myself. Boils were nothing to fear.

Two days later I noticed another one. On the side of my thigh. It was small, in its early stages, but I knew what it was.

An afternoon or two later I was sitting, as usual, out the back, watching the sun go down. An event occurred. A yacht sailed into view, about a mile offshore. It was the first boat I'd seen, close in, since we arrived. It was small and black against the sun, but it seemed to be angling towards land. I remembered our duty to protect the coast against hunters, smugglers, illegal immigrants. Australia for Australians, that was the Cobourg motto. I went over to inform Vince.

I hadn't seen him for four or five days. I knocked on his door. There were no lights on in the hallway. I went in, down to the living room. There was a lamp on at the desk. Paper in the typewriter, black print covering half the page. Vince wasn't at his stool. He was lying on one of the couches, asleep. His shirt was open, his face was heavy with growth. There was a glass of port on the floor beside him. The ceiling fans whirred over the silence.

'Vince?' I said.

He woke up. Stared at me dimly. 'What?'

'There's a yacht out there. Close in. I thought maybe it was going to land.'

He pulled himself up and sat forward. Coughed muck out of his throat. 'What sort of yacht?'

'I dunno. A small one.'

'And what am I supposed to do?'

'Uh . . . I just thought I should tell you.'

He looked at me. 'Well I can't go out and *meet* them can I. Not unless you've got a spare boat.'

'I guess not.'

'Anything else?'

'No.'

He reached for the glass. 'See you later then.'

I got out of there.

TWENTY-NINE

Next morning Kevin was barking on our front verandah. He lived with us almost full time now. Whatever the mood was in Vince's house, the dog didn't like it. He slept in Wayne's room. Wayne didn't mind the fleas or the ticks in his bed. On the other hand, Wayne was unlikely to get up and see what Kevin wanted. That sort of thing was a control freak's job.

I got up, wrapped a towel around myself, went out. I assumed Russel would be there, Kevin didn't bark for anyone else. It wasn't Russel. It wasn't even anyone black. It was four people, white. Two men and two women. I stared at them stupidly.

'G'day,' one of the men said. He looked about fifty or sixty. Wizened, heavily tanned, bearded. 'We were sailing past, decided we'd land.'

'You know,' grinned the other man, 'Saw your light on, thought we'd drop in.'

It took me some time to realise he was talking about the lighthouse. It was a joke. He was younger than the other man. He had sleek black hair and a tight, naked chest above his shorts. I was suddenly conscious of the holes in my towel and the way my belly hung over the top. And the large, ready-to-burst boil on my leg.

I said, 'Was that your yacht sailing around last night?'

The old man nodded. 'It's alright if we land here, isn't it?'

'I don't know.'

They exchanged glances. It wasn't much of an answer, but then I'd never had to deal with visitors before.

'You the only one here?' he went on, 'We knocked at the other two houses but no one answered.'

I was waking up a little now. It seemed about mid-morning. 'There should've been someone there. They might all bo asleep.'

We went through the introductions. The old one was Angus, the younger one Greg. The two women had been hanging back, talking to each other. They looked around twenty. Their names were Gail and Jennifer. They were English. Backpackers. The four of them had set sail from Darwin a few days ago. They were on their way around the northern coast to Cairns. They had anchored in the bay, rowed to the beach in their lifeboat, then walked up the track.

'So what's the story here?' Angus asked.

I explained about Wayne and me and the weather station, and about Vince and Russel and the national park. Then I went inside, put some clothes on, and took the four of them over to Vince's house. I hammered on the door, called. Eventually Vince came out. He didn't look well. I made the introductions again. I half thought Vince might throw them off the place. Instead he brightened up, even sounded cheerful.

'How long you here for?' he asked them.

'Just the day.'

'Well, we might slap up a bit of a barbecue. What d'you think Gordon?'

'Sure.'

Vince invited them into his house. I went back to my own. Wayne had just got up. I went through the details. Who they were, what was happening.

'Are we invited to this barbecue?'

'I guess so. God knows why Vince wants to have one. He's hardly been in a barbecue mood lately.'

'There were two women you said. English backpackers.'

'Yes.'

Wayne laughed. 'The horny old bastard—can't you see?'

We wandered over after midday. Vince, Angus and Greg were out under the tree, setting-up a table and chairs, drinking beer. They all seemed to be getting along. The women, they said, were taking advantage of Vince's shower and its hot water system. There was no sign of Russel or Eve. Wayne and I opened beers of our own.

'Vince tells me you blokes don't get many visitors round here,' said Greg.

'No, not many.'

'Just the local blacks, that right?'

'Uh-huh.'

He grinned. 'Bet you were happy to see a couple of white women.'

'Well . . . '

'Wouldn't mind being a fly on the wall in that shower eh? Or a bar of soap.'

He laughed. Angus laughed. Wayne and I glanced at each other, sat down. Greg started telling us about himself. It seemed he was a businessman from Perth. He was on holiday. He'd hired Angus and Angus's yacht for a cruise around the coast of Australia.

'Then while we were docked in Darwin we thought we'd like some female company. We asked around at a few backpacker hostels and came up with Gail and Jennifer.'

'And how's it gone so far?' I asked.

'They haven't come round yet, but they will. It's a long way to Cairns and it's a small, slow boat. They've got nowhere to hide.'

We sat there, drinking. Gail and Jennifer emerged from the house, freshly showered. They cracked open beers, sat down, got introduced to Wayne. They gave out a few details. They were both from London, both out of England for the first time. They'd planned the trip for years, waiting until the Bicentennial. Expo was on, and all the other things. They were here to see Australia at its best.

They were getting it. Five Australian males, a hot afternoon in the scrub, and alcohol. It had undertones of gang rape. Now that there were women around, we men were all puffed-up, alert, jockeying. Even Wayne. Even me. It made no sense. I wasn't in any way attracted to Jennifer or Gail. They were tanned and fit and bland. I'd never liked backpackers. Never liked the look, or the attitude. But competition was in the air. The need to impress.

Vince was the main aggressor. He was a ranger, it was his station, he was all competence. He was telling the women stories about his days in the outback. The Rock. The Simpson Desert. Greg and Angus could see he was a man to be reckoned with. They kept up with him, told stories of their own. Wayne and I were easier to dismiss. We had no stories to tell and no authority. And anyway, I had a boil.

None of it mattered. Jennifer and Gail weren't interested. They were polite to Vince, tolerant of Angus, openly revolted by Greg. I supposed it was nothing new to them. They'd been travelling around Australia for months, they said. Hitchhiking from Sydney to Melbourne, Melbourne to Perth, Perth to Darwin. Working here and there in truck stops, cafes, farms. They would've faced worse by now.

The afternoon passed. We men grew drunker and louder. The women were treated to slaps on the back, touched knees, various innuendos. Towards dusk, Angus and Greg made noises about getting back to their boat. Vince insisted they stay. He had plenty of spare beds. It was decided. Angus and Greg, in turn, insisted on at least going back to the boat to get some of their own drinks. Vince agreed. The three of them climbed into the Toyota and drove off down to the beach. That confirmed it. Wayne and I were so harmless we'd been left alone with the women.

We sat there. We weren't harmless. We were men. And this was our chance. We had twenty minutes, maybe half an hour. That was long enough for anything. For clothes to come off. For fast, meaningless fucking. People did this sort of thing, didn't they? All it took was someone to suggest it.

Wayne spoke. 'So what's it like, on the yacht with Angus and Greg?'

'Terrible,' said Jennifer, 'We should never have come. All they've gone on about for the last three days is sex, sex, sex. They're pathetic. They've got no chance of getting it.'

'They seem pretty confident.'

'Tough. We made sure we got our own cabin. With a lock.'

I swilled my beer. I was going mad. I remembered it was time for the evening weather observation. I headed off to the shack. There were *People* magazines open all over the desk. I looked at them for a moment, then stacked them all up, threw them under the table.

When I came out again Wayne and Gail and Jennifer had vanished. I heard laughter coming from our house. I envisaged various scenarios, stopped myself. It was a disease. I walked over. They were all in Wayne's studio, looking at his canvases. It was the first time I'd seen them myself, for a while. There was nothing much new.

'What about your writing,' Jennifer asked me, 'What exactly are you doing?'

'Very little.'

'Didn't you say something about a horror novel before?'

'It was meant to be. I sort of gave up on that idea.'

'Ever tried fantasy? I read a lot of fantasy. And science fiction.'

'No.'

It was back to art. I took no part in the discussion. I was beginning to feel slow after all the afternoon beers. Vince and the other two men returned. They had a bottle of fine scotch and some champagne. A party was called, over at Vince's house. Wayne headed off with the others. I stayed behind.

Somehow it seemed pointless. I was bored with all the bravado, the muddled thoughts of sex. I really didn't want anything to do with Gail or Jennifer, and yet there was a longing for the physical. To just *fuck* a body. It was insane and it wouldn't happen. I'd only get drunker and slower and more impatient with myself. With everyone. Then it'd turn to bitterness. Easier just to stay away.

I moved around the house, listening for the sounds of music and voices from the party. I couldn't relax. What was wrong with me? They were just people, Gail and Jennifer. I should've been glad to see them. It wasn't as if Cape Don offered much else in terms of society. Maybe that was it. It was all too pressured. It should've been casual, an encounter, but it was overloaded by loneliness. Frustration. I was too far gone.

I went to bed and stewed. I masturbated. I tried to think about Gail and Jennifer. About any woman. Nothing came. No woman would have me.

THIRTY

I rose at nine. Wayne was up much later, badly hungover. I asked him how things had gone. His memories were hazy. Too much scotch and champagne. But he had images of Angus and Greg chasing the women around the room. Of attempted hugs, gropes, kisses. Of Gail and Jennifer finally getting angry. Of arguments over the sleeping arrangements, who would have which room and which bed. Of the women barricading themselves in, Greg and Angus hammering on the bedroom door.

'What was Vince doing?'

'He was pretty quiet. After a while he just sat on his stool and drank port and looked sad. I think he realised the girls weren't interested. Not in him, anyway.'

'What about you?'

'Not in me either. Not in anyone.'

'Did Angus and Greg get through the door?'

'Not last night.'

I sat for a while on the front steps. Vince wandered by, hungover, back to his old self. He said the visitors had got up and left about eight that morning. I thought about the four of them, stuck on that little yacht again. It was depressing. One small lock on that cabin door and Angus and Greg to deal with. And after last night I wasn't even sure I had the right to feel superior.

But they were gone and Vince had other news. There'd been a radio call from Darwin.

'Someone else is coming,' he said.

'Yeah?'

I wasn't very interested. I was sick of visitors, they disturbed things. This would be our third in quick succession. First Danny, then the yacht . . . maybe that was ominous. Bad portents always came in threes.

I said, 'So who is it this time?'

'His name's Barry. He's a ranger.'

I nodded, waited.

'He's the one who was here before me.'

I sat up. This was something. The man who'd gone mad, driven to it by life at the lighthouse.

'Is he coming back to take over again?'

Vince shook his head. 'He's coming for his dog and his personal property. Then he's leaving forever.'

We considered each other. We knew what it meant. Cape Don had broken him.

Barry flew in on a specially chartered plane. Vince picked him up from the airstrip. The first Wayne or I saw of him was when he arrived unannounced at our front door and yelled down the hall.

'Hey! You two *artistes* have got my dog!'

We were sitting, with Kevin, on the back verandah. Kevin leapt up and bounded along the hall. We followed. Barry squatted down and batted Kevin's head.

'So, Kevvie boy, you missed me?'

He didn't look like someone recovering from a nervous breakdown. He looked very fit. Solid, tanned, with a rich black mustache. He was in full uniform. Ironed shirt, tight shorts, big black boots.

'I'm Barry,' he said, 'I'm here for my stuff.'

We gave him our names.

'You're both painters they tell me.'

'Wayne's the painter,' I said, 'I'm a writer.'

'Yeah? Real fucking art community this place is now. Listen, I got some scuba gear and a few other things stored in that room there. You guys haven't touched any of it, have you?'

'I'm using it as a studio,' Wayne said, 'We moved some things out of the way, that's all.'

He wasn't pleased. 'I better take a look.'

We all went into the studio. Barry looked at the scuba tanks and the spear gun and the stacks of chemicals. Now he was angry.

'I had all this arranged y'know. I knew where everything was. You had no business touching it.'

I said, 'We haven't *used* anything.'

He surveyed the other half of the room, the studio. The paint on the walls and floor, the canvases themselves. '*This* is what you've been doing?' he said, 'I thought they said you were a painter.'

'Well . . . ' said Wayne.

'You make money outta this?'

'No.'

Barry shook his head, turned back to his gear. 'Don't touch anything else. Those scuba tanks, just bump 'em wrong and they're fucked. I'll load it all in the truck tomorrow.'

He headed off. Kevin lingered on our verandah a moment, looking at us, looking at Barry. Maybe he was remembering all the ticks Wayne had pulled off him. The bed he'd offered. The food we'd given.

Barry glanced back. 'C'mon dog.'

Kevin went.

Barry was to stay for three days. On his first night Vince held a dinner for us all. Russel and Eve were invited, but declined. It wasn't much of a meal. Vince was looking bad. Drunk, dirty, tired. Barry was the only one of us with energy. He swigged back beers, sucked on Marlboro Reds.

'You been keeping Russel busy?' he asked Vince, 'Got him mowing the grass?'

Vince was struggling with a glass of scotch. 'I haven't *got* Russel doing anything.'

'He'll mow it alright. It's the only thing the lazy bastard *will* do. He's shit scared of snakes. Hates long grass.'

'I wouldn't know.'

We sat around after dinner, listening to Vince's music. Barry couldn't sit still. He roamed about the room, looking at things. The maps on the wall, the chart of aircraft silhouettes.

'Can't say I envy you Vince,' he said, 'Stuck here for two years. The bastards tried to pull that on me too. I didn't mind six months or so—I got some fishing in, some diving—but not two years.'

Vince gave a sour look to Wayne and I. 'I haven't done any fishing.'

'Why not? *Great* fishing out there.'

'The outboard on the boat, it's stuffed.'

Barry shrugged. 'I'll have a look at it tomorrow. I wanna get out on the reef one last time. Pity the cruiser's not here.'

'What exactly happened to the cruiser?'

'I took it. Once I realised they planned to keep me in this shithole forever, I jumped in the cruiser and sailed straight to Darwin. Told them I wasn't going back. I'm too senior for a one-man post. It was command of a proper station or I quit.'

'And you got it?'

'Sure. And the cruiser was due for a service anyway. They kept it there. Thought you'd have it back by now.'

Vince drank, said nothing.

Barry turned to Wayne and I. 'What about you two? Done any fishing yet?'

'No,' I said.

'I'll take you out, when I've fixed the outboard. What about crabs? Big muddies around the mangroves. You gone after them?'

'No.'

'What've you been doing all this time? You finished your book yet?'

'Not exactly.'

'How many you got published?'

'None.'

He laughed. 'So where d'you get off calling yourself a writer?'

He went off in search of another beer. The rest of us looked at each other. There seemed nothing to say. We'd all been lied to, this man had no problems, he was in complete control. It was worse for Vince. The Commission had suckered him. Nervous breakdown, emergency replacement . . . it was all bullshit. He stared into his scotch glass, swirled the ice. We waited for Barry to come back.

Late next morning he was knocking on our door. He'd fixed the outboard motor, he said. It'd taken only a few minutes. Vince had missed something obvious. So, were we ready to go fishing?

I said, 'We have to do the weather in a couple of hours.'

'Get Vince to do it. He's not interested in fishing anyway. C'mon, you can't say you've seen the Territory if you just sit on your arses all day.'

So we went. We gathered a few reels and lines, then drove down to the bay. The boat was there, with the outboard re-attached. We shoved off and climbed in. Barry took the wheel, gunned the motor and we were on our way. Wayne and I sat forward, hunched on the small bench. We weren't enthusiastic. I had no real interest in fishing. I didn't even like fish very much.

It was overcast, the ocean grey. We powered along at speed. The bay widened out and we hit a low, smooth swell. I looked back at the coast. Eventually I could see the lighthouse. Its lower half was hidden by trees. There was no sign of the houses or any other part of the compound. It looked insignificant, small. Passing by I would hardly have thought there was any reason to stop and visit.

Still, we were out on the ocean. There was fresh air, salt spray and the call of the sea. I began to feel better about things. I stood up with Barry at the wheel, got the wind in my hair, stared out at the flat horizon. It was the Arafura Sea. The great Asian archipelago. If we kept heading north the next stop was East Timor. Or Indonesia. China. It wasn't even very far. Two days, three days. Even a boat of this size might make it.

We got about a mile out. Then Barry pulled back on the throttle, looked at us. 'You guys know anything about fishing?'

'No.'

'See up ahead, where all the birds are?'

We looked. There appeared to be a reef, a dark line just under the water, awash with white foam. In a wide arc around it were seagulls. They were hovering, diving, riding on the water. 'Where the birds are,' Barry explained, 'The fish are.'

He started inspecting the lines and the reels. He selected two, gave one to Wayne, one to me. I looked at the reel. The line. The hook.

'What about bait?'

'Don't need any. There's a whole school down there, feeding. They'll snap at anything bright and shiny.'

We approached the reef. The seagulls lifted, wheeled away. Barry stood in the centre of the boat, steering, watching. Then he gave the command to throw in the lines.

I unravelled a few metres and tossed the hook over. Wayne did the same on the other side of the boat. I studied the water. I couldn't see any fish. I couldn't see anything. We chugged in a broad circle around the rocks. My line trailed away behind. No one spoke. I wondered if I should be slowly drawing the line in. Lure the fish. I didn't do anything. I stared at the distant coastline.

'Hey,' Wayne said.

Barry cut the engine. 'Got one?'

Wayne was staring at the line jumping around in his hand. 'I think so.'

'Well go on, pull the fucker in.'

Wayne began tugging in the line. It looked heavy, digging into his fingers. The fish started circling. Wayne went with it, stumbled around, arms and legs waving. Barry yelled advice. I sat in my corner, rocking up and down. Finally we could see it, a large, silver fish in the water. Barry took hold of the line. Together he and Wayne managed to heave it over the side. It flopped about on the bottom of the boat, a foot and a half long, all scales and muscle. Wayne danced, keeping his feet out of its way. He sucked painfully on his fingers.

'Well,' said Barry, 'Pull the hook out.'

Wayne stared at the fish. 'How?'

'Just stamp on its head and rip the hook out.'

'I'm not wearing shoes.'

'It won't *bite*.'

Wayne shuffled, looking for a good angle. He lowered his foot gingerly, caught the fish around the tail, lost it altogether. Blood was pumping out of its mouth, the eyes bugged. Barry finally strode over and dropped one booted foot directly on its head. I could hear the jaws crunch. He grabbed the hook and worked it out. Then he dumped it in the bow cavity. 'There. That's how it's done.'

The fish bounced a few more times, gulping, then lay still.

'What sort is it?' I asked.

'Queenfish.'

'It's big.'

'Big? That's nothing.'

Then there was a tug on my line, and it was my turn.

We pulled fish out of the sea for about an hour. There were two types, Queenfish and Trevally. We had sixteen when Barry decided it was time to quit. The floor of the boat was spattered with blood and muck. I didn't know the correct terms of weight or measurement, but all the fish were large. I was glad it was over. My arms were tired. There were cuts on my fingers. And I was bored.

We motored back towards the bay. I smoked a cigarette. Wayne sat next to me, silent, staring out. He'd enjoyed it even less than I had. Barry had been hard on him. Wayne just didn't have the knack. He pulled the line the wrong way, let it slip, couldn't get the hook out clean. Barry didn't believe it. Everyone could *fish*. What sort of idiot *was* Wayne.

We were halfway in. Then Barry saw something. He turned the boat. We looked. It was a lone platform of coral, about a yard wide, just awash with water. We circled around it. From certain angles it looked as if there was no coral there at all, just ocean. Barry was excited. 'I've got an idea for a photo.'

He'd brought his camera. It was a big and expensive one. He outlined the plan. We'd pull up next to the coral and he would climb out. Then Wayne and I would pull away in the boat and get a photo of him standing there. The idea was that from the right position, it would look as if he was standing unsupported in mid-ocean. It was the sort of thing, he said, you sometimes saw in *People* magazine.

Which settled that question.

'They're all yours?' I said, 'The *People* magazines around the lighthouse?'

'Yeah. They'd love a trick shot like this.'

We idled in, bumped up against the coral. I took the wheel, Wayne took the camera, and Barry climbed out. We moved away. Barry stood there. Alone, on a tiny wave-washed platform, a half mile from shore, in shark and crocodile infested waters.

'Leave him there,' said Wayne.

I played with the wheel, bounced the boat around. The waves seemed bigger suddenly. 'I'm not sure I can get back there even if I want to.'

'What's his fucking story, leaving us in charge of the boat? Doesn't he care about his life? About ours?'

'*People* magazine. They love that trick photography.'

We were at the correct angle. Barry waved and yelled. Wayne took photos. Then it was time to get him back. It took me about fifteen minutes. I charged in too fast and had to swing away, or came in too slow and got washed off course. Barry shouted abuse and instructions. Finally we had him. He shoved me aside, took the wheel. Got his camera off Wayne.

'Hope you took the bloody lens cap off.'

Wayne didn't answer. The boat turned for home. We sat up front again, waiting for the day to end, sixteen dead fish at our feet.

THIRTY-ONE

The day wasn't over. We beached the boat and deposited the fish in the back of the Toyota. Then Barry announced it was time to go after crabs.

'Crabs?' I said.

'Sure. The tide's going out. The mudflats are there. Let's go. Better get your shoes on Wayne. The bastards'll take your toes off.'

He strode off, following the beach towards the mangroves and the mud. All Wayne had was a pair of old tennis shoes without laces. He pulled them on.

'I don't want any crabs,' he said, 'Why do we have to catch crabs?'

'Don't ask me.'

We followed him. Off the beach, into the mangroves. Wayne pointed to some marks in the mud. 'Are those tracks?'

They were. There was the furrow with the clawed footprints either side, just like I'd seen before. But these were new. Two sets. They led from the water into the darkness of the mangrove.

'Hey, Barry,' Wayne said, 'Aren't they crocodile tracks?'

Barry looked back, nodded. 'Don't panic. If a croc comes at you, you can always paint it.'

Wayne stared at him. I wasn't too happy myself. I was no expert, but the tracks didn't look very old. They just looked big. I moved away from them, out into the mud. Wayne came behind more slowly. I had better shoes than he did. I was wearing ankle-high boots.

'How do you catch crabs anyway?' I asked Barry.

'Easy, fuck the wrong woman.'

'Seriously.'

'Just pick them up. The crabs that is, not the women.'

He was a charmer alright. We waded about. The mud sucked and pulled at my boots. The flat was bordered mostly by mangrove, and on the far side was the mouth of the creek. A slow current oozed out, black. The mud got deeper. It was reaching my knees. Walking was difficult. My boots were coming off. It was fine for Barry. *His* boots were calf high and tightly laced. He was striding from spot to spot, peering at the muck.

I stood still, examining the situation. We were maybe ten yards from the mangroves. Sandflies buzzed, wood creaked, small waves lapped. Wayne had stopped too. We watched Barry.

I said, 'Have you ever caught crabs here before?'

'Nope.'

'Have you ever tried here before?'

'Nope.'

'How do you know they'll be here?'

'I don't.'

I looked at Wayne. He looked at me. We both looked at the crocodile tracks.

We could die with this man.

Barry had crossed the mudflat and was standing in the

mouth of the creek. 'I don't think there're any crabs here. But I've caught barramundi in this creek before. I should've brought the lines.'

'So what now?'

'Well, we could go out to the headland and get some rock oysters.' He glanced at us. 'Hey, I wouldn't stand there too long. Those crocs are territorial you know.'

'Fuck.' I went to move, couldn't. I'd sunk. The mud was over my knees. I could feel my foot sliding out of the boot. 'Shit.'

I looked at Wayne. He was in trouble too. We should never have stood still. From there I looked to the shore, to the mangroves. Anything could be hiding in there. Anything about fifteen-feet long, low, covered with thick hide and endowed with a huge, man-killing mouth. And fast. I'd heard about how fast. I remembered being told once that if I was ever being chased by a croc I should run in diagonal spurts. Crocodiles were supposed to be slow at changing direction. Was that true? Did it even matter when I couldn't move. I tugged furiously at my feet.

Barry was cutting across the far side of the flat, back towards the beach. 'What's the problem?'

'We're stuck.'

'Just rip your feet out, it's no place to hang around.'

'Then why the fuck are we *here*?'

I was panicking I knew, but there was no stopping it. I ripped my foot out, leaving the boot behind. Then the other foot. I turned and dug in the mud. The boots had vanished. I glanced repeatedly at the shore. It'd come in an explosion of speed. I'd have maybe three or four seconds of terror before the end. Fuck Barry, fuck the boots. Were they worth my life? I found one, heaved it out. Then the other. I took off, running in big, high, running steps towards the beach. I poured the mud from the boots as I ran.

Wayne was ahead of me. Bare feet. No shoes in his hands.

Barry was waiting, smiling.

'You really should've worn better shoes.'

Wayne was furious. 'You didn't *tell* us.'

'Isn't it obvious? This isn't downtown Brisbane. C'mon, we'll check out the rocks for oysters.'

He marched off. He couldn't be real. He was a curse. A punishment for something we'd done, something we didn't even know about. All we could do was follow. He took us up through the bush and then out onto the headland. It was a broad shelf of rock, pocked and barnacled, exposed by the tide. We waited and watched while Barry clambered around, poking at things with his knife.

'Here we are,' he said.

We went over. He had two flat shells. He pried one open, gouged out the mussel and slurped it down. 'Beautiful.' He opened the next one, looked at us. 'I don't suppose either of you two are game?'

'Not me,' I said.

Barry looked at Wayne.

Wayne looked right back. He'd been pushed far enough. 'Okay,' he said.

Barry dug out the oyster. Wayne took it, sat it on his tongue, swallowed. It went down. It stayed down. I was impressed. Wayne had struck a blow. It wasn't until we got back to the Toyota that he began vomiting.

Barry and I watched him.

'Maybe it was off,' I said.

Barry shook his head, got in behind the wheel.

We drove home, got out. Wayne still looked a little queasy. His face was red. Anger or embarrassment, I didn't know which. He headed straight off for the house.

Barry began throwing the fish out onto the grass. 'I'll get these buggers filleted. We can have a barbie tonight.'

'Okay.'

'Hang on. Half of these are yours.'

'Mine?'

'You know how to fillet fish don't you?'

'No.'

'Shit. Come on in. I'll show you how to do the first few. Practice is the only way.'

I watched and learned how to fillet fish. I ended up doing eleven of them, in the sink of Vince's kitchen. It was trickier than it looked, filleting fish, and even less fun than killing them. In the end I was covered with scales and muck. The heads and tails and backbones went into the garbage. I thought about the Chinese and their soups, back in Brisbane. I missed the Chinese. What was left of the fish I stacked in the fridge for the barbecue. I wasn't looking forward to it. I was sick of the sight of fish. Sick of the *smell* of them.

I went home and checked on Wayne. He was fine.

'That thing was fucking disgusting,' he said, 'I could feel it moving in my stomach.'

'Ready to eat fish with Barry tonight?'

'I'm not going. He's a prick.'

'If I'm going, you are.'

We showed. It was a warm, still evening. Things were set up outside, under the tree. Vince and Barry were already seated, drinking. There was salad and bread, and the fish were all wrapped in foil, ready to go.

Barry grinned up at Wayne. 'How you feeling?'

'I'm fine.'

We sat down, opened beers, lit cigarettes, said nothing. Barry talked, Vince listened.

Eventually I said, 'Are Eve and Russel coming?'

'We asked,' said Vince, 'but no.'

I looked over at their house. I supposed they were making a statement of sorts. They'd lived with Barry before. What had the lighthouse been like then? What if Wayne and I had arrived six months earlier and struck Barry as our ranger instead of Vince. I watched Vince pouring down his scotch. The round red face, the thick stubble, the belly poking through the shirt. Suddenly I loved him.

Then there was Kevin. He was sitting watchfully in the dirt at Barry's feet. He seemed a sharper, meaner dog. He'd already forgotten Wayne and me.

I said, 'Have you always owned Kevin?'

'Yep.'

'Why does he hate Russel so much.'

'Don't you worry about that. Kevvie hates whoever I tell him to hate.'

We were lucky alright. Under Barry, Cape Don would've been a prison camp.

Time passed. The fish were thrown on the barbecue and we ate. Despite everything it was delicious—big juicy fillets baked in vinegar and butter. Not even half of what we caught that afternoon was being eaten. Barry talked about fishing trips of his past. And not just fish. He'd gone after things like turtle and dugong. He'd also eaten goanna, snake, wallaby, crocodile. Everything the national park had to offer.

I said, 'I thought only the Gurig could hunt around here.'

'It's alright. I'm square with the big bossman. Allan Price. You met him yet?'

'No.'

'He'd love you two.'

We settled into drinking. I found myself trying to keep pace with Barry. Wayne was matching it as well. We had to prove we could do *something* as well as he could. Drinking was our only strength. It was a mistake. Barry slammed down beer after beer. I couldn't keep up. My stomach was swelling, bloating.

Barry's wasn't. It didn't seem to touch him. He drank and smoked and sneered at us. He started pestering Wayne about art. Even there Wayne couldn't win. Barry knew what he was talking about. His main interest was photography. He even had a book due out soon, in conjunction with the Commission. Photos and accompanying text concerning one of the wetland national parks, south of Darwin.

Wayne was struggling. He tried to explain himself, what his theories were, why he was having trouble with his painting at the moment. Barry tore it all apart. Wayne tensed up, got more extravagant. Nothing he said was very coherent. And he was looking his worst. Dense curls of blond hair, white skin, thin hunched shoulders. He had nowhere to argue from, no certainty. Barry was bigger and tougher and had no doubts about anything.

I was getting too drunk. The atmosphere was making me ill. It was ugly, nearing some sort of violence. From time to time Vince or I tried to steer the conversation to other things. It didn't help. Even Barry was drunk now, and he was focused. The fishing had started it, then the crab-hunting, the oyster. Wayne was the victim for the night. Barry got on to the idea of Wayne doing portraits of the Cobourg locals.

'I can't believe they'd ask a kid from Brisbane to do it.'

'I didn't want it,' said Wayne, 'I'm not even going to *do* it.'

Barry was hardly listening. 'What the hell are you two even doing up here? There's people in Darwin need a job.'

'My father fixed it up.'

'Oh Jesus, your *father*?'

It went on. It was both Wayne and I now. Did we know anything at all about the Territory? We didn't. Did we plan to stay up north when the job was finished? We didn't. Had we seen anything of the Peninsula at all? We hadn't. We were wanting in everything. Dump us alone in the bush and we wouldn't last three days. Give us a broken-down engine to fix and we were helpless. Barry didn't even like the way I smoked. I didn't inhale properly. I sucked on it like a girl.

'It wouldn't be so bad if you could really paint, or you could really write. But what would you write about, what would you paint about? You've got no guts, no experience, you don't know anything. Why would anyone listen to anything you two had to say?'

I couldn't think of any answers. He was right. We didn't know anything. Wayne was silent, staring at the ground. In the end we simply got up and walked home. Once we were inside I realised Wayne had tears in his eyes. He went into his studio, switched on the music. I sat on the back verandah. I felt low and dirty. And stupid.

Barry had got to me. I hated him and his opinion meant nothing, but he had got to me. What *did* I think I was doing up there? Did it matter that I'd just hidden away in my room these last few months? Would a real writer do that?

Maybe it really was a farce, me thinking I could write novels. Certainly I'd had doubts about it before, periods when I hadn't written anything. But the idea that I *never* would was something new. It was disturbing and depressing. It was failure on a whole new scale.

I made an effort. I went in to Wayne. He was sitting on the floor, looking at his paintings. Barry had got to him too, seriously. Somehow that was even worse. I hadn't thought anything could get to Wayne.

'C'mon,' I said, 'Just because we're useless in a place like this, and to someone like Barry, it doesn't mean we're completely fucked. How would he survive in Brisbane?'

Wayne's eyes were dry. 'They'd worship him. They'd make a TV show out of him. He's good-looking. He can do everything. He's the great Australian dream. Believe me, they'd take him over us any day.'

We sat there.

It was true. They would.

THIRTY-TWO

Barry flew out the next day with his scuba gear and his spear gun and his dog. We were finally left in peace. There were no more visitors. It didn't matter. The damage was done. Cape Don had been unmasked. It was an abode of the defeated.

Over the next few weeks Wayne took down his canvases and stayed away from the studio. He painted nothing, sketched nothing. It was over. There wasn't going to be any exhibition. I understood, a little, of what he felt. There wasn't going to be any novel either. I went through the pages I'd written. They were very bad. Worse than I'd imagined. Barry had ruined it for the both of us, revealed an ugly truth. No one was ever going to be interested. We were wasting our time.

I strayed around the house, wondering what to do. I smoked a cigarette every two hours or so. Even they were beginning to annoy me. I could smoke them comfortably, but I still had no real taste for nicotine. I wasn't a smoker. I smoked for image. It was another pretence. My mind was going into a loop, picking my life to pieces. This wasn't supposed to be happening. Even my body was a problem. It was the boils. The one on my thigh hadn't been too bad—it'd grown, popped and passed—but now there was one growing on the cheek of my arse. It was big and painful and I was sick of boils.

Vince was no better. He stayed with his port and his scotch. It'd been a downhill few weeks, ever since Danny had left. Barry couldn't have helped. He'd fixed the outboard with appalling ease. He'd caught fish. He'd done everything Vince couldn't. There hadn't even been any nervous breakdown. Barry had just taken the cruiser and left. Demanded a new job, got it. A man of action, a man in charge of his own destiny.

It must've been the last straw. One Friday afternoon the supply plane arrived and I drove out as usual with Vince. While I unloaded the boxes I heard him talking to the pilot. He was organising a flight back to Darwin. He said he wanted to see Commission headquarters about getting a transfer. If Barry could do it, so could he. He'd had enough. He wanted out. Fast.

I shouldn't have been surprised. I was though. And disturbed.

'What'll you tell them?' I asked, on the drive home.

'That they made a mistake.'

We got back. I starting stocking the groceries in the fridge. Wayne came in, flicked through his mail. I told him about Vince.

'Good,' he said, 'Least someone is getting outta here.'

'Maybe. But Vince was the last person I thought it'd be. What're *we* supposed to do.'

Wayne didn't answer for a minute.

'He's not the only one,' he said.

I looked at him. He handed me a letter. It was from the

Queensland Department of Transport. Wayne's painting of roadworkers had won their Expo competition. The prize was five thousand dollars. The money would be awarded at a gala dinner, in Brisbane. They wanted him there. They were willing, the letter said, to fly him to Brisbane for the event, all expenses paid, economy class, return. It was in one week. Could he possibly attend?

Vince called a dinner to discuss the situation. All five Cape Don residents were present. I took a stool for once, because of the boil. I was worried about it. How was I going to pop one that I couldn't even see? I was depressed about other things too. Vince was going. Wayne was going. I wasn't.

Wayne himself was subdued about the prize. He could certainly use the money, but he'd never liked the painting, so he saw it as no great victory. Getting away from Cape Don was the main thing. Vince, too, was in a morbidly hopeful mood, now that he'd made the decision to leave. Wayne would fly out on the same plane as Vince. On Monday.

'Are you coming back?' Vince asked Wayne.

'He'd better,' I said.

We'd already gone through it. There was no way I was letting Wayne out of his remaining contract. The job was his, after all, not mine. We'd worked out that he'd be gone just over a week. It was strange though, the idea of Wayne simply flying to Brisbane for dinner, then flying straight back again. It brought the real world too close, destroyed the sense of exile and distance. If there wasn't at least remoteness to define Cape Don, then what was there?

Either way, Wayne was jetting off to success and I was being left to handle the weather on my own. All the observations. Every three hours. Night and day.

Vince wasn't sympathetic. 'I had to do it before you guys

got here. It's a shit way to live, but you've only got it for eight or nine days.'

Vince, too, would be gone at least that long, if he ever came back at all. Russel would be in charge of the station. I would be in charge of the generators. Everyone seemed content with the arrangement. Everyone but me. Vince and Wayne grew progressively more cheerful as the drinks went down. They'd never been the best of friends, now they were getting along fine. Vince was impressed about the prize. Wayne might not have known much about engines or anything else, but he'd won five thousand dollars for his artwork. He couldn't be all bad.

Five thousand dollars. I was trying not to think about it. It was more money than I ever dreamed of having. I was happy for Wayne but deeply envious. I would never win any prizes. What had I done? Not even a chapter in two years. Knowing how to change the generators was all very well, but where was it going to get me? I drank and felt my boil ache and struggled to remain civil.

Russel and Eve were the only ones who didn't seem to care. Russel was polite and indifferent, Eve was silent and guarded. The same as ever. Art awards didn't impress them. I wondered if anything we did ever would. I watched the two of them, sitting there, watching us. It occurred to me then that Vince and Wayne were celebrating their departure from a place that Russel and Eve called home.

It was something I hadn't thought about. Whatever happened, in two months, six months, a year, we three whites would be long gone. Russel and Eve would still be there. Someone else would be inviting them over for dinner. And someone else again after that. All transients. And if I couldn't be bothered getting to know the Chinese back in Brisbane, why should Russel and Eve bother getting to know us? We had our own homes, and sooner or later we'd always go back to them.

Wayne was also watching Russel and Eve. He was quite drunk now. Cheerful. He said, 'What about a video Russel? I hear you two've got a video over there, and some movies.'

Eve shot Russel a startled glance. Russel was on his seventh or eighth beer, looking sleepy. He shrugged and nodded. 'Yeah, we got movies.'

'You gonna invite the rest of us over to watch one some day?'

'Maybe.'

'Why not tonight?'

I said, 'It hasn't gotta be tonight.'

'What's wrong with tonight?' Wayne asked. 'Tonight's fine with you isn't it Russel?'

Russel looked up at Eve. She was frowning, gazing off down the hall. She didn't say anything. He smiled uncomfortably. 'Okay.'

'Not me,' said Vince, 'I've got resignation letters to write.'

Wayne drained his beer. 'What've you got to drink over there?'

'We'll bring our own,' I said, 'We can go back to our house and get some.'

Russel nodded again. He wasn't looking so happy about it now. Wayne and I got up and headed out across the compound.

'What did you do that for?' I said.

'Do what?'

'Invite yourself over to Russel and Eve's?'

'I didn't invite myself. They asked.'

'They didn't ask. You forced them into it.'

'They could've said no.'

'You didn't give them a chance.'

'It's only for a movie.'

'It's their house Wayne. We shouldn't just charge in if they don't want us.'

'Russel didn't seem worried.'

'He's drunk. Eve isn't.'

'Well it's too late now.'

Indeed it was. We stocked up with more beer and cigarettes, then went over and knocked. Russel came to the door and took us in. Their house was the same design as the other two, but more spartan. In the living room there was only one couch, one chair, and the TV. Nothing on the walls, no other furniture, the floorboards swept smooth and clean. There was a video machine on top of the TV, and several stacks of videos on the floor.

Eve was curled up in the chair, her arms folded. She nodded at us. Russel stood there, tall and awkward. He waved his hand towards the videos. 'Which one d'you want?'

We squatted down to check them out. I felt bad. This was an invasion. There was nothing the four of us could talk about. Something stood in the way of casual conversation. An ignorance. A dislike. I didn't know. We were limited to single sentence statements. Nods. Shrugs.

The videos, as Wayne had said, were exclusively martial arts and westerns. We chose a western. *Shane*. Neither of us had seen it before. I assumed Russel and Eve had seen them all. That made it worse. Russel took the cassette and loaded it up, pressed play. None of us said anything. Wayne wanted a movie, we were getting one. We sat on the couch, our beers between our feet. Russel settled on the floor, leaning back into Eve's chair. The movie started.

We sat there for the next two hours. I didn't know what to make of it. All I saw were images, unconnected passages of dialogue. Nothing had any meaning. I was out of the habit. Preoccupied. From time to time I glanced at Russel and Eve. Russel seemed to have fallen asleep. Eve was watching the screen, her head resting on her hand, resigned. Had we chosen the longest film we possibly could?

It was dreadful. I drank beer and smoked and waited. I cursed Wayne. Finally Shane rode off into the mountains, the boy calling after him. It wasn't the ending I wanted. I'd been hoping he would die. Tumble off his horse into the dust in the final scene. I also hated the boy. Inane and whining. Deserving of a movie death.

We stood up, stretched. Russel woke and yawned. 'Finished?'

'Uh-huh,' I said.

'One movie'll do eh?'

'Yes. Thanks for having us.'

The nod. The shrug.

'Thanks Eve,' I added.

Her expression was flat. 'I'm going to bed.'

We gathered up our warm beer and ventured out into the night.

'Satisfied?' I said.

Wayne nodded. 'That was horrible.'

'What'd you expect?'

'Why can't we talk to them? Why does it feel so impossible?'

'It might've helped if they'd *wanted* us there.'

'It's not my fault.'

'Whose is it then?'

'Right, it's always me. I do everything wrong.'

'Yes, most of the time you do.'

He looked hurt. 'Thanks a lot.'

'Forget it.'

'What am I supposed to do?'

'Go back to Brisbane.'

'Thank Christ too. I'm sick of being told how useless I am.'

'You could try at least.'

'I *have* been.' We were back at the house, on the front steps. 'Why do you think I mentioned the videos in the first place? I was trying to be *friendly*.'

He vanished into his bedroom. I went to the kitchen. Swapped a warm beer for a cold one. Sat on the back verandah. I lit a cigarette. My fourteenth or fifteenth for the night. Hard core.

I felt lousy. Wayne didn't deserve me coming down on him like that. What was *wrong* with me? I sat there. Scared. I was beginning to hate the things I was doing. I'd been bored with what I was before. Gone through times of self-pity and loathing. But this was different. This was the emergence of someone cheap and petty and bitter.

I drank. I smoked another cigarette. Nausea bloomed. Too much nicotine. It didn't matter. I smoked another one. Sucking on it, hard. Then I stood up, leaned over the side of the verandah and vomited. I fetched another beer, forced it down. Wayne came out, got himself a drink. He stood on the verandah a moment, looking out. I couldn't say anything to him. He said nothing to me. He went away.

On Monday morning I drove Vince and Wayne over to the airstrip. The plane was there. They said goodbye, climbed in and flew away. I drove home. Another boil had appeared, in my armpit. The one on my arse was already causing me serious difficulties. I felt grimy and diseased. Clean, healthy people didn't get boils. And what was in my head was worse.

That afternoon Russel appeared at my door. He'd been on the radio to Araru. An elderly cousin was dying, over on Croker Island. The clans were related in an important manner. He and Eve had to attend. I drove the two of them down to the beach, wincing at the bumps. They fuelled-up and motored off, out of sight. They'd be back, they said, in a week or two. It depended on the cousin. I drove home again.

Dusk came on. It was warm and still. There were no lights on in Vince's house, no lights in Russel and Eve's. No lights in Wayne's studio. No lights, even, out on the ocean.

I was alone with the boils.

THIRTY-THREE

Sleep was going to be the problem. I rolled around in bed that night, awake. The two boils ached. I could feel a third developing on my hip. It didn't matter which angle I lay in, they hurt. And then there were the observations. After I finally fell asleep I was woken by the alarm at quarter to three. I was back in bed by five past three, asleep towards four, up again at quarter to six. Asleep again by six-thirty, up at quarter to nine. It wasn't restful. I liked sleep. I needed it in good eight, nine hour stretches.

It wouldn't happen. Not if I got all the observations, and I was determined to get them all. It was a matter of pride. I needed an achievement. Everything else about my life might've gone wrong, but I intended, at least, to do this one thing. I would run Cape Don, smoothly and competently, and I'd do it alone.

Still, it would be dull. I spent most of the second day reading, perched awkwardly in a chair. I'd long since finished my own collection of books. I was into Vince's store of Le Carré and Graham Greene. I wrote part of a letter.

I smoked cigarettes. I took care of the generators. I sat on the verandah and stared. The day passed. No yachts sailed by. No planes flew over. Everything was quiet.

I turned to alcohol. Maybe I couldn't handle drinking alone back in Brisbane, but now there was no choice. I started on the beer. It turned out to be only a matter of perseverance. The drinks went down slower without conversation, but they still went down. After five or six it grew easier, and then very easy. My brain circled and thought and kept itself occupied. The evening developed. I didn't need company.

I went to bed drunk. Even then I couldn't sleep properly. Every three hours the alarm was ringing. The months of heavy use had told on it. It'd lost its sharp tone, the springs were going. It was down to a death rattle. When I rolled out of bed for the 9 a.m. observation I was thinly hungover and tired. The boils throbbed. Outside, the day was bright and fine as always. I glared at it, got dressed. It occurred to me I needn't bother. There was no one to notice me, naked or not. And clothes irritated the boils.

I rejected the idea. I wasn't big on nudity. Mine wasn't much of a body and I liked it better clothed. The day ticked by. I lay on the bed reading, suffering the boils, starting every three hours at the alarm. At one stage I dozed and was woken by an aeroplane engine. I went out, but the sound was already fading. I couldn't see the plane. I took the Toyota and drove to the airstrip. There was no one there. I drove home, got out of the car.

I stopped. I could hear voices. I looked around. They were coming from the weather shack. I went over, looked in. It was the radio. I stared at it. I didn't understand. The radio wasn't switched to one of the public channels. Wayne and I usually flicked it to an empty one, between observations. Otherwise we'd be listening to people all day, the public channels were in constant use. I'd never heard anyone on this channel before, it was supposed to be dead air. But the voices were there. Loud, blaring, male. There were two of them.

'There's someone else here.'

'Where are you?'

'I'm here. I've told you'

'I can't see.'

'There's someone else here.'

'Who?'

'I don't know.'

'Where are you?'

'I don't know.'

It kept going. There were sounds I couldn't identify. Snatches of other words. The voices were toneless, made flat by static. There was something disturbing about it. Senseless. I switched it off. I walked out into the compound. Looked around. Nothing.

Another night passed with the alarm clock. I was keeping up with all the observations, but I was feeling the lack of sleep. Things were beginning to blur. My head was slow, my eyes felt grainy and inflamed. But I couldn't actually sleep. No matter how tired I was, I could always hear the clock ticking beside the bed, knew it would go off in one hour, two hours.

And the boils were getting worse. There was one in my groin now. I was sprouting the things everywhere. I finally abandoned my shorts, they were rubbing in painful places. I walked around naked from the waist down. It didn't help much. The boils kept bumping things. Chairs. Walls. The mattress. I plastered bandaids over them. I watched my penis for the inevitable signs. It would happen right at the tip. The biggest boil yet. I'd probably get an erection squeezing it. And it'd come bucketloads of semen-ridden pus.

I remembered Wayne's marijuana. I hadn't smoked any for weeks. The supply had dwindled down to about a quarter of a bag. Wayne had left it behind, confident of finding more in Brisbane. That night I drank bourbon and smoked several joints, laced with tobacco. I could inhale the stuff more deeply now that I was a smoker. There was no more coughing.

The marijuana helped the pain. It didn't help the mind. I reeled around the house, confused, leering at things. I sat in Wayne's studio and stared at the old paintings. They were nauseating. I heard a phone ringing, started up and went out to answer it. I stopped. Gazed around the darkened compound. The only sound was the generator, humming in its shed. There were no phones at Cape Don.

I went back to the bourbon. I walked around the house. I didn't like the empty rooms. The buzz of the fluorescents. I sat on the back verandah. It didn't work. There was no peace. I felt restless, full of nervous energy. There was no way to spend it and no distractions. No Scrabble, no one to talk to, no TV. I thought about going over to Russel and Eve's house to watch videos. I couldn't do it. Their house was dark and closed. Their presence was still there, even if they weren't.

I drank, grew very drunk. At two forty-five a.m. I hobbled over to the shack. These walks at night I was finding the worst, out in the open with nothing but the lighthouse beam overhead, and the pale streetlights glowing along the paths. The houses around me were empty, the bush was empty. It was nothing but darkness for thirty, forty, fifty ks in any direction. In all the world there was only this small circle of dim light, and only me, walking across it.

I stopped ten feet short of the shack. Swayed. Stared.

The door was blocked by a giant lizard. It was huge, a good eleven or twelve feet long. It was a dinosaur. Mottled grey in the light spilling out from the shack. Sinewy. Ugly. It was up on its front legs. Its mouth was open, red tongue half out, eyes glaring at me. I glared back.

What the hell was it? A big goanna? A monitor lizard? We stood there, unmoving, eyes fixed on each other. The night hung still around us. Then the lizard moved. It swivelled and ran off around behind the shack. I followed. It wasn't there. I heard loud, rustling sounds, branches snapping in the scrub. There was no scrub there. There was nothing behind the shack but the cliff, dropping straight down. There was nowhere it could have gone.

I stood there, breathing hard. The sound of a phone ringing, that was one thing. Giant lizards, that was another. Something wasn't right. I entered the shack, sat at the desk. I looked at the radio. Static. Empty air. I thought about the voices I'd heard. What if I heard them now. What if they spoke to *me*. I waited, dreading it. In the corners the spiders sat in their webs and watched me. The radio didn't speak. I started the weather, finished it. Outside again I played the torch all around the shack. Nothing. I walked back to the house, very carefully. Listening. Watching.

The house was waiting. Deserted rooms. I went into my own and shut the door. Shut even the French windows. I didn't know what might be outside. I lay on the bed, my limbs distorted and painful. I set the alarm for two hours and forty minutes time. Stared at the ceiling fan. Didn't sleep.

Next day the supply plane arrived. I was on the verandah when it flew over, saw it do the circle. I put some pants on, drove out. The pilot seemed solid and real and cheerful, and I was very glad to see him. Last night didn't mean anything.

'Just you now is it?' he asked.

'Just me.'

'Sure you don't wanna jump on board? Get out like all the others?'

'I'm alright.'

And I was. But then I drove home. Cape Don clamped down around me again. I stacked the food in the fridge, opened a warm beer, walked up and down the front verandah. There was something nagging about the view. I'd been looking at it too long. I put on some shoes and went for a walk. It was painful and slow because of the boils, but it seemed important to get away from the house.

I explored the scrub at the far end of the point. It narrowed to a strip maybe fifty yards wide. On either side low cliffs fell down to the mangroves. The bush was littered with junk. Drums, bottles, sheet iron, unidentifiable rusting lumps. A dump. It was dreary and hot. I needed to piss and shit. I couldn't do it. I felt watched.

Finally I emerged to a small clearing at the very tip of the point. Below me was a wide strip of mangrove, and beyond that the ocean. The air was hazy, the sea flat and pale. In the clearing itself there were two circles of cement, four or five yards across, with large holes in the centre.

I knew what these were, they were the remains of the gun emplacements. Vince had told me. In World War Two the army had stationed some men at Cape Don. They were supposed to be guarding the channel against a Japanese invasion fleet. I lowered myself gently and sat on the cement. Lit a cigarette.

I remembered the story. The men had spent most of the war here, slowly rotting. There was nowhere for them to go, nothing for them to do. After a while they'd fallen to fighting amongst themselves, or to wandering off into the bush. Someone had been killed in one of the brawls. Another three men disappeared in the scrub, were never seen again.

There were some names inscribed in the cement. I didn't look at them closely. I didn't want to know. The clearing was lonely, brooding. I walked back through the bush. Most of the junk, I supposed, was the army's. Things had fallen apart. Halfway down one slope I noticed a small, concrete bunker. It was overgrown and half-buried in dirt. I thought about climbing down. Didn't. There would be nothing in it. It looked dark. A hole into the earth. I went back to the house, and emptied my bowels.

The walk hadn't helped. I felt ill. I was surrounded by decay. Over the next two days I alternated between drinking, and short, useless snatches of sleep. I avoided getting stoned, but it made little difference. Between the boils and the observations and the fatigue I was losing grip. I heard more phones ringing, more planes flying over. I'd drive out to the airstrip and there'd never be anything there. At night I'd hear faint classical music coming from Vince's place. Things crawling around under the house. Iron creaking in the roof. I'd suddenly realise that the sound of the generator was gone. I'd have to shake my head and slap my ears until I could hear it again.

I contemplated abandoning the observations, at least the night ones. There was genuinely no need for me to be doing them. Even the Bureau back in Darwin could hardly have cared during the dry season. Night after night the conditions were identical. No clouds. No wind. No real variation in temperature. It wasn't *weather* at all. But I couldn't do it. The observations represented order. They strung out, one after the other, they were beacons. All I had to do was make it to the next one, and I'd get by.

But there came a night, finally. I was out of stamina. Out of bandaids. I had five active boils. My armpit, my back, my shoulder, my groin and my hip. The sheets of my bed were spotted with blood. Every itch on my skin felt like a new one rising. I was going to die from boils, I understood that. I'd given up on clothes altogether. It made me feel uneasy and foolish, but it was necessary. The boils had picked the worst possible pressure points. I was bursting them as soon as a head appeared, but new ones replaced the old. I could think of nothing else to do with the things.

It was around midnight. I'd been smoking small joints throughout the day. I'd also been drinking steadily, without any real awareness of amounts. I was dealing with a running hangover, four or five days old, the body had no more use for alcohol. I was shaking, sweating. I needed something to do. An escape. I thought about reading. I was out of books. I'd finished the last one that I'd borrowed from Vince. I needed more.

I put on a shirt. I took the torch and a can of beer and went over to Vince's house. It was all darkness inside. I could hear the whirr of the ceiling fans. Soft movements from the bedrooms. I knew there was no one there. I edged along the hall until I found a switch, flicked it. Fluorescents blinked into life. It was only Vince's house.

I made it to the living room and the bookshelves. I squatted down, looked. I didn't know why I wanted more books. Books were the last thing I needed. I suddenly felt an utter hatred for every writer who had held on long enough to finish something. I never would. The hatred was physical, it was a sickness. I went through the titles. I pulled out Sartre. Herman Hesse. More Graham Greene. Hemingway. I dropped them, threw them away. They were evil. Then I saw a sex book by Norman Mailer.

I looked at it. It was called *The Prisoner of Sex*. I flicked through the pages, came to a section about the female orgasm. Stop it, I thought. Not this. Not now. I'd read far too many books about sex. They hadn't solved anything. All they'd done was confuse me, fucked me forever.

I threw Mailer away. I saw a bottle of Vince's port on the desk. I sat there, swigged from the bottle. I went over and picked up Mailer again. I lay on the couch. I read what Mailer had to say about fucking. About good fucks and bad fucks. I lost track of the context. I saw something about the most beautiful fuck ever. I lay back, let the words swim. The most beautiful fuck ever. The most beautiful fuck in history. *In the world.*

I dropped the book. Anger came from somewhere. I grabbed my prick. I'd give Mailer the most beautiful fuck in the world. I clenched and pulled. The erection came. There was no thought of sex in my mind. It was nothing but brute force. I jabbed and jabbed like a dog. I sweated and rolled, exhausted, maddened. I pulled off my shirt. The boils rubbed on the couch. Broke, bled. I worked at it, teeth gritted, fucking the pain. It wouldn't come. My prick was raw.

I stopped, furious. I was panting. I sat up. There were spots of blood on the couch. I headed for the bathroom. I needed to throw up. I needed more bandaids. I went in, switched on the light. I was facing the mirror over the sink. It was large. It reflected my body as far down as my knees. I hadn't seen myself for months. There were no mirrors in my house, only the one on my desk. That one was covered with books and letters and sheets of paper. This was something else entirely. I stared at myself in the fluorescent glare.

I was hideous. Huge and round and white. Streaked with grime. My erection poked out from under my belly. It was tiny. Ludicrous. There was a bandaid tangled in the pubic hair. And there were boils everywhere. Red pus oozed from their heads. My eyes were pink, my face covered with a dirty, ginger fuzz. It was disgusting. I was a monster.

I reeled away. I forgot about the bandaids, they weren't going to save me. I made it to the front door, looked across the compound. I couldn't go out there, couldn't cover that much open space. Not looking like this. Not *feeling* like this. I debated, hesitated, swore at myself, finally hurried across. It was like broad daylight in the centre of a crowded street. I was exposed. I was visible. Someone somewhere was watching this and they were sickened by it. I got to my front door, hid in my room.

I lay rigid on the iron bed. My hands gripped the sheets. I was in crisis. Terror. I wasn't going to make it. From outside I could hear the generator. It was impossibly loud. The sound of it filled my head, rose and fell. It was loose, out of its shed, circling the house. I knew it wasn't real. It wouldn't stop. It was coming down the hall, huge and lumbering. It was right outside my door.

I got up. I had to sleep. I went out to the kitchen, found my supply of antihistamines, found some wine. I washed down four of the small red tablets. I looked at the tinfoil sheet. I took four more. Then four more again. I went out to the front verandah and stared at the compound. I told myself there was nothing and no one there. That the generator was secure in its shed. Then I went back to my room. I lay down, pulled the sheet up over my body. Waited.

The antihistamines swung in. It was a long, dazed night. At times I slept, but the dreams jolted me out of it. Vivid dreams. Fucking. Screaming. I shifted and feared. Dawn arrived. I was still in the grip of the drugs. I gazed at the light stupidly. Planes were flying over again. I dozed. Woke. There were noises from the back verandah. Clunks. Mutters. They stopped. Finally I rose and went out. The verandah was empty. I had known it would be. I walked down the hall, opened the screen door at the front.

There was a black man sitting there, on the steps. He was smoking a cigarette, eyeing me.

'Which one are you?' he said.

'Uh . . .' Nothing emerged. I could only look at him. He was old, white-bearded, heavy-browed. Stern. I'd seen him somewhere before.

'Didn't you hear the plane?' he went on, annoyed, 'I had to walk here from the strip.'

I stood there, naked, boil-ridden, lost. I realised who it was. Allan Price. Chairman of the Board of the Gurig National Park.

'Excuse me,' I said. Then I went back inside to get some clothes.

THIRTY-FOUR

I got dressed. I thought *Allan Price*. At a time like this. I was doomed. I went back out. He was still there.

'Sorry about that,' I said.

He shrugged. 'Which one, the painter or the writer?'

'I'm supposed to be the writer. Gordon.'

He gave me a long, unimpressed look. Even dressed, I didn't feel like much to see. 'Woke you up eh?'

I nodded. 'I didn't hear the plane. I didn't know you were coming.'

'Where's Russel? Where's Vince?'

I explained where Vince was, where Wayne was, where Russel and Eve were.

He frowned. 'No one told me. You know how to run this place?'

'The weather station. And the generator. That's all.'

He nodded, stared off. There were a couple of battered bags at his feet. I wondered where he had come from, why he was here. Time passed in silence. I stood there. Was I supposed to be doing something?

I said, 'Uh . . . would you like a beer?'

'Beer?' He measured me up again. In some way I must have been satisfactory. 'Yeah. Thanks.'

We sat on the steps and drank slowly. The house and the compound and the lighthouse, they were all fading back to normality. There were no noises, nothing was watching me. The generator was a distant hum. I sipped from the can. I thought about the night before, at Vince's place. I'd left bloodstains on his couch. I'd left my shirt there, books all over the floor.

I stopped thinking about it. I waited. Allan Price didn't speak, didn't even glance at me. I thought of things to say, didn't say them. Finally he took a long pull from the can and smacked his lips. He sighed, looked at me. He'd come, he said, from a Land Council meeting down in Arnhem Land. He hadn't been around Cobourg for several weeks. That's why he was out of touch.

'The others are due back in a day or two,' I said.

'Don't matter. I'll get Russel on the radio. Get him over with a boat. How you bin going here?'

'Oh. Good.'

'You like Cobourg?'

'I haven't seen much. Only around the lighthouse.' I remembered who he was. 'It looks like good land though.'

'Oh yeah, good land. Good life. Where you from?'

'Brisbane.'

He nodded. 'Bin there. Canberra too. Sydney. Did the whole bloody tour, talkin' to authorities. When we were settin' this place up.'

'The national park?'

'Uh-huh.'

'You were on Croker Island before that, weren't you?'

'Croker. Meningrida. All over. Used to live right here

even. You seen those old shacks down in the bush? We lived down there.'

'Vince told me. He said they had a school in this house.'

He laughed. 'Shit yeah. Never did much good. Kids were wild, y'know.'

I got more beers. Allan seemed in a better mood. I felt better myself. Dazed, but functioning. I asked him questions about Cape Don, the compound, the house. What else did he remember?

He remembered the old lighthouse-keepers. Who they were, how they'd spent their time. How two of them had once gone wild, duelled it out with rifles. Sex was the problem. One of them had caught his wife fucking the other one on the lighthouse steps.

'Anyone get killed?'

'Nah. Hopeless bloody shots. Then the wives stepped in. They were big women, them wives. *They* nearly killed each other.'

He remembered the army too, during the war. How he and his people would swap meat and wild honey with the soldiers for their rum. How the gunners would lob shells out at the reefs, for practice.

'What about the men who disappeared.'

He shook his head. 'We looked. Followed their tracks to a swamp. After that, nothin'.'

I listened, felt all the tension draining away. Allan wasn't what I'd been expecting. There was still a severe and ominous air about him, but it wasn't directed at me. He seemed to appreciate the questions, enjoy the stories. He chain-smoked his rolled cigarettes, coughed occasionally, spat. I smoked my Winfield Blues. Felt sane again. The beer ran out. I'd drunk most of it over the last few days. Allan stood up. An hour or so had passed.

'What you doin' now?' he asked.

'Nothing.'

'Come on down the bush then. I'll show you these shacks we had. Haven't bin there in a while.'

'Uh . . . if you want. You sure you don't have other stuff to do?'

'Nah. I got plenty of time.'

I put on some shoes. I realised it was almost midday. I remembered the weather. I'd missed the last three observations. I explained this to Allan. He waited while I did the readings. On the radio the Darwin operator asked what had happened to me, where'd I'd been. She sounded concerned. I made excuses. Then I followed Allan down off the plateau into the scrub.

We walked. It was strange. Twenty-four hours earlier this would've been impossible. A nightmare. And I still had the boils and I still needed sleep, but everything had changed. I stumbled after Allan through vines and low bushes and rough clearings of broken stone, and felt good. Confused about exactly where we were headed, or how far away it might be, or what we would do when we got there, but good.

Allan set a steady pace. He moved easily, despite his age and bare feet and eternally lit cigarette. The plateau fell well behind. We were in level, thick forest. Away to the right I caught glimpses of the ocean. Even the sand of a beach. It was a different world. Fertile, tropical, almost rainforest. Birds called and things scampered away in the undergrowth. I asked Allan about giant lizards.

'Saw one eh?'

'Yes. At night. Near the weather shack. It was bigger than I was.'

'That big? Must've been an old fella.'

He seemed to think it was no great event. Finally we came across the shacks. There were three of them, tin roofs and tin walls. They were old, rusted, leaning. The ceiling of one had collapsed. Vines and trees swathed them in greenery. There were a few drums around, some bottles, nothing else. Allan was wandering from shack to shack, peering in, shoving branches out of the way.

'How many of you lived here?' I asked.

'Thirty. Forty.'

'Bit crowded.'

'Only went inside in the wet. Slept out bush in the dry.'

'Why here?'

'Nowhere else we were allowed to go. Government made this a reserve. They wanted us kept outta the rest of the place. Dunno why, *they* didn't know what to do with it. We could buy flour off the keepers up at the lighthouse. Some of them were okay. Then they took the lot of us over to Croker. That was that.'

I looked in the shacks. They were small and dark and festooned with webs. One still contained a three-legged table.

I said, 'At least you've got it all back now.'

He shrugged, nodded. 'Too late for some of this lot though. Died over on Croker.'

I fell silent. There was little else to comment on. Whatever had been there was gone. Except for Allan himself and the things he remembered. And whatever those things were, or what they meant, he didn't say. After a time we headed back.

'How long you here for?' he asked me, when we were almost home.

'Under two months left now.'

'That all?'

'It was only a six-month job.'

'But you can stay longer, if you want.'

'I suppose we could.'

He thought for a while. 'Well, you come over to Araru. Take a look.'

'Araru? Me?'

He nodded, serious. 'Gotta see the place, meet a few people. No good stuck over here.'

'When?'

'When the others get back. You can come with me and Russel.' He looked at me over his shoulder. 'You don't look too good. How long you been alone here?'

'Not much more than a week. I don't think I handled it too well. I'm not used to isolation.'

'This place . . .' He shook his head. 'Russel shoulda known. Round here, not a good place to be alone, a bloke like you. Bad things eh. Make you go crazy.'

'Seriously?'

He paused. 'When you come out this morning, looked like you thought I was a ghost.' He laughed, began climbing up the hill to the lighthouse.

Allan went off to Russel and Eve's house. He said he planned to sleep. I went back to my own place. I cooked myself a big meal of steak and vegetables and orange juice. I showered, squeezed one of the boils. I found a razor and shaved off the beard. Then I slept, six hours straight. It all seemed simple. I woke up around nine, did the observation. There were lights on over at Russel and Eve's house. The place was occupied again.

And I had only one more night, then hopefully Wayne would be back. Maybe Allan was right. Maybe Cape Don was an evil place to exist alone. On the other hand, maybe it was just lack of sleep and the boils and too much alcohol, too much pot. When I thought about it, nothing else had changed. My life was still going nowhere. I wasn't going to do any writing. I didn't even want to do any *reading*.

The sense of relief faded. Depression returned. Things

weren't going right here, it'd been a mistake to even come. I wanted to get back to Brisbane. Back to the pubs and television and old friends. Back where I didn't get boils and the only sounds at night were traffic and police sirens and the Chinese talking. But it was all still months away.

Next morning I went over to Vince's house and cleaned up the books. I flipped the couch cushions over to hide the spots of blood. They weren't as bad as I'd thought anyway. A few hours later a plane did the circuit. Allan came out of his house and watched it too. Together we drove out to the strip. The plane was waiting there. It unloaded both Vince and Wayne. They squinted in the sun, looked exactly the same as when they'd left. My family.

Vince was surprised to see Allan. We all got in the car, drove back to the lighthouse. Vince and Allan talked in the front, Wayne and I sat in the back. Wayne was silent. Staring out the window.

'So how was Brisbane?' I asked.

He thought. 'Really weird. It felt all wrong. I couldn't relax.'

'Who did you see?'

'Madelaine. She asked how you were. Everyone else. They kept on wanting to know what Cape Don was like, what we'd been doing. I couldn't tell them anything. I dunno why.'

'What about the award dinner?'

He shrugged. 'I mean, it made no sense to suddenly be at something like that after being here so long. And I'd forgotten how bad my painting was. It was shit, the whole thing. How did you go here?'

'I lost it a little. Before Allan showed up. What about the prize money? *That* must have been okay.'

'Yeah, that was okay.'

But he didn't sound convinced. He went back to looking

out the window. I was surprised. How could he have not enjoyed Brisbane? Brisbane was *everything*.

We got back to the compound. Allan went into Vince's house to use the park radio. He was making his call to Russel, organising a boat. Wayne and I stayed outside with Vince. He seemed tired. Depressed.

'I might as well tell you Gordon,' he said, 'I've already told Wayne. I'm not leaving.'

'What happened?'

'They said they appreciated my situation, but that there were no other positions open and that no one wants to replace me here. I'm not surprised. Word's got around. Stay the fuck away from Cape Don.'

'So what happens now?'

'Another six months at least. Maybe a year.'

'I'm sorry,' I said. And I was.

He sighed. 'At least I might get the cruiser now. They know I'm pissed off. I said that if the cruiser wasn't here within three months I was quitting, regardless. They promised it would be. And new parts for the generator.'

'Do you believe them?'

'No.' He made an effort, became a ranger again. 'So, any problems here while I was gone?'

'Russel had to leave, but that was all. I didn't break anything.'

'Did you get all the weather?'

'No.'

He nodded. 'No one can. I nearly went mad when I tried to do it alone. Believe me.'

'I do.'

Allan came out. He'd tracked Russel down at Croker Island. The cousin there wasn't dead yet. Russel would have time to come over with the boat next day, pick up Allan, then spend a day or so at Araru. He looked at me.

249

'You feelin' better yet?'

'Sure.'

'You'll be coming too then.'

It wasn't a question. He was the man in charge, and he'd made the decision. For some reason, after that one afternoon we'd spent together, I was wanted.

THIRTY-FIVE

By late next morning Allan and I were packed and waiting down at the bay. I'd borrowed a sleeping bag from Vince, thrown a few other things together. Asthma drugs, cigarettes, a half-full cask of wine. I wasn't sure how long I'd be gone. Allan didn't say, I didn't ask. It seemed best not to worry. Russel and Eve arrived about noon, ran the boat up on the beach. They nodded at me. I assumed they'd known I was coming. Allan and I loaded in, and we shoved off. We headed east, out of the bay, into the ocean.

The day was sunny and blue and warm. The boat powered up to speed, bucked across the waves. I looked back, watched the lighthouse fall away behind. With it went Cape Don, the houses, the writing, the observations, everything. It was a failure and there was nothing much left to be salvaged, but at least I knew that much now. Things could progress. I was finally heading somewhere different.

I lolled in the stern and lit a cigarette. I watched the ocean and the coastline, blew smoke into the wind. *This* was what smoking was for. Travelling. Eve was also sitting in the stern. She seemed cheerful. She looked across at me and actually smiled. It was quick and small, but it was there, and it made her face almost unrecognisable. I wasn't sure what to do. I smiled back. Allan, standing with Russel at the wheel, called me forward.

'You see that?' he said.

He was pointing to a large reef. I nodded.

'Crab dreaming place,' he said, 'Lots of dreaming places around here. Dingo, stingray, snake.' He waited, watching me. 'You know what dreaming is?'

'No. Not really.'

'Cape Don. That's a dreaming place.'

'Yeah?'

He laughed. 'Yeah. Big lizard dreaming.'

'You're kidding.'

'No, no joke. *You* know. Mean old fella, big lizard. Plays tricks in your head. But Cape Don's not so bad. Some of these other places around, they're more dangerous. Only Gurig go there. No rangers. No tourists.'

I nodded.

He looked at me seriously. 'If I show you, you'll stay away then eh?'

'Of course.'

He was satisfied. He began pointing out places along the coast, explained a little of what they meant to the Gurig clans. It wasn't exactly secret knowledge. There was a map on Vince's wall, back at Cape Don, which marked some of the more sacred areas, along with warnings to stay clear. Anyone could read it.

And Allan was only talking in general terms. First he showed me a large, forested point of land, surrounded by reefs. Somewhere back in the bush was a giant banyan tree. It was an earthquake spirit tree and would cause disaster if interfered with. The Cobourg Peninsula did get earthquakes from time to time, Allan said, but only small ones. The last big one had happened before he was even born. And only he and Russel knew exactly where the tree was.

Then there was a long white beach that had an influence on the weather. If someone drew certain signs in a certain place in the sand, strong winds would blow. Even worse, placing a banyan stick in the sand and talking to it in a certain way would cause the skies to darken and a cyclone to come. Very few people knew the words or the signs, but the beach itself was still forbidden.

'Have you ever called a cyclone?'

He smiled at me. 'Don't think I could eh?'

'I dunno.'

'No, I never called one. Big things cyclones. But one was called, once. By mistake.'

He explained. It had nothing to do with the beach. An important set of rocks on another part of the coast had been interfered with. A woman visiting from another tribe had been searching for oysters there, not knowing the law. The cyclone that came was heavy with rain and the Peninsula was severely flooded. Deaths occurred. And it was all long, long ago.

'You know, I've seen some of these places on a map,' I said, 'At the ranger station.'

'Yeah, we made that map. For the rangers. It's all these tourists. They don't know anything.'

And there would be more tourists soon. He told me that the park board had recently voted for the building of a small resort. It was over on the east side of the Peninsula, not far from the present camping grounds. Room for maybe twenty or thirty visitors.

'You don't mind people coming?'

'No. Long as it's done right. Our people need the jobs.

This resort, it'll be run by us. We'll give 'em tours. And there's a bit of white history around too. People should see it.'

'The settlements?'

I knew, from the maps, that further along the coast there were ruins from the colonial days. There had been two attempts by Europeans to settle Cobourg in the early 1800s. They were amongst the first white settlements in the whole of Australia, outside of Sydney. Long before Darwin was founded. When the whole northern half of the continent was still unknown territory. Both had failed utterly in the face of starvation and disease and Gurig resistance. Apparently there were still a few buildings and foundations left, fireplaces, junk, some gravestones.

Allan nodded. 'Cyclone got 'em. Lot of them died. They waited for more people to come. Nothing. So they went home. Lucky for us.'

'I guess so.'

'There's others too. You heard about the Macassans? They were coming here before Captain Cook even.'

Vince had told me a little. Muslim fishermen from the city of Macassar, in what was now Indonesia, had been visiting the peninsula decades earlier than any whites. They were hunting trepang. Sea slugs. They sold them in China, where they were a delicacy.

'They camped along the coast,' Allan said, 'You can see where. We still got stories about 'em. They stayed here for months sometimes. They weren't like the whites. They only wanted sea slugs. It was all friendly.'

'Vince told me some of your people even went back overseas with them.'

'Yeah. This one bloke, he went. Got another boat from there, kept going. Ended up in England. Came back years later. Spoke English. Before any whites even got here. You believe that?'

'It's a little hard.'

'True though. You're a writer. Write a book about *him.*'

Then Eve was yelling and pointing out to sea. I looked but couldn't see anything. Russel and Allan could. Russel turned the boat.

'What is it?' I asked.

'Turtle,' Eve grinned, hanging over the side. The boat zipped and plunged, slowed down. Finally I caught a splash ahead. Then we were over it. I saw a dark-green oval shape, large, flippers working, gliding away to the depths. I watched. The turtle, I knew, was something significant. It was the official symbol of the Gurig National Park. The sign of a sea people. Russel circled the boat and there it was again, shimmering far below.

'What're you going to do?' I asked Eve.

'Nothin'. We're just showing you. You ever seen a turtle?'

'No. Do you catch them?'

'Not today. Only sometimes. Turtle's special. They're good eating but.'

The turtle veered off. Russel let it go, turned the boat east again. The sea was wide and empty and blue. I settled back in the stern. Water splashed over the side. Allan, Russel, Eve, all of them looked back at me from time to time. Expectant in a way. Was I enjoying myself? I had no idea why they were bothering with me, why they cared whether I was happy or not, but I was. I lit another cigarette, offered them round. We skimmed over the ocean.

We arrived at Araru half an hour later. I wasn't sure what I'd been expecting, but it was nothing like Cape Don. It was different country altogether. There were no swamps, no mangroves, no dense scrub. Instead the settlement was on a long, white beach, open to the sea. Beyond the sand was dry grassland, thinly scattered with gum trees. There was a shack visible, a shed, and some campsites. No houses. No compound. No lighthouse.

Russel ran the boat up onto the sand. There was already another boat there, and some petrol drums. We climbed out. About a dozen people were coming over to us, men, women and children. They were all Aboriginal. Allan and Russel and Eve began talking with them in Gurig. I looked around. The shack was maybe a hundred yards back. Here and there were blankets spread under trees, canvas awnings strung between the trunks. There were fireplaces, eskies, boxes of stuff. And vehicles. There was a four-wheel drive parked near the shack, a Landcruiser, and the bodies of several others around the place, stripped and rusting.

Allan was waving me over to one of the campsites. Everyone was sitting down, in the shade. I went over and sat. Introductions were made. Some of the men I already knew. Davie. Long Bob. Jerry. And Con, the one Wayne had shared the joint with, back at Cape Don. The women, though, I'd never met. Vonnie. Cathy. Hilda. And Dulcie. Dulcie. The name was familiar from somewhere. She looked about thirty, big, smoking a cigarette.

I said, 'Is that your name written on the wall in the house at Cape Don?'

She looked at me for a moment. Then she laughed. 'The school? Hah. I'd forgotten about that. How high am I? Miss Andrea made us do that.'

'She was the teacher?'

'Uh-huh. Poor thing, she never looked very happy.'

'I'm living in that house now.'

'Yeah? Good luck. I hated the place.'

The others laughed. I sat back, waited. Conversation flowed around me. Most of it was in Gurig. I smoked cigarettes and watched. After a while Allan and Russel and the other men went off towards the shack, talking. I stayed with the women. Three young children ran about, screaming and playing. Eve chased after them. I realised there were no teenagers around. Only the kids and the adults.

I lay back, stared at the sky. I began wondering exactly what I was supposed to be doing there. Nothing was happening. Maybe nothing would. Still, it was better than weather observing. The day was fading into afternoon. There was a warm breeze. The sound of ocean nearby. I decided it didn't matter what I was doing there. This was fine.

The men came back.

'C'mon,' Allan said, 'We're going fishing.'

'Oh. Okay.'

I got up. Allan and Russel and I climbed back in the boat. I saw that the rest of the men were piling into the Landcruiser, and that they had several guns. Allan noticed me watching.

'They're after meat,' he said, 'We're after fish.'

We sailed off south along the beach. The sun sank low. Eventually the beach gave way to mangrove. We came to the mouth of a creek. Russel steered us slowly inwards. The creek narrowed, split into two channels. We went along the thinner one. The mangroves closed in, all twisted black trunks and branches, mud glistening in between. Sandflies rose in clouds. Allan handed me some insect repellent.

I said, 'What sort of fish are we after?'

'Barramundi.'

There were lines and reels in the boat, but they weren't being unrolled. Allan and Russel had thin wooden spears. I'd seen this sort of thing on television before, but never first-hand. I was surprised anyone still did it for real. I looked over the side. The water was clear, only a foot or two deep. The boat slowed to a stop. We waited in silence.

Russel nodded to me, 'Here.'

I looked. There was a fish down there, drifting around above the sand. It wasn't very large. I didn't know what Barramundi looked like. Russel raised his spear, studied the fish. I remembered things about water and refraction. Did you aim in front, or behind? Russel drove down with the spear. There was a splash and a flurry. The spear came out again. There was nothing on the end of it. Allan laughed.

'Big Barra there Russ.'

Russel shrugged, smiled.

They fished until it was almost dark. It was very quiet, only the odd word from Allan or Russel, the bubble of the motor. Moisture dripped from branches. No one speared any fish. I didn't much care. I was staring out to either side of the boat, watching the mangroves. The creek wound through them, curling in slow loops, dividing again and again into new channels. There was no end to it.

Eventually it was too dark to see the bottom. Russel began threading his way out. I had no idea where we were. Allan scrabbled about in the bottom of the boat, found a torch, flicked it on. He shone it around. Ghost shapes stood out, flecks of deep green.

'Keep a lookout Gordon,' he said, 'Bit of luck we'll show you some crocs.'

There was no moon yet, just the dim stars. The channel was only faintly visible, twisting and turning. Allan stood in the bow. From time to time he searched the shoreline with the torch.

'You'll see the eyes first,' he told me, 'Big, orange eyes.'

And then there they were. Up ahead. Two glowing points that disappeared in a blink, appeared again. Then another set. We eased forward. Allan kept the torch on. Finally I could see them, two crocodiles. They were crouched in the mud at an open section of the creek bank. The nemesis of my Cape Don dreams.

We passed only a few yards away. They weren't very big, only nine or ten feet. Nor did they lunge at the boat or slither off into the water. They lay dead still in the circle of light and watched us. All the fear I had stored up, it had nowhere to go. The crocodiles fell behind. One set of eyes blinked out, then the other.

Allan was at my ear. 'Just little fellas, eh? Step in that mud but, just you and them, then they're big.'

We returned to Araru in full night. I could see fires burning. There was an electric light in the shack, and I could hear the thin whine of a small generator. Yells were exchanged across the water as we landed. The other men'd had more luck. They'd shot and slaughtered one of the banteng cattle, there was plenty of meat.

We all gathered around one of the fires. There was a large hotplate over the coals. On a stretch of canvas there were huge sections of freshly cut meat. Bones were showing, hairy skin still attached around the joints. Blood pooled beneath. There was also salt and butter. Various bottled sauces. Loaves of bread. Old soft drink bottles full of water.

I waited. Ants and other insects crawled over the meat, feasting. Then the women swept them away. They started slicing off chunks, throwing them on the hotplate. A cask of wine appeared and began doing the rounds. We sucked from the nozzle. Small sips. The women looked at me, gestured at me to take food. I snatched some slices of the meat from the fire, some bread. The bread was stale, but the meat was hot, crisp on the outside, warm and bloody on the inside. I was hungry and it was superb.

Then the women began throwing other, smaller cuts on the hotplate. I assumed these were choice pieces. Liver.

Kidneys. I saw the heart. It was huge and whole. Blood still oozed from the arteries. It sizzled, rolling around the plate for a while. Then it was pulled off by one of the women. It was Dulcie. She gripped it in her hand, took a huge bite, right into the muscle. She chewed, juices dripping down her cheeks. She looked around the group, caught my eye.

'Gordon,' she said, offering the heart, 'You want some?'

I thought, hesitated, shook my head.

She laughed. Everyone laughed. The heart did the rounds.

The night aged. The meal was finished, the spare meat carted away. The group sat around the fire, talking, sipping on the cask. Occasionally the talk switched to English, and I was asked a few questions, but not often. People began drifting off to other camps, or the shack. Allan came over to me.

'You sleep here, okay.'

'Okay.'

'If you walk around at night, keep off the beach. Crocs there sometimes.'

'Uh-huh.'

'So, you like it here?'

'Yes. I do.'

'Good. Cobourg's not so bad eh. Maybe you might wanna stay, over at that lighthouse.'

He went off. I was more or less alone, no one else was bedding down close to me. I opened the sleeping bag and spread it on the ground. It was too warm to get inside it, I lay on top. People wandered around for a while, then everyone was settled. Silence fell. I watched the glowing remains of the fire. Stay on at the lighthouse? What had Allan meant by that?

I didn't dwell on it. I rolled on my back and looked at

the stars, billions of them, bright in the sky. I felt full and satisfied and tired. Even the boils felt better. Maybe salt air was all it took. Maybe it was just the escape from Cape Don. I didn't know. I didn't care. Everything about my life seemed distant and small. I listened to the breeze, and the sea, and the odd, soft mutter from the other camps. Then, at some point, I slept.

THIRTY-SIX

Everyone was up early. The morning was bright and cool. People went here and there, cooking their breakfasts. I ate, then lay in the shade, waiting for nothing. My mind was blank. I didn't think about Cape Don, my writing, anything. Only the ground under my back, and the low boom of the surf. No one came near me. Finally I was bored.

I got up, explored the camp. First the shack. It was very simple in design. Tin walls, post frame, concrete floor. There was a large room that contained a freezer, a table, some chairs and a two-way radio. Off that opened three small bedrooms. The floor of each bedroom was covered with mattresses. Probably twelve or fifteen people could squeeze in there, if it was the wet season and there was nowhere else to go.

Outside there was the generator, a pump at the head of a well, a toilet and a shower. And further off, all the derelict four-wheel drives. I asked Allan about them. He said that while there were no real roads to anywhere from Araru, there were a few bush tracks. They led to important sites and some good hunting grounds. It was hard on the vehicles though, so none of the four-wheel drives lasted long. New ones were delivered by a big ocean-going barge from Darwin. They were expensive.

He took me back to the shack and dug around in a box under the table. He came up with a bunch of papers. He showed them to me. They were bills. For food, petrol, transport. Social Security statements. Old tax forms. Some for individual people, some for the Gurig people in general.

'You know about this stuff?' he asked.

'No.'

'Pain in the arse eh.'

I nodded. I'd known, I supposed, that things couldn't be as simple as they looked around Araru. Money still had to be made. And there had to be a school around somewhere, either at Black Point or on Croker. And medical services, and some way of organising banking. And lawyers and accountants, for park business. And a store too, of some sort. For the bread and the butter and the wine and the cigarettes.

'We owe a lot of money,' said Allan.

'Do you make enough to cover it?'

'We will, once we get this resort. Have to get training though, for the business side.'

I nodded.

He looked at me. 'Never know. Someone like you might wanna work in a place like that.'

I was surprised. I said, 'I don't really know anything about business.'

He shrugged. 'Well, years off yet.'

He left it at that. I went back outside, sat. I was confused. I couldn't see why Allan was talking to me about these things. I was young, I didn't know anything, and I was from Brisbane.

Time passed. Then around midday there was a stir in the camp. A boat was pulling up on the beach, another dinghy. It held two aboriginal men, one of them quite old. They climbed out and talked with Allan and Russel. It seemed important. Allan then spoke to everyone else in Gurig. They all headed off, started collecting their gear.

Allan came over. He told me that the two men had come from Croker. It turned out that the old cousin over there had finally died. Everyone at Araru was needed over at the island, to begin the funeral rites.

'How far is it?' I asked.

'You can't go. It's private.'

'Oh.'

'Not tonight anyway. Maybe later. You stay here.'

'Oh . . . okay.' I was alarmed. Left alone again. Cape Don had been bad enough, but at least I'd had my own house, and books and a stereo. At Araru there was nothing.

Allan was grinning. 'Not just you. Con, he'll be here too. He's Tiwi, not Gurig. This funeral's nothin' for him. And Hilda. She's from inland.'

'Alright. How long for?'

He thought. 'I'll come back with Russel, get you tomorrow. See what we can do with you then.'

'Would it be easier to just drop me back at Cape Don . . .'

'No, you stay here. One night's not enough.'

'Okay.'

Croker was miles away, right over the other side of the peninsula. By boat, it would be two hours from Araru at least. It seemed a lot of travelling back and forth. Still, it was Allan's decision, not mine. I watched while everyone loaded themselves into the three boats. Con came over and stood with me.

'Just you and me,' he said.

'And Hilda.'

'Bring any of that gunja?'

'No.'

'No worries, I got wine hidden, back in the bush. We'll get pissed tonight, okay?'

'Okay.'

They were ready to leave. Allan came over again. He was carrying a rifle, a .303 with a scope. Allan gave it to Con, along with handful of bullets. They spoke together for some time. Allan was serious, Con was nodding, smiling. Then Allan went back to the others, and the boats pushed off into the surf. They motored up and headed north.

'What's the gun for?' I asked Con.

He swung it round, aimed at my head. 'We might need it.'

The afternoon was slow. Con and I sat on the beach and talked and smoked. It wasn't an easy conversation. Con spoke for a while about Cobourg and Melville Island, but mainly it was about Darwin and his time in prison. The men he'd fought, the women he'd fucked, the people he'd fooled. I had little to say in comparison. I'd never been in prison, was useless around violence. Still, there was no one else for company. Hilda was about somewhere, but I hadn't seen her.

Towards dusk Con went off and brought back two casks, one of claret, one of port. We started drinking, watching the sun go down. The wine was flat and hot and again we drank it straight from the nozzle. I wasn't enjoying it, but the sooner I got drunk, the sooner I might get to sleep. Sleep seemed like a good option. Once it was fully dark, Con told me we should move away from the water. There was the chance of crocodiles.

We took the casks and wandered up to the shack. The generator and the lights were on. Hilda was inside, sitting at the table. She was a large woman, young, with wide dark eyes. I'd seen her with the other women, talking and yelling, but now she was dead quiet, watching us warily. Con said something to her, not in English, laughed. She didn't reply.

There was an electric frypan on the bench. It was greasy from old meals. Con rummaged around in the freezer and came up with a joint of meat. We sliced off cuts and cooked them. We passed the casks back and forth. Hilda had a few pulls, ate with us, didn't talk. Outside was the great, empty night. Inside the shack it was close and hot. The hours crawled by. I grew drunk. Con was drunker.

'You ever killed any banteng?' he asked me.

'No.'

'You wanna?'

'Now?'

'Yeah. Now. We got the gun.'

Hilda said something in Gurig. Con snapped back at her, shoved her shoulder. She went quiet. He shoved her again. Waved his hand towards the bedrooms. Yelled at her. She got up. Went.

Con hefted the cask. Grinned at me.

'Don't worry 'bout her. We'll go later.'

'Sure.'

We drank. The night was getting cheap and evil, I could sense it. The bad wine, the hot small room, Hilda, none of it was what I really wanted to be doing. We were deep into the port. Mumbling. Sweating. I was wearing shorts and a T-shirt, Con was just in shorts. His fat belly hung over the top.

'That Allan Price,' he said, 'He likes you.'

'I don't know why.'

'He don't like me.'

'Why not?'

'Reckons I shouldn't be here.'

'Oh.'

'Fuck him. Big fucking man.'

'Well he is, isn't he?'

'Not on Melville he's not.'

'Uh-huh.'

I wasn't keen to hear this. I drank, walked around the room. Con went on. He didn't like Allan, didn't like Cobourg, didn't like anything. I was beginning to hate him. I found a stack of old magazines. I began flicking through them. After a time Con got up and followed Hilda into the bedroom. There were some indistinct sounds. Thumps. Con laughing. Nothing from Hilda.

I sat there, drunkenly flicking pages. There were copies of *People*, *Woman's Weekly*, *Penthouse*. I ended up with the *Penthouses*, staring at the pictures. Soft focus, pale bodies, wrapped in silk and pastel colours and smiles. They were ludicrous, impossible. Especially in this little tin shed, tired and dulled with alcohol. I went from page to page, drinking more port, deeply bored. When I looked up Con was standing in the bedroom doorway, staring at me.

'You like that stuff?' he asked.

'Not really.'

'Turn you on?'

'No.'

He curled his finger. 'Come over here.'

'Why?'

'Come on.' He was nodding in towards the beds. 'Just look.'

I got up, went over. I looked in. There was no light in the bedroom, but the light from the main room was enough. Hilda was lying on one of the mattresses. She was naked. Her eyes were wide and white, looking up at Con and I. Her arms were at her sides. I saw large, flattened breasts.

A round belly. The tangle of pubic hair, her legs held together.

'You want her?' Con asked.

'What?'

'Go on, she's yours. I told her.'

'What are you talking about?'

'Just get a suck from her, eh. Give her a bit of white cock.'

'No.'

'Why not? I won't look.'

'It's not that.'

I was still staring. Hilda was watching us, her eyes flicking from Con to me, back to Con. She made no move to cover herself. She seemed afraid. Submissive. Her dress discarded at her feet.

'Don't you like her?' Con asked, confused, 'She'll do it.'

'No.' The idea of actually going in, fucking her like that . . . other men could do it maybe, without even thinking. Con obviously *expected* me to do it. Maybe even Hilda did. It could happen. Her big legs spread, me in between. Her sweat. Her smell. Her wide lips, taking in my prick, sucking. I thought about the women, the night before, biting into the bullock's heart. The juices on their cheeks. Suddenly I was appalled, sickened.

'No,' I said again.

Con wasn't pleased. 'Don't you like women?'

I had to get away. I fumbled for excuses. Anything. I said, 'I can't. I've got a girlfriend. Back in Brisbane.'

'So?'

I babbled. 'So I don't wanna sleep with anyone else. She's more than just a girlfriend. We're engaged. We're getting married when I go back.'

'Gettin' married? You never said.'

I shrugged, smiled hopelessly at him. Smiled at Hilda.

She still gave no reaction. I tried not to look at her body. Her legs, her hips, the wide mattress all around her.

'I'm sorry,' I said, to no one. I turned away, grabbed the cask from the table, walked out into the night.

'Gettin' married eh?' Con called after me, laughing. I walked over to where I hoped my sleeping bag was, found it eventually in the dark. I felt ill and disgusted. Engaged? Getting married? Was that *all* I could think of to say?

I lay down. The sky reeled horribly. Too drunk. Hilda was still in my head. Big. Passive. Fearful. Of Con. Of *me*. There was something in me that liked that. The fear. Something that *wanted* her to just lie there, let me fuck her like a corpse. I hated it. I sat up again, drank from the cask, lit a cigarette. I watched the shack. There was no sound but the buzz of the little generator. I waited. Finally Con appeared in the doorway of the shack. He looked out. He had the rifle.

'Gordon!' he yelled.

I didn't answer. He walked away from the shack, looked around. Eventually he came straight over to me, stood there, swaying slightly. In the darkness I could just make out that the gun was pointed my way.

'It's got a bullet in it,' he said.

'Okay.'

'Where's the cask?'

I handed it up to him. He drank from it, single-handed. Then he dropped the cask, lifted the rifle to his shoulder and fired. It made a loud, flat crack. He was aiming, vaguely, towards the ocean. He reloaded, shot again. Then again. Then he sat down. Seemed to look at me. Seconds went by.

'Why *did* Allan give you that?' I asked.

His dim shape leaned back, leaned forward. 'You dunno a fucking thing, do you?'

'No.'

'I could kill you.'

'I know.'

'I could kill anyone.'

I said nothing. My mind was freezing up. It seemed a particularly pointless time to die.

'You ever been out in the open, a place like this before?' he said.

'I'm from Brisbane.' It was all I could think of.

'You never know,' he said, 'you could be sleepin', anyone could find you. Anyone could come up, slit your throat.'

We sat there. The night, the ocean, the endless bush, in every direction.

'Bad people out there.' Con's voice was low, serious, directed straight at me. 'Just walking around. A man comes up to your fire. From nowhere. You don't know who he is. What he wants. What he *is*.'

I coughed. Said, 'Yes.'

'Maybe he's not a man at all.'

I didn't reply. I didn't know how to. I stared at his silhouette. Suddenly it moved. Something heavy and cold landed in my lap. It was the gun. Con was standing up.

'Those banteng'll be out now,' he said, 'Let's go.'

We were in the Landcruiser, jolting along a sandy trail through the scrub. Con was driving, drunken and fast, slewing all over the road. I was in a daze, the last hazy stages of fear and alcohol. Sucking at the port, peering out. The world was nothing but the glare from the headlights. The gun was in my lap. It was loaded. Ready to kill.

Then the scrub cleared and we were on a stretch of open grassland. Its borders disappeared off beyond the range of the lights. Con upped the speed, charged across, throwing us around the cabin. Finally, on the fringe of visibility, I could see what looked like cattle. Dozens of them. A herd.

'That's them,' Con said, 'Banteng.'

The animals were staring at us. They were light brown, sharper and fitter looking than most cattle I'd seen before. We bore down. The herd took fright and bolted. Suddenly it was a chase, a nightmare. Con swinging the wheel, yelling at me to shoot for the shoulder. The cattle leaping, stumbling, fleeing. The smell of exhaust and gun oil and dust. It couldn't be real. I wasn't doing this. We were alongside the herd, twenty, thirty yards away.

I lifted the rifle, took aim at a flash of brown, fired. There was noise, recoil, the cattle streaming away. Nothing. I'd missed. Con was swearing, the Landcruiser skidding as he tried to get behind them again.

'Reload!'

I reloaded, fumbling with the bullet. Death was moments away. Con was driving blindly. There'd be a tree stump, or a sudden gully, and that'd be it. The banteng were in view again, zigzagging. I rammed the bullet in, flicked the bolt. Somewhere in my mind I remembered that international hunters would pay thousands of dollars for this privilege.

'I can get you real close,' Con said.

We slid up beside them, to their right. They jagged to the left, Con followed them. Suddenly we were only six or seven feet from the nearest one. It was right outside my window.

'Shoot,' Con was screaming, 'Shoot!'

It was a split second thing, I knew, before they veered off again. I raised the gun. The broad brown hide of the animal filled the sight. It was impossible to miss. As soon as I fired it would rear or stumble or fall, and Con would heave the truck up, circle back to the carcass. Maybe another shot would be needed, but eventually it'd be dead. A huge knife would appear from somewhere and Con would be slicing through the skin, gutting it, skinning it, carving off great joints and cuts of meat from its rump. There'd be blood and shit and rising steam. Blood on my hands, my legs. Meat. Food. Thrown on the hotplate tomorrow morning.

'*Shoot!*'

I pulled the trigger. There was a click, then nothing. The Banteng swung off. I jiggled the bolt, pulled the trigger again. Nothing. I banged the rifle against the door, pulled the trigger yet again. It didn't work. I looked up. A line of bush appeared and the herd charged for it, vanished. Con pulled the Landcruiser up in a long, dusty slide. Looked at me, dumbfounded.

'I'm sorry,' I said, 'It didn't fire.'

'You loaded it?'

'Yes.'

I had the bolt open, but it was too dark in the cab to see. I got out and went round in front to use the headlights. I looked in the breech. The bullet was there, but not quite fully slotted in. There was a reason for that. The bullet was backwards. The dull lead point stared up at me.

'Holy shit,' I said.

'What?' said Con, from the cab.

I didn't answer. I was thinking of all the times I'd pulled the trigger, of banging the gun against the door. It could've gone off. It could've blown up in my face. I'd put the fucking bullet in *backwards*.

I dropped the rifle, stumbled away. How close had it been? How close had it been all night?

'What?' Con yelled after me, 'What's wrong?'

'Nothing,' I answered.

I stopped, stood still. I felt nauseous, hot, full of adrenalin. I looked up at the distant, blurred sky. I heard the clumping of the banteng in the bush, their snorted, breathless lowing. Panicked. Exhausted. Lucky to be alive.

International hunters, I thought.

A thousand fucking dollars.

THIRTY-SEVEN

I woke to pain and sand and dazzling sunlight. I sat up. The hangover moved in. The asthma. The headache. I looked around. I had no water. No painkillers. I got to my feet. The sky, the ocean, the trees, everything was there. It was another beautiful day at Araru. I wanted nothing to do with it. I wanted my bed, the ceiling fan, and darkness. I headed off to the shack to find something to drink.

I spent the rest of the morning lying in the shade under a tree. Con and Hilda wandered into view from time to time, but left me alone. I was glad. I had nothing to say to either of them. I ran through the previous night in my head. All of it seemed ugly. Something to forget. I dozed. Grew hungry. I thought about cutting slices of meat off those big, hairy joints. Couldn't face it.

Sometime after noon, a boat motored down along the beach and landed. It was Allan and Russel and Long Bob. I watched them pull the boat up the beach. I wondered where they'd be taking me next. More fishing? More hunting? Back to Croker with them? I was tired of it all. Cape

Don and its comforts seemed years away. I got up and went over. Allan pointed to the Landcruiser.

'Who moved that?' he demanded.

I looked. The Landcruiser was parked next to the shack, where Con had left it the night before. I couldn't remember exactly where it had been parked the previous day.

'Con did,' I said.

Allan nodded, spoke to Russel and Long Bob in Gurig. He was angry. I followed them over to the shack. Con came out, smiling. The others began yelling at him. He faltered, said something. Allan cuffed him over the head, then pushed him back into the room. I stood at the door, bewildered. They shoved Con back and forth, shouting. Hilda stood at the bedroom door and watched.

Allan found the rifle, and the remaining bullets. There were only three. He held them in his hand, thrust them at Con. Con talked back, sullen. Then Hilda spoke. Occasionally either she or Con gestured towards me. Everyone's looks were hostile. Something was wrong with the fact that we'd been shooting, and driving the Landcruiser. I waited. Finally they dragged Con out again, shouldering me aside. Hilda came and stood with me in the doorway.

'What's happening?' I asked.

'Con. He got no right driving or shooting round here, them banteng aren't his. Allan told him stay put last night. Do nothin'.'

'What'd Allan leave him the gun for then?'

'Just in case. Not to take you shooting.'

I thought. 'Did you tell Allan about last night? In the bedroom?'

She shook her head, her eyes on Con. 'Not his business. This's enough.'

They had Con on the ground now. Russel and Long Bob were holding him down. He wasn't struggling. Allan had two thick chunks of wood. He put them under Con's left arm. One near the elbow, one near the wrist. Then he stood up, took aim, and stamped down hard.

'Shit,' I said.

Hilda gave me a short look. 'You stay out. Lucky it's not you.'

Allan peered at the arm, stamped his foot down again. Then again. On the third time, Con screamed. Allan stopped. He kneeled and examined the arm, seemed satisfied. He spoke to Con for a while. Then they let him go, walked away. Con sat up, cradling his wrist, staring at it.

Allan came over to me. His face was still stern. It was my turn.

'I'm sorry,' I said. It was weak. Pathetic. I didn't want my arm broken.

'That Con,' Allan said, 'I told you he was Tiwi, not Gurig eh?'

'Yes.'

'He does nothin' here, if we don't say he can. Not you either. You know that?'

'Yes.'

'Them banteng—we live on them. For food, for money. Not too many left. What you gonna do if you hit one last night?'

'I dunno. I didn't think.'

He shook his head. 'That Con, he's stupid, too much grog, gets in fights. Not you. Thought maybe you had sense.'

I looked at the ground.

Russel came up. He and Allan headed off, talking. I went inside, sat down. I flicked through the magazines. Hilda watched me. She brought out a joint of meat and began cooking slices. She offered me one. I declined. I was feeling terrible. Sick. Guilty.

Allan finally came back. He ate, talked with Hilda. He

looked at me. 'Better get your stuff. Russel can take you back to Cape Don.'

'Alright.'

I went out, walked over to my sleeping bag. I rolled it up, gathered my things together. Then I sat waiting. I was being kicked out. I deserved it. I was a fool. Russel was over talking with Con, inspecting the injury. Then he went into the shack, came out again, walked over to me.

'You ready?'

'Uh-huh. How's Con's arm?'

'Little break. We'll take him to Black Point later, get it looked at.'

We walked over to the boat.

'I'm sorry about last night,' I said.

Russel shrugged. 'You don't know better.'

We pushed the boat off, climbed in, and headed west. It was a silent trip back. I sat in the stern and smoked and didn't feel any pleasure from it. Not from the wind, or the waves, or the spray. The hangover and my empty stomach verged on seasickness. Finally we were at the bay. Russel dropped me at the beach, said goodbye, turned around and headed east again.

I watched him go, then shouldered my gear. I began the long walk through the bush, back to the lighthouse.

THIRTY-EIGHT

It was the end. Yet another one. I was through with the Cobourg Peninsula. Whatever chances it might have offered, I'd thrown them away. From now on it would be only the lighthouse and the weather observations. Until our time was served.

I made it to the compound, found Wayne in his bedroom. He was surprised to see me. I'd only been gone two days. I gave him the sorry details. I didn't mention Hilda. I went over and reported in to Vince. He was angry about the hunting episode.

'I'm not surprised Allan freaked,' he said, 'Those banteng are a prime resource. And they all hate that idiot Con. I thought you knew that.'

'No.'

'Well, least Allan didn't kick you right out of the park. He could've you know. *I* could too.'

I nodded. I was very tired. 'It might be a favour if you did.'

It would never be that easy. There was a full six weeks to

277

go, no one was getting out early. I went back to´the routine. It was hateful now—the compound, the weather, the whole process of existence at the lighthouse. I ate. Showered. Cleaned my teeth. Shaved. The last of the boils went away. I didn't know why. Nothing had changed in my diet or lifestyle. Maybe they'd just had their time.

I packed away the writing gear. All the paper and the ink. I wasn't going to be using any of it. Not now, not ever. I wiped dust of the surface of the mirror. I looked into it. There, I thought, Is a man in trouble. Then I flipped the door over, mirror facing down. It'd all been crap in the first place.

I took to spending my time on the back verandah, staring out. I listened to music. Wayne's tapes. They were louder and more violent than mine, and that was good. I smoked steadily. That was good too. I had it almost completely now, the habit, the addiction, the style. At least I'd got *that* out of the six months. The asthma was playing up a little, but there were no regrets. The cigarettes demanded only health, gave everything in return.

Otherwise there was nothing but Scrabble. Wayne and I still played our one game every night after dinner. I won them all. It was effortless. I was clocking-up scores of over four hundred. Two things, then, that had saved me at Cape Don. Smoking and Scrabble. I would be grateful to them both forever. Then one night Wayne refused to play anymore. He'd never really liked the game, losing every night. Now that was finished too. I couldn't blame him.

Time crawled. There were things that could be done, I knew. The whole national park was still waiting out there. It could be walked, looked at, fished. I couldn't rouse myself. Russel and Eve finally returned from Croker, but it made no difference. I'd lost interest in anything or anyone to do with the Cobourg Peninsula. Allan made no more visits. Nor did Con or any of the others. Maybe everyone had seen it was futile.

Time kept crawling. I wandered around the house feeling hot, bored, mindless. The Scrabble set sat unused on the dining table, the tiles in position from our last game. I sat down one afternoon to pack it away. The board was stained with tomato sauce and gravy, pencil and ink. A hardened board. I toyed with the letters, made words, messages, scattered them again. The minutes ticked by.

Eventually I balanced one of the tiles on the end of a knife, studied it. Plastic. Had they ever made letters out of ivory? Or marble? Or gold? I had a cigarette lighter with me. I lit it under the knife, warmed up the tile. The tile began to smoke, melt, and finally to burn. I dropped it onto the board, lifted another one with the knife. I lit it as well. It was decided. I'd spend the afternoon burning the tiles.

I did another three or four, dropped them, flaming, into a pile on the board. A small, steady fire developed, oozing black smoke. I dangled new tiles over it till they dripped. The fire grew. The room was big and airy enough, the smoke wasn't a problem. I started tearing up the box, adding it to the flames, bit by bit. Then it was some *People* magazines. There was no joy in it, no fascination. Just the passing of time.

Wayne came out, looked.

'What are you doing?'

'Burning the Scrabble set.'

'But you love it.'

'I know. It has to die.'

He nodded, watched for while. The flames tried to creep out, away from the board. I patted them out. Wayne went off, came back with some papers and scraps of canvas from his studio. He sat down on the other side of the table. Built the fire. It came to me that I should go and get the few pages I'd actually written, burn them too. I couldn't be bothered. I didn't want to move. We watched the fire. Smoke billowed around the room, blown by the ceiling fans. We stopped adding things to it. The Scrabble board was all gone, but the flames kept going, getting fuel from somewhere.

Then the table gave way. A circle in the middle dropped to the floor, taking the fire with it. We'd burned right through. Ash and flames drifted across the floor. We stared at them. Would it matter if the house went up? No one wanted it anyway. We waited. The fire burnt itself out. We were left with a pile of ash and a round ball of plastic slag. We examined the hole in the table. There was still plenty of room around the edges for the dinner plates. It had never been a table of any grace or beauty anyway.

No harm done.

Wayne began clearing out what was left of his studio. He stacked the finished canvases in his room. There were about a dozen. I didn't know what he thought of them. He didn't talk about art anymore. Something in him had changed since his visit to Brisbane. He'd become very quiet. Listless. He sat in his empty studio and listened to his stereo.

I found I was worried about him. During our Friday night sessions he drank slowly and silently, staring out. There was no more marijuana, no more attacks on the bourbon, no arguments. I'd talk about Brisbane, the things I'd do when we got back there. Wayne only nodded, smoked his cigarettes. In the past he'd been the one longing to go home. Now he didn't seem to care.

I cared. I wanted Brisbane. Every day that went by, stretched out into its three-hour segments, I hated Cape Don. Sitting on the front steps, smoking, I'd stare at the lighthouse and the sheds and the wide circle of dirt. I'd feel a fury build-up inside. It was a disaster, a massive waste of six months of my life, and I was still *stuck* there. I wanted nothing but for it to end.

Finally, I took it out on the dining room. The wreckage in Wayne's studio gave me the idea. Amidst all the junk and the pesticides, there were several cans of house paint. Red and black and green. There were also the leftover tubes of Wayne's oil paints. At least one of us, I decided, would paint something. I got all the gear out, set it up in the dining room, started on the walls.

It wasn't art. It was revenge. Deranged cartoon super-heroes. Ludicrous nudes. Meaningless jumbles. I was no artist. Even if I had been I wasn't doing it to create, I was doing it to destroy. The room was ugly, I made it uglier. It was all I had to say. Wayne watched. After a time he splashed on stuff of his own, carelessly. Even when he wasn't trying he couldn't help himself. *His* was art.

I said, 'You are gonna paint again aren't you, when we get out of here?'

He shook his head. 'I'm getting a job.'

'Like what?'

'A cleaner. I'll clean things.'

'You're hardly a neat person Wayne.'

'I'll learn.' He looked at me. 'I'll get *organised*.'

I stopped painting. Instead I took a small brush and a pot of black paint. I began writing lines up there. Short pieces. Rubbish. Some of it in poetry form. I was no poet either. I knew nothing about rhythm or pace. It was bitter. Things about packing tape and shitting and bad mastur-bation on slow afternoons. Someone might stray into the house one day, years after we'd gone, and wonder who had bothered. And why.

Wayne observed it all. 'Some of those aren't too bad.'

'You kidding?'

'I'm not saying it's *good* or anything. Is that the sort of stuff you normally write?'

'Hell no.'

He looked up the wall. 'Just as well, I suppose.'

We were down to the last three weeks. Vince came over. He'd been on the radio to Darwin. He told us that we were not going to be offered a renewal of our original contract. We were not considered to have been a success. The Met. Bureau weren't happy. We'd missed too many observations, filled out the field-books in a shoddy fashion. The Commission wasn't happy. We'd damaged a park vehicle and lived like pigs and a senior ranger called Barry had reported that we were fools. The Gurig people had expressed no opinion one way or the other, but certainly they had made no request for us to stay.

'*I've* got nothing against you guys,' said Vince, 'But I know you wanna leave anyway.'

'Who'll do the weather?' I asked.

It seemed the job had already been advertised in the Darwin paper. There would be interviews. Vince, as commanding ranger of Cape Don, would fly to Darwin to join the interviewing panel. The panel would also include someone from the Met. Bureau, as well as one of the Gurig people. Hopefully this time they might get someone more suitable.

It seemed a lot of work just to find a weather observer, but it was their problem now, not mine. Vince flew out with the next supply plane. A week inched by without him. I ran the generators. Vince returned. I drove out to the strip to meet him.

'Find someone?'

They had. Vince filled me in as we drove home. Our replacement would be a twenty-nine-year old woman called Stacy. She had just returned from overseas, a backpacking tour through the Middle East. She needed work and she was ready to start as soon as Wayne and I finished.

'Why only one person?' I asked.

'I'll help her out. Do a few observations. It'll be fine'

'Did you tell her what it's like out here?'

'Yeah. She said isolation was no problem.'

'And did you tell her about the house she'll have to live in?'

'She won't be living in your house. I'll give her a room in mine.'

'Oh.'

I thought about that. About what Wayne and I had been given when we first arrived. And about what Vince had been going through, alone in that big house of his, all these last, useless months.

I said, 'How many people did you interview?'

'Eleven.'

'And was this Stacy the only woman?'

Vince looked at me for a long time. Then he looked away. 'Yes.'

THIRTY-NINE

Stacy flew in with the supply plane. It was three days before Wayne and I were due to fly out. I went to the strip with Vince to meet her. I was thinking again about first impressions of the place, what hers might be, what mine had been, half a year before. The red rectangle of dust, the dry bush, crows calling in the distance. It hadn't looked like much, and for me, at least, that's what it had turned out to be. I found myself getting ready to pity her. The thought of going through it all again. Six long months. It was impossible.

We pulled onto the runway. The plane was there, and the pilot, unloading the grocery boxes. There was no Stacy. Then I spotted her. She was off behind the plane, in the middle of the strip, taking photographs. We stopped, climbed out. She lowered the camera and came over. She was tall and thin, deeply tanned. She had dark, shorn hair and was dressed in loose shorts, singlet, and sunglasses.

'Hullo Vince,' she said, 'Great colours here. That red and that green.'

'G'day Stacy. This is Gordon. One of the observers you're replacing.'

'Hi,' I said.

'You gonna teach me all the tricks?' she asked, smiling. There was a touch to her accent I couldn't place. The Middle East perhaps.

'There aren't any tricks.'

She laughed, turned to Vince. 'This place is great. I saw the lighthouse from the plane. I loved it.'

Vince did his shrug. 'See if you say that in a few months time.'

We loaded our groceries and her luggage into the Toyota. All she had was a backpack and an old suitcase. I remembered all the junk Wayne and I had carted over. And not even come close to using.

We drove back to the lighthouse. Vince and Stacy were in the front. Vince pointed out things along the way. Types of trees, general vegetation. It was more than he'd done for Wayne and I on our first day. In our first ten weeks. We swung up into the compound. Looked. The lighthouse, the sheds, the houses. The same as they always were.

Stacy laughed. 'Streetlights. And paths. It's beautiful. It's like an old military post of the British Raj or something. In India.'

I gazed about. It was true.

Vince pulled up outside his house.

'Dinner tonight Gordon,' he said, 'You and Wayne'll be there?'

'Sure.'

'How about we all meet at the weather shack for the 6 p.m. observation. Show Stacy what she's in for.'

I nodded, looked at Stacy. 'How many of the observations do you plan to do yourself?'

She glanced questioningly at Vince.

'Oh,' he said, 'We've got plenty of time to work that out.'

Everyone was at Vince's for dinner. One final time. Wayne and I. Russel and Eve. Vince. Stacy. There was plenty of alcohol. Wayne and I hadn't ordered much food for our last three days, but the drinks order was unchanged. We planned to make the remaining hours at Cape Don as painless as possible.

The mood was high. Even Wayne seemed better. Beer and wine and scotch flowed. Stacy moved around the room, looking at everything, asking questions. She was serious, fluent, enthusiastic. She wanted to know all about the national park. She sat herself down between Russel and Eve. They smiled, seemed cheerful. She talked to them both, got conversation out of them both. I was amazed.

And they had things in common. It turned out Stacy had worked on a station around the Kimberly region, years before. Eve had once visited relations in the same place. Both she and Stacy knew a little of the local Aboriginal language. They ran through what they remembered, made comparisons with Russel. Vince joined in with his expertise of inland tribal languages. The four of them went through vocabularies and origins. I sat there watching. I was beginning to see what Vince had meant, regarding Stacy, by the term 'someone more suitable'.

The night developed. Towards nine o'clock we all headed out for the weather observation. It was Stacy's second look. She'd done her one-day's training in Darwin, the same as we had. She seemed to know everything there was to know. In the end it was only a matter of practice. I could hardly believe that at first it had taken me twenty minutes to do it all. These days I was doing it in five or six.

I asked her how Lawrence was, back at the Darwin Met. Bureau. It turned out that he and Stacy had got along wonderfully during the day. They'd even gone out for drinks, after the lessons were over.

'What did he say about Wayne and I?'

'He said he liked you.'

'But as weather observers?'

'Well . . . apparently you guys had problems.'

'It's alright, we know we did.'

'I'm not saying I'll do any better.'

'Somehow I think you will.'

Then it was back to the house. Stacy started asking Wayne and I about our lives. The painting, the writing. We did our best to explain why none of that really applied any longer. She refused to believe it. She wasn't into reading all that much, but she loved art. Historical art in particular. She told us about the things she'd seen on her travels. In Egypt, Turkey, Jerusalem, up to Rome for a while. She and Wayne talked theory.

She was a smoker. The cigarettes she smoked were strange. They came in a small, red pack and smelled sweet. They were called Gudang Garams. I asked her about them. She said they were an Indonesian brand, and they were made of cloves mixed with tobacco. The nicotine levels in them were so high they were barely allowed in most western markets. That was why the cloves were added. They anaesthetised the throat so that the poison flowed down smoothly.

She offered me one. I took it, lit up, inhaled. It was beautiful, like inhaling honey. The cigarette itself was thick, and burnt very slowly, crackling. God only knew what was in it. It didn't matter. By the end it was sickening. My lips started to gum up. My stomach turned.

'You smoke this all the time?' I asked.

'Sure. Nothing hits like these babies do.'

I still had things to learn, it seemed, about smoking. I

lay back on the couch, listened while Stacy talked. Her travels were extensive. She'd been everywhere, done everything. It became clear to me. She was going to love Cape Don and the Cobourg Peninsula. She'd get out, she'd explore. She'd meet Allan Price and she wouldn't fuck things up. She'd be all over the place, doing all there was to do, within weeks. Even Barry would've been impressed. I was impressed.

Vince too. Late in the night, instead of the usual booming classical, he dug out some tapes he'd recorded in Central Australia. Snatches of aboriginal language, songs, music. We listened to old man dreaming chants and the clicking of sticks. I remembered Araru, the night and the stars and the fire. The mutter of voices. Suddenly even Cape Don didn't feel like Cape Don anymore. It wasn't just the dust, the boredom, the concrete lighthouse. It was older. I remembered the lizard. What Allan had said. Big Lizard dreaming.

Then it was gone. I was at Vince's house, on his couch, drunk, and soon I'd be gone altogether. It was too late to be thinking about the things I'd missed. The conversation had dropped away. Stacy was asking Vince whether she should get up for the early-morning observations. He was saying no, Gordon and Wayne could take care of it. Gordon and Wayne stood up, made their goodnights.

We headed out. The compound was waiting there. The streetlights, the lighthouse beam, the hum of the generator, the warm, still darkness. A pale moon hung above it all. I'd only have to look at it twice more.

'Weird, isn't she,' said Wayne.

'Stacy?'

'All that energy.'

'Yeah.'

Energy.

We strolled towards our house, lacking it.

FORTY

Our second-last night. Wayne and I were on the back verandah, drinking. We'd been there all afternoon, already half drunk. Stacy came over, with two bowls of soup.

'It's pea and ham,' she said, 'I made it for Vince. Thought you might like some.'

We'd eaten, but the soup looked good and it seemed decent of her, so we ate it. Stacy took a beer from the fridge and set-up a third chair on the verandah. She was due to take over the weather observations at 9 a.m. next morning.

'Good view you guys have.'

'Yes,' I said.

'House is a wreck though. How come you live over here?'

'We weren't invited into Vince's.'

'Oh.' A pause. 'He seems very nice, Vince. I hope the two of us can get on.'

'I wouldn't worry. He likes you.'

She thought. 'Look, I know the question of fucking is going to come up sooner or later, but whatever plans Vince might have, I'm not here for the sex.'

We all thought about that.

'He's been alone a long time,' I said finally, 'But I don't think he'll try to rape you or anything.'

'He must have been alone a *very* long time. He's painfully shy when it's just the two of us.'

'So what d'you plan to do while you're here?'

'Oh, nothing. Look around a bit. I've been travelling too long. I want a rest.'

'Well you'll get that.'

'Good. I'm not here to do anything special. I'm not creative like you two. Wayne, can I see some of your paintings?'

Wayne wasn't at all enthusiastic, but they headed off to his room to view the canvases. I sat and drank. I thought about Stacy and Vince, together in that house for the next six months. Vince on his stool with his scotch and port and classical music. Night after night after night. I liked Vince, but living with him? I didn't envy her.

As for the sex, who knew. Vince *had* been alone a long time, maybe it was on his mind, maybe he really did have plans. But then after a few months at Cape Don maybe it would be on Stacy's mind too. Nothing was ever certain. Wayne and I had been alone too long too. What right did she have to think *we* were trustworthy, that *we* wouldn't make moves.

I supposed maybe we wouldn't. It felt odd, having someone else sitting there on the verandah with us. Vince, Russel, Eve—none of them had ever sat there. For six months it had been our spot, just Wayne and I. It hadn't always been good, and lately it had been pretty bad, but still, we were like an old couple, spinster aunts. We were bound to each other. We were no threat to outsiders, to Stacy.

I thought about Wayne and me. We were not, even after

all the time together, good friends. Any sort of friends at all. Often enough we'd caused each other nothing but annoyance. But somehow I couldn't quite dislike him. I pitied him in a way, felt superior. Even protective. Both of us might be failures, but I'd survive in the practical world with an ease that he'd never have. Despite his five thousand dollars.

None of it mattered.

We were just about through with each other.

After a while Wayne and Stacy came back. She'd liked his paintings. Wayne still didn't. We sat and drank beer. It was pleasant there on the verandah. A breeze was blowing, it was cool. Perhaps even approaching chill. This was deep winter in the Territory. I thought of my leather jacket. It was by no means necessary, but it was a chance to wear it. And it was a festive occasion. Our second-last night.

I went into my room and dug it out. I put it on. It was far too heavy—thick and black and zippered. It looked ridiculous with shorts, bare feet and a T-shirt. Still, I was pleased. I hadn't brought it all this way for nothing. I went back out on the verandah.

'Hey, cool,' said Wayne.

Stacy was smiling. 'That's one mean jacket. Isn't it a little hot?'

I pushed the sleeves up as far as possible, 'No. As long I don't move around too much. Don't work up a sweat.'

We sat and drank. Wayne and Stacy went off for the 9 p.m. observation, came back. I moved around in my chair. The jacket *was* too hot, but it was the first time I'd ever worn it without feeling self-conscious. It was so out of place that it couldn't be taken seriously. And besides, I was a smoker now. Dangling a cigarette from the lips gave you all sorts of credibility.

'Do you guys smoke pot?' Stacy asked after a while.

'Sure,' said Wayne, 'But we ran out weeks ago.'

'I've got some, back in the house.'

'Well good.'

'Is it alright if I invite Vince? I don't wanna leave him alone over there.'

Wayne nodded. 'I'm not sure he smokes though. He might not approve of it in his national park.'

'Vince? He's an old hippy, can't you tell? Of course he'll smoke.'

She went off. Ten minutes later she was back, Vince in tow. He had a bottle of scotch and was smiling, tight-lipped. Out of his own territory he seemed sad and vulnerable. We squeezed a fourth chair on the verandah and he sat down. Looked out.

He said, 'I've never been over here at night before.'

I felt guilty. We could've asked him to at least *one* dinner at our place. I said, 'We always thought your house was better for entertaining.'

He nodded. 'I notice you've got a hole in your table anyway.'

'It was an accident.'

'What about all the stuff on the walls?'

'Does it matter?'

'No.'

Stacy brought out a large bag of marijuana and began rolling. She mixed it with tobacco from the clove cigarettes. Vince watched but said nothing. When it was ready he took his turn and sucked in a long, almost relieved drag.

'You know,' said Wayne, 'We had bags of the stuff when we first arrived here.'

Vince eyed him. 'Then it's lucky I didn't know.'

It was my turn. The cloves in the mix made it smooth and sweet tasting. It was an improvement. I took big puffs, held them down in my lungs. Wayne broke out the bourbon.

The night began to grow hazy. The conversation flowed between the other three. That was fine. I always had trouble with conversation when I was stoned. The others didn't seem to. They laughed, talked, sounded happy. I drank bourbon and stared out at the stars.

Another joint went round. More bourbon. I was getting very drunk. Stuttering when I spoke. After a long time I felt a faint stir of nausea. I poured myself a drink, then got up and wandered down the hall. I wanted space and air. I went down the front steps, out into the compound. I walked over to the weather shack, looked in. I had only one more observation to make, the 3 a.m. It was finally all over.

I went in, sat down, listened to the wails from the radio. There were no voices. Maybe there never had been. I looked at the spiders. The instruments. After six months the room was almost exactly as we had found it. Dust in the same places. Old leaves and other rubbish in the corners. The same posters on the walls. We'd left no mark at all.

I looked at the clock. One a.m. How had it gotten so late? I went out, gazed up at the sky. The moon was brighter tonight, the stars pale, the lighthouse beam faded to nothing. The nausea wasn't going away. I had trouble standing up straight. Why did I always do this? Drink too much. Smoke too much. It always went beyond pleasure into illness. There was no control. I walked some more, sipping at the bourbon.

I ended up coming round the side of our house to the back. I looked up at the crumbled verandah. The other three were still there, talking.

Vince saw me. 'What are you doing down there?'

'Just looking around.'

They went back to their conversation. I didn't listen. A few yards from the verandah was a rectangular wooden arch, the base of it set in concrete. It was all that remained of the back stairs. I stood beneath it, leaning on one of the posts. I watched Wayne and Vince and Stacy. I was depressed. I didn't know the reason.

I raised my hands, caught hold of the crossbeam. I swayed back and forth, testing my weight. I liked the way the jacket moved around my shoulders. I felt big and impressive. Strong. I lifted myself, lowered myself. Very strong. I lifted myself again, raised my legs, flipped myself upside down.

'Gordon, what are you doing?' It was Wayne's voice.

I curled my head around. They were all looking at me.

'It's alright,' I said, 'I can do this.'

I hung there. Then they were talking again. I kept hanging. Then suddenly I didn't feel strong anymore, only stupid. This was the sort of thing five-year olds did, for attention. I went to uncurl myself. I fell. I slammed into the ground. There was a slap of pain from my head and neck and shoulders. It was bracing, it cut nicely through the alcohol.

'Shit,' Wayne said, 'You okay?'

'I'm fine. I'm just gonna lie here a while.'

'Okay.'

I lay there. This was ridiculous. I never did things like this. I got up again. Found my glass, handed it up through the verandah.

'Could I have some more bourbon?'

'You sure?' Vince asked.

'I'm sure.'

They filled my glass. I wandered off again, towards Russel and Eve's house. Their lights were off, they'd be long asleep by now. I went on by, down to the water tank. I looked up at it, at the ladder that climbed the frame. It hit me again. I couldn't help myself. I climbed up the ladder. Something in me was determined to do these things. It was difficult, I was climbing one-handed, keeping my drink level. I swayed and slipped, clung on. I got to the top, sat on the platform. It was higher than I'd thought. I looked out. The distant ocean was silver beneath the moon, the bush and the mangroves a blur of grey and black.

I could see the others on the verandah. I felt sure they couldn't see me. That was comforting. I didn't want to be seen. I stayed there, sipping on my drink. I smoked a cigarette. I muttered to myself, even sang. Then I noticed Vince standing up. He appeared to be saying goodnight to Wayne and Stacy. He disappeared inside, then appeared again out front, heading towards his house. Wayne and Stacy remained alone on the chairs. I watched until I finished my drink. Smoked another cigarette.

Time to get down, I thought. I needed more bourbon. Towards the bottom of the ladder I missed a step and fell the rest of the way. This time I landed on my back. The jolt of pain was sharp and clear. Good, I thought, getting up, *Good*.

I turned towards the house, looked at the verandah. Wayne and Stacy were gone. There were just the four empty chairs, slightly askew, and a collection of beer cans and glasses. It was a terrible, ugly sight. I didn't know what to do. I hurried round to the front of the house, up the stairs, down the hall. The dining room was empty. I went out to the verandah. No one was there. I went back inside, down the hall. The door to Wayne's room was closed. I stared at it. It couldn't be.

I went back to the fridge, found the cask of wine. I opened it, poured a glass. I felt a sick fear. It *couldn't* be. Back out to the verandah. I sat down. Drank. I looked over towards the water tank. The platform at the top was easily visible. They would've all known I was there. They would've seen me, clutching my drink, curled around myself, sulking. In my leather jacket.

I got up. I stared down the hall. The ceiling fans whirred. Open that door and come out, I thought, Open that door and *come out*. Nothing happened. I began creeping down the hall. I hated myself for it, couldn't stop. What did it matter what they were doing in there? It had nothing to do with me. But it did. Wayne was in there. Wayne had *everything* to do with me.

I got to the door. Listened intently. I heard nothing. Were they even in there? Maybe they'd gone for a walk. Maybe Stacy had gone home and Wayne had simply gone to bed. I waited. There was a mutter, Wayne's voice, and then a low laugh, female. The world froze. My heart thumped painfully. I kept listening. More mutters, more laughs, something hitting the floor. Then silence. Then moving sounds, and then, very faint—an intake of breath? A gasp?

I couldn't stand it. I backed away. They were in there, they were doing it, they were fucking. How *could* they be. It was horrific. I got back to the verandah, quaffed wine. I was breathing fast, panicked. I tried to rationalise things. If they saw fit to fuck for an evening, it was their good fortune. I wasn't involved. I didn't need to feel anything.

But it wouldn't go away. I drank more wine. Had a cigarette. Thought. It made no sense. Why was I doing this to myself? I had no interest in Stacy, no sexual interest. I hadn't even thought about her that way, until now. How could I be jealous of Wayne for something I didn't want. So *furiously* jealous.

But my mind wouldn't stop. The images kept coming. The big double bed in Wayne's room. Clothes coming off. Stacy, slim and naked, laying Wayne down. Wayne, slim himself, that long expanse of soft, white skin along the bed. The muscles in his chest stretched out, his arms over his head. Stacy sliding down, her hands running from his face to his neck, down across his breasts, to the dip of his stomach. His penis.

I could see it. Pale, slim, erect. Her fingers moving lightly up the shaft, down. Her mouth hovering near it, her hands moving, fingering his balls, tugging, gathering them in. Fine white hairs around the sac. Then her mouth coming down, lips parting around the head. Swallowing it lightly, her tongue barely touching. Wayne stiffening, hardening. The heat of his prick, soft, hard, *him,* filling her mouth, my mouth . . .

No. It was too much, far too much. I was shaking. I had an erection. For who I didn't know anymore. I got up. I took one of the kitchen chairs, carried it inside. I hurled it down the hall. It bounced and clattered, rapped against Wayne's door. Come out fuck it, *come out.*

He didn't. They didn't. I couldn't stay there. I went out, past his door, out into the night. I staggered across the compound. The lighthouse, the streetlights. I spotted the track. It plunged down into utter blackness, the jungle. I took it. I was walking fast, almost running. I needed to exhaust myself. Suddenly my legs were gone. I hit the ground, hard. I was drunk, appallingly drunk. I was up again, reeling along. Gravel, I thought. I'd probably scratched the jacket.

Good. The jacket was ridiculous. Shiny and new and ridiculous. It needed scratches. It needed to be worn down, beaten. I began to run. Really run. Down along the track, jet black on either side. My legs went again. I hit the stones, skidding, cracked my head. The pain was knife-keen and beautiful. I saw it all suddenly.

Pain was the key. There was something huge inside me. Something dark and tight and swollen. A giant boil. Pus-ridden with denial. Pain was the only way to burst it, get

rid of it forever. I was up again, running. I fell. Deliberately
this time. I threw myself at the ground, felt gravel tearing
on skin. It still wasn't enough. I did it again. And again.
Running blindly. Battering at the shit in me, feeling it rise,
ready to gush, to spew out . . .

I stopped. I was sprawled in sand. It was soft, useless.
I was at the bay. I stood up, swaying, stared at the sea. It
seemed darker now, the silver was gone. The mangroves
were all around me, waiting silently. Everything hurt. My
lip was swollen, bleeding. I hadn't got there. There was no
release. Nothing had worked.

I gulped air. The mangroves watched. Waves lapped on
the beach. Time passed. There was nothing in my mind.
Eventually I was cold. I began walking home, slowly. I
stepped carefully and didn't fall over. I didn't want to. The
pain wasn't good anymore. I reached the compound,
climbed the stairs of our house. Wayne's door was still
closed. I didn't care. I went to my room, shut my own door,
and fell into bed.

FORTY-ONE

Pain. I awoke to it everywhere. Every joint, all down my left side, my mouth. My head. Inside it there was a hang-over headache, outside it was something like concussion. And asthma too. I hadn't taken any of the drugs. I sat up, coughed and wheezed and winced. Nausea swung in. I hung there, stupefied. A body couldn't feel this bad. I looked down at it. I was still fully dressed. I eased the jacket off, examined the leather. I began, dimly, to remember. There were scuff marks on the elbows, down one side. No serious damage.

Then I saw blood on my T-shirt. I lifted it. It came away crustily from my left side. The skin was all red, a massive gravel rash. I'd pulled away the scabs with the shirt. Blood was oozing out in long, wide welts. I pulled off my shorts. Another red scrape ran along one thigh. My knees were the same. Jesus Christ, I thought. Jesus fucking Christ.

I looked around, out the French windows. It was full daylight, maybe around mid-morning. I blinked at it. Nothing was making much sense. I thought about the weather, remembered it was Stacy's job now. Then I remembered Wayne and Stacy. Everything that I'd done. The chair I'd thrown, the way it bounced down the hall. I sat there, feeling the full weight of self-disgust. Then suddenly I was thinking about the observations again. I'd been on the 3 a.m. I strove to remember. Had I done it? No, I hadn't. I'd missed my very last observation.

The nausea swelled again. I fought it for a moment. Then I was up. Through the French windows, out onto the verandah, on my raw knees, hanging over edge. Vomiting, naked, bleeding in the hot, bright sun.

Later I made it out into the kitchen. Wayne was there. He looked ruffled and tired and ill. He looked me over in turn. I assumed I was worse.

'What happened to your knees?' he said.

'I fell down. On the track.'

'Did you throw a chair at my door last night?'

I nodded. I was hunting around the kitchen for Panadol. 'Sorry. I went a bit crazy.'

'You were really pissed. What were you doing up the water tank?'

'I don't know.' I found the Panadol, took three. The water swished dangerously in my stomach, then settled. 'So, you and Stacy have fun last night?'

Wayne shrugged, smiled. 'Well, we were both pretty pissed too.'

'Did she take over the weather at nine?'

'Yep. I missed my six. Either way, we're finished with it.'

Indeed we were. I went back to bed and suffered for a time, then gave up on sleep. I began packing. I threw the alarm clock in the rubbish, stacked things in boxes. I moved very slowly. I progressed onto the dining room. Wayne was packing up his own gear. We put the boxes on the front verandah. We were silent. I didn't want to ask him any more about Stacy. I didn't want to know anything about the previous night at all.

I recovered enough to get some toast down. The asthma remained bad. I had a cigarette. At the first few puffs I gagged and coughed up heavy, dark phlegm. After that I felt better. The body was an impressive thing. I lay on the bed, watched the ceiling fan spin, dozed. Late in the afternoon Vince came over, caught me on the front verandah.

'You guys gonna be ready tomorrow?'

I nodded. Our plane was due around midday.

'You alright?' he asked, 'You were *way* out of your depth last night.'

'I know.'

'Well, hope you're okay for tonight. I'm cooking up a special one for your goodbye dinner.'

I'd forgotten that. A goodbye dinner. I wasn't going to be allowed to crawl away from Cape Don quietly. 'We'll be there,' I said.

He went off. I wondered if he knew about Wayne and Stacy. I doubted he'd care anyway. Wayne didn't matter to Vince, Wayne was leaving. I went inside, sat in the bathtub under the slow, warm water, and waited.

We were at Vince's by seven. We had the very last of the beer and the wine. I didn't drink much. I wasn't up to it. The headache seemed to be getting worse. I sat on the couch, not talking often. My bottom lip was badly swollen, my words felt slurred. I'd fingered all of my scalp. There were several large lumps, but no splits.

The meal was the standard roast. Vince was lively enough, but everyone else seemed low. Even Stacy. She smoked steadily, didn't speak. She and Wayne barely acknowledged each other. Maybe they hadn't had it so great, after all. I kept watching the clock, even though there was no need. At twenty to nine it was Stacy who got up and went out to the weather shack.

At eleven I packed it in, made the goodnights. I walked back across the compound. I didn't look at anything, see anything. Once in the house I took more Panadol, the asthma drugs, and went to bed. I lay there for some time, trying for sleep. It was maybe an hour or two before I heard Wayne come in. By the sounds of it, he was alone.

By eleven the next morning we were fully packed. Our gear was loaded into the Toyota. We'd given all our leftover food to Vince and Stacy. I wandered through the house, checking for anything we'd missed. I felt almost healthy again. The headache was gone, most of the major aches. I should've been feeling very good. It was another beautiful day, and we were getting out at last. By nightfall we'd be in Darwin, in a bar, in the real world again.

I didn't feel good, only depressed. The house didn't help. It had never looked occupied, even with all our stuff around, now it looked completely derelict. The lone table with its scorched hole in the middle. The chairs out the back. My desk with its mirror facing down, the single iron-framed bed. Wayne was walking about the place, taking photos with Stacy's camera. I supposed in several years I might've wanted some reminder of the place. I didn't just then.

Vince was with the Toyota. 'Might as well come and wait over at my place,' he said, 'No need to hang around here.'

We went. We sat on his front verandah, in his deck chairs. The four of us, staring out, waiting for the plane in the sky. The plane was late. Midday went by. Then one o'clock, then two. It was one last, drawn out piece of agony. Cape Don's way of saying goodbye. At half past three the plane appeared and did the circuit. We stood up, made for the stairs.

Stacy hung back. 'I won't come. I'll say goodbye now.'

'Okay,' I said, 'Good luck with it all here.'

'Thanks.'

I went down the stairs, left Wayne to say whatever he wanted to. Russel and Eve were coming across from their house. It wasn't to say goodbye. Russel was coming with us. He had business of some sort in Darwin. He had one small bag, threw it on top of all our rubbish. Then Vince and Wayne came down. We got in. There was only room for the three of us, none for Eve. She said goodbye to Russel, and then, quite distinctly, to Wayne and to me. Vince started up the engine and we rolled down the track. The bush closed in. Cape Don was gone.

The plane was waiting at the strip. It was a twin-engine, twelve-seater. We weren't the only passengers. A couple of Commission officials were on their way back from Black Point. We loaded our stuff in, crowding the plane. The two officials were both weighty, middle-aged men. They laughed at us. Then everything was on board. It was time to go.

'Well,' said Vince, sticking out his hand, 'This is it.'

I shook it. 'Thanks for putting up with us.'

'It wasn't so bad. Don't forget me though. Send me a bottle of port at Christmas.'

Christmas, I thought. It was over four months away. I felt an acute and utter pity.

Then Wayne shook Vince's hand, said goodbye and thanks, and we were through. We climbed on board with Russel, took our seats. It was only my second time in a plane, but there were none of the nerves of the first time. The plane was too big. And it was the end. I wasn't going anywhere I hadn't been before.

We taxied slowly up the runway. Wayne, Russel and I were sitting in one row of seats, facing the two officials. They were in a jovial mood. They tried to talk to us.

Especially to Russel. He was, I supposed, an important man in Gurig terms. They joked, asked Russel questions. Somehow they sounded patronising. Russel gave only monosyllabic answers. So, in our turn, did Wayne and I. The three of us, for the one and only time, in accord.

The plane turned. I caught a glimpse of the Toyota out the window, Vince standing beside it. Then the engines surged and we accelerated down the runway. Red dust and olive scrub streamed by. We tilted, lifted off, began climbing. Once above tree level we turned into the sun. It was westering, throwing the sky into orange glare. There was nothing clear to be seen out the windows, but I kept looking. Finally the plane turned a little and I saw, already far off to the right, the lighthouse.

It was just a black sliver, no features. I thought briefly of Vince winding his way back along the track. Of Stacy waiting there. Of the radio crackling in the weather shack. Of the ceiling fans spinning in our house, in empty rooms, over no one. The lights off. The shadows deepening.

I stopped thinking about it, turned away from the window. We flew in silence towards Darwin.

FORTY-TWO

It was dark by the time we had all our luggage unloaded. We were on the tarmac outside the Northwing terminal. The woman from the office was waiting. So was my car. It was freshly washed and, she said, the tank was full. She also handed me a new set of keys.

'I lost the old set on the beach,' she said, 'But thanks again. I didn't drive it to Alice Springs or anything, but it was very handy.'

'That's alright.'

She headed off. The two officials were long gone, in a cab. Russel too. He'd been picked up by a carload of relatives. He'd said goodbye and shaken our hands. Wayne and I were alone and in Darwin. The night was warm, there was the sound of traffic in the distance. We loaded the car. It was tiresome. Again, we should've been excited. We weren't.

We drove out of the airport, into town. It was a Monday night. I waited for some sort of culture shock at the sight of the traffic and the buildings. It didn't come. It felt like

any Monday night. Drab, lacking in promise. We went to
the same hostel we'd stayed in before, booked a room. We
sat there for a minute.

'What now?' said Wayne.

'The pub, I suppose.'

We headed out. Ate at Kentucky Fried. Wandered along
the mall. We ended up in the Victoria Hotel. It had been
refurbished in our absence. The chicken wire was gone.
There was new carpet and new colours. We sat and drank.
Eventually a band came on. They weren't very good. The
crowd was small. Wayne and I spoke to no one else. Hardly
spoke to each other. We sat it out until one a.m., then went
back to the hostel. Nothing else appeared to be open. We
went to bed. It was not how I'd imagined our first night
would be.

Next morning we attended to some business. I closed my
cheque account. I'd sent maybe seven or eight cheques to
Darwin from Cape Don, I didn't expect to need it again.
We visited the Met. Bureau offices and got the last of our
wages. I looked for Lawrence, didn't see him. We went to
the Nightcliff supermarket and payed what remained owing
on our account. Then we got back in the car and took a
last look at Darwin.

We had talked, once, about staying in the North for a
while, on holiday. About not going straight back to Brisbane. About seeing some of the Territory. Kakadu. The
Katherine Gorge. Maybe even getting across to the
Kimberly. Neither of us mentioned it now. We found the
highway, headed south.

It took four days. We skipped Katherine, but otherwise we
stopped at the same towns as we had on the way up, and
in the same hotels. And between Mt Isa and Longreach we
took the direct route, not the scenic. We had no interest in
scenery. At night we sat in the hotel rooms eating take-

aways, drinking beer and watching TV. It was good to see a screen again, but there were only two stations out there, and neither had much on.

Even the news was dull. Both the papers and the television. We'd heard basically nothing for six months, but overall the world seemed to have kept fairly quiet. The only thing I was interested in was the football season. It was well progressed. The new Brisbane Broncos, it seemed, had started well in the NSW League. They'd won their first five or six games straight. Now they were fading badly in the latter half of the season. Finals didn't look likely.

Otherwise we slept and ate and waited for the road to roll by. At Tennant Creek our friends with the cocktail lounge in their hotel had disappeared. The lounge itself was closed. In Longreach we saw that the Stockman's Hall of Fame had been completed and was now open for business. We didn't go in. Wayne overheated the car once more, the same way, and I got annoyed. We argued, then stewed about it for a few hours. There was a deep and final weariness between us. I looked with something like real hatred upon Wayne, and he looked the same way back at me.

Finally it was Friday evening and we were back in South-East Queensland, nearing Dalby. We were arguing again. The problem was that I wanted to stop over at my parents' farm, spend the night. Wayne wanted to push on to Brisbane. I could see his point, we were so close, it was only another three hours. I gave less than a fuck about his point.

'You can see your parents anytime,' Wayne was saying. He was almost in tears with the frustration. 'Let's just get this over with, get back to *Brisbane*.'

But it was my car and I was driving it. At Dalby we turned north, drove out to the farm. My parents weren't

1988

---

home. The house was dark, their car wasn't in the garage.
I hadn't called ahead. It was freezing, standing there in
the dark. We were in winter. If anything felt alien, it was
that. The cold. I'd forgotten that weather could even be
that way. Cold weather, cold welcome.

'Well?' said Wayne from the car.

'In a minute.'

I went inside. My parents never locked the house—some
of the doors didn't even *have* locks. I walked around. The
place was chill, empty. I picked up the phone and dialled
my sister in Brisbane. She was surprised to hear from me.
Was I due back already? I said I was, asked if she knew
where Mum and Dad were. It turned out they were in
Brisbane. Visiting the family. I went back out to the car.

'Okay,' I said to Wayne, and started up.

The very last stretch. It was back through Dalby, up to
Toowoomba. Then down the range, across the Lockyer
Valley, over the low Brisbane hills. It was almost midnight.
And there it was. The glow in the sky. Orange streetlights.
Outlying suburbs. It was beautiful. The highway turned
onto the six-lane arterial. We came in through Oxley and
Annerly, flowing with the traffic. Then the city highrises
were in view, alight, multicoloured. Brisbane. It was
impossibly beautiful.

I drove across to Hamilton, pulled up outside Wayne's
parents' house. He went inside to wake them, I started
unloading. Wayne came back with his mother. She was in
a dressing-gown, excited, asking questions. We stacked all
his stuff on the footpath. Then it was finished. Wayne's
mother went back inside to get some food going. I sat on
the hood, lit a cigarette. Wayne lit one too.

'Where you gonna stay tonight?' he asked.

'At my sister's.'

We smoked for a moment. I looked out over Brisbane.

308

There was a strange beam of light, arcing across the sky. It came from somewhere behind the bulk of the CBD.

I said, 'You'll be right getting this stuff inside?'

'Sure.'

'Okay then.' I got up, opened the car door. 'I'll see you later.'

He nodded. I started up, put it in gear, drove away.

I steered through the streets. I was tired. I headed for Louise's place. On the way I passed along the top of the Kangaroo Point cliffs. I stopped. If there was any single view of Brisbane, maybe it was this. I left the car, walked to the edge. There was the river and the city centre. Then the botanical gardens with their small mangrove patch and their mudflats. And beyond all that, glimmering, were the buildings and pavilions and sails of the 1988 International Exposition.

I stared. The great event itself, four city blocks of it. It was quiet at the moment, closed for the night. I didn't really know what was in there, what it was all about, but right in the middle was a tall, slim tower. I knew its name. It was the Expo Skyneedle. It was meant to be a giant piece of sculpture. At the very top it had a powerful light. The light was revolving, it's beam sweeping across the sky. It was what I'd seen from Wayne's place. It was strong. Solid. Silent. Stretching out over Brisbane, over everything.

I turned away, went back to my car.

FORTY-THREE

Brisbane again.

I went through the process, caught up with everyone. Family members. Friends. They all seemed pleased to see me. They asked questions about Cape Don, about the Cobourg Peninsula, about any writing I might have done. I said what I could about the former two. I said Cape Don had been interesting. Worthwhile. I mentioned the fishing. The crocodiles. The boils. I said that, as far as the writing went, it hadn't quite worked out.

But the questions didn't last long. There was no reason why they should. Other people I knew were returning from overseas after being away for years. From holding down jobs in Europe. From having disappeared into India. Indonesia. They had better stories than a patch of scrub on the coast.

And Brisbane felt strange. It wasn't the way I'd left it. At times, in the evening, I could hear the popping of the fireworks from the Expo site. Or the droning of the blimp that constantly circled the area. The streets were full of

tourists. The papers were full of Expo events and Bicentennial news. Live acts. Free concerts. Parades. My mother
had given me a season pass to Expo, I'd have to use it
sooner or later. But every day seventy or eighty or a
hundred thousand people packed themselves in there. The
thought of it appalled me.

I waited. The last of my money dwindled away. I wasn't
sure what to do. I thought about applying for the dole. I'd
never been on it. I didn't like the idea. Finally I wandered
into the public bar of the Capital Hotel, my old workplace.
I sat at the counter, ordered a beer. I didn't see anyone I
knew. Then the bottle shop manager walked in.

'Gordon,' he said, 'You're back.'

'Uh-huh.'

'Right, can you start tomorrow? The guys I've got out
there now are hopeless.'

'I didn't come in here looking for a job.'

He laughed. 'That's bullshit.'

I nodded. It was.

I went and saw Madelaine. She said she'd already seen
Wayne, so she knew all there was to know.

'What are you doing now?' she asked.

'Back at the bottle shop.'

'What about the writing?'

'I don't think so. Is Wayne painting?'

'No. He's got a job.'

'Cleaning?'

'How'd you know? Have you seen him?'

'No. I don't think I'll be seeing much of Wayne.'

'How *did* you and him get along up there?'

'What'd Wayne say?'

'He said at least you didn't come to blows.'

'No.'

And I supposed that was something.

I needed somewhere to live. My sister's place was free, but it was only temporary. I drove over to New Farm, went up James Street and parked outside William's place. The house had been painted, in pastels, green and red. A couple I didn't recognise were doing some carpentry on the front stairs.

I asked them about William. He was gone, they replied. They'd purchased the house from him about four months ago, had been renovating ever since. They didn't know where he was now. They were forwarding mail to a post office box. I left them to it. I didn't ask about the Chinese. I hoped they were doing well, but I wasn't going to live with them again.

I began looking at small, single bedroom flats. I kept to the New Farm area. I couldn't afford anything I saw. The suburb was slowly going up-market. Sixty a week was my maximum. I lowered my standards, began looking at small, dingy places. Two-room flats, boarding house conditions and old men lolling on the front steps. Finally I pulled up outside a place down near New Farm park. It must've once been a sizeable Queenslander with big verandahs. Now it was all shut-in and subdivided. I walked down the hall. The sign outside said to apply at flat three.

I knocked. An old black man answered, asked what it was about.

'The flat,' I said.

He peered at me. Coughed, hawked up some phlegm, swallowed it.

'Emphysema,' he said.

He got the key, showed me the flat, number eight. It was the best I'd seen for the money. Two large rooms, half of one partitioned to make a small kitchen. It was dark and old. Toilets and bathroom were down the hall.

'I might take it,' I said.

'Yeah? Come back to my place and I'll give you the forms to take to the agent.'

I followed him back. He walked with a slight hunch, but also with a wiry toughness. He invited me in. There was an old radio and a TV and stacks of paperback westerns against the walls. He hunted around for the forms.

'You'll be the youngest bloke here,' he said, 'Mostly it's just us old bastards. Get a padlock for your door. Locks are fucked. Pricks stealing all the time. You want a drink?'

'Okay.'

He poured a couple of glasses from a cask of red. Asked me my name. His, he said, was Vass. We sat and drank and he told me more about the place, what to expect, what rules to follow. I thought about another old black man, three thousand miles away, Allan Price. Vass was nothing like him, but I'd wandered into Vass's territory just as I wandered into Allan's.

Respect, I thought, *respect*. The place wasn't much, but it was his home and I wanted to live there. And there was something about Vass himself that I liked. An old bitterness that sounded almost fond. I finished the drink. Had another. Got up. 'I owe you a beer,' I said.

'Damn fucking right you do.'

I moved in. I worked in the bottle shop. I talked to the old men in the house. Watched TV. I thought about nothing, planned nothing. When I got drunk the old bitterness was still there. The old fear. I saw it all around me in the old men. They were my future.

I began writing. Only small things. Poems. Maybe two or three a week. I had no hopes for them, never expected anyone to read them. I wrote about sex. I wrote about the old men and the things they said. I didn't write about Cape Don. Christmas approached. I remembered Vince and the bottle of port he'd asked for. I didn't send it.

Then it was New Year's Eve. I went to a party to celebrate it, with friends. It hadn't been the same with them either, since Cape Don. There was a distance. I felt uncomfortable in large groups. Had trouble following everyone's conversations. At midnight the cheer went up. I watched people kissing each other. I watched the women. None of them kissed me. I didn't want them to. I didn't know what I wanted. From women. From men. Anyone.

I went outside, stared up. There were only a few dim stars visible in the sky. It was 1989. Australia was 201. Parts of it anyway. And I was 22. It didn't seem significant anymore. Nothing was going to happen. At any age. I lit a cigarette. One pack a day now. The asthma getting worse.

I went home and slept. I showed up for work two days later. It was a quiet afternoon. Hungover. A new barmaid had started at the pub. I met her behind the bar. She was reading a book. I said hello. She said hello back.

Her name was Cynthia.